This Book is a work of fiction.

All of the characters, organizations, and events portrayed in the novel are either products of the authors imagination or are used fictitiously. Its not about you.

TRICK OF FAE

THESE HALLOWED HILLS SERIES

Quick Quill Publishing

© 2017

ALSO BY S.L.MASON

THESE HALLOWED HILLS SERIES

TEST OF FAE

THORNS OF FAE

TWIST OF FAE

TRAITS OF FAE

DEDICATION

To my daughter, Gillian and my son Jack.

For inspiring my dreams and this book.

Remember, just because you've never seen it. Doesn't mean

it doesn't exists!

TABLE OF CONTENTS

CHAPTER 1

Tuatha Dé Danann, Elves, Fae, fair folk, fairies—I used to believe in them. All those fluffy cotton candy stories they feed little girls. They sounded magical and wonderful, with wings floating around. Every story you've ever heard about a fairy is a lie. They do have magic, but they're not magical. They are every bit as evil, conniving, manipulative, and barbaric as humans. They just hide it behind a beautiful face and pointy ears. The Fae live for power and conquest. Greed rules them; it is in their veins. Their vanity is really what started all of this. No human has ever become a Fae. No Fae has ever become human. We are two different races, incompatible, or so I'd been led to believe. I should back up and start from the beginning.

This is how all fairy tales start.

Once upon a time, there was a girl. I'm that girl, and my name is Sarah.

It was Tuesday. I remember it was Tuesday because I always go to youth group on Tuesdays. It was a chance for me to hang out with my friends, play sports and games. I love games, any game, I love to compete, win. Plus, I didn't have to worry about my parents giving me a hard time if I stayed out late. I was supposed to leave youth group before ten and be home by ten-thirty. The walk home from church didn't take long, but I took my time about it.

Sometimes my girlfriends would walk with me. That's when I had girlfriends. That's when I had any friends. I lost my friends. I'm not an asshole. They didn't leave because they hated me; they're just dead. Lots of people died.

———————

The sun was fading from the sky. It was summer twilight when it didn't get dark till ten o'clock at night. I'd left church a little later than I had intended, and I walked home in the growing gloom. The last few wisps of sunlight disappeared. Off to the side, I caught the edge of a man-shaped shadow dash away into the darkness. The only sound to follow the wisp in the gloom was the neigh of a horse. I shook my head; that's silly! Horses don't live in the burbs. The echo of hooves clapping on cement rang down the side road. A moment later a loud crack cut the air and a round, flat, dark objects appeared in the sky. Beings rode them like it was straight out of a comic book. They appeared tall and well-built with long white hair.

I stood transfixed by a sound in the background, not a sound, a song. Three blocks down the street, one of these things landed. Twenty beings jumped off, and from a distance, they looked human. The longer I stared, the more little differences I picked out—the willowy gait of their walk, the lightness of a jump, or the floating quality of a step.

An inhuman song emanated from their lips, and the descending darkness increased the luminescence of their skin. My body stood locked in fascination.

One of them brandished a long thin object from behind him. Light from a streetlamp flashed off the edge. There was only one thing that shone in the light with such clarity—steel.

Was he carrying a sword? I mean it was 2020 for god's sake. People didn't run around brandishing swords. Whoever he was, he was armed with a menacing stance. The volume of the singing increased, along with the beating of my heart. He turned away from me, freeing me from my trance.

I bolted one block over and shouldered my way through a bush. Shouts called after me, along with the sound of feet thumping on the pavement. With a pounding heart in my chest, I ran, pumping my legs up and down as hard as I could. At the end of the block, I threw on an extra burst of energy to cross from one block to the other, avoiding the overexposure of the street. The outside air filled with screams. But the next alley was clear all the way to my parents' back gate. My feet skidded on loose gravel as I latched my hand onto the gate handle. I pressed the lever down, yanking it open and then pulling it closed behind me. Gulping in the air and pinching my side stitch, I hurried to the back door of the house, only to be met by the smell of fresh gun oil and a black barrel.

9mm is always a good choice for home protection. This 9mm was a familiar fixture in our house. The clicking of the safety was muffled by a gruff voice.

"Oh my god, Sarah. Thank god, it's you." My father said, while two big meaty arms pulled me in for a hug. The low whimpering from my mother lingered in the background.

"Dad, what's going on?" I asked, shivers running over me as my chest shuttered for a breath.

With a low voice, my father replied, "It's some kind of invasion. It's happening everywhere; it was all over the news. These creatures are attacking everywhere at once using the dark of night." He holstered the 9mm.

I looked from my mother's wide eyes to my father's creased brow. My mother's incessant lip biting irritated me. "I saw some of them a couple of blocks away, they chased me," I whispered, while trying to catch my breath.

My father moved from one light to another, turning them off, including the television.

CHAPTER 2

Screams drifted in from outside. They could've been down the street.

"Allison, take Sarah upstairs. Hide in your cupboard; you know which one." Dad ordered, and pushed to me to follow.

I laid a hand on Mom's forearm. Her body stiffened. Her unseeing eyes met mine as trembling took over. We picked our way up the stairs following the shadows. Keeping my movements slow, I held my breath to keep the creaking of the stairs at bay by lifting and lowering each foot, toe to heel.

With every sound, my heart leaped. I couldn't force myself to breathe deeply. I didn't want anything to hear me.

The sound of my father moving furniture drifted up through the floor—scrape, silence, scrape. My mother jumped, letting a little whimper escape with every bump. She latched onto my arm with an iron grip.

I didn't mean to look out the window, but I couldn't help myself. Whatever was out there, wasn't human. I needed to look at it one more time to be sure. But the street was still, and the creatures missing. The muffled whimpers of my mother pulled me back. She clawed at me with her free hand. We moved into my parents' bedroom and climbed into the over-sized cupboard. The bottom was lined with a mat and pillow. It had a lived-in feel to it.

I shut the door, closing off the rising screams that only grew ever closer.

I pulled out my phone and touched the screen illuminating the interior of the cabinet and seized the news feed icon. The web link revealed my first real look at three of them.

Each had white hair and a swimmer's build, with long limbs, broad shoulders, and narrow hips. Their eyes were every shade of the rainbow. One wore a gold breastplate like something out of medieval times. His eyes were the color of fresh flowing blood. A sound issued from his mouth, clawing at me. Words scrolled across the screen, detailing the death tolls in cities across the continent. A drone followed the creatures, filming the wholesale slaughter in the streets.

"Mom, are you seeing this? When I first saw them, I froze. I couldn't move, like hitting pause on a movie." I asked, and turned the phone to her, illuminating her face in a ghoulish fashion.

She wasn't looking. Her mind was far away and she spoke in a distant, almost lost voice. "They said some were shot down with bow and arrows. I watched one reporter's head get cut off. He didn't move, didn't flinch, didn't do anything to get away. It is their way." she trailed off to a whisper.

What she said sounded crazy and didn't make any sense.

"I don't know. Maybe the sounds stopped them? One of them was making some sound. I was standing next to the bushes. Maybe he didn't notice me? But somehow I snapped out of it and got away." I said, then tilted my head back and rested it on the wall of the wardrobe.

That was what it was. Maybe they're using sounds to control us. I seized on the idea.

"Mom, do you have earplugs?" I demanded, then used my hands to turn her face to mine. The light from my cell lit us from below, giving our faces a hollowed, monstrous appearance.

"Your father might have some in the nightstand. Sometimes he has a hard time sleeping with my snoring." Her listless reply didn't hinder my resolve.

I crept out to my father's nightstand. Pulling the drawer open, I rifled through and found a set of plugs. Who knew the old man had a whole gross of them. I'd never noticed my mother's snoring. Then again, my bedroom was across the stairs.

I put a plug in each ear. It didn't kill the sound, but it stifled it. It was flat with no tone, like it was coming from a tunnel. I handed a set to my mother.

"It makes the sound stop," I said, and did my best to not shout while tapping my earlobe. I didn't care if my mother thought I was crazy. Maybe I should've grabbed foil from the kitchen and fashioned it into hats. The truth was I'd just seen creatures that looked suspiciously like a cross between an elf and a fairy, hacking people to death, and apparently, they were singing while doing it. Crazy was already here.

The moment my father crept in, I handed him a pair of earplugs.

He waved me off and said, "No, I want to hear them coming."

"What if hearing is what gets you killed?" I replied, then explained my theory to him. After a few minutes, he shrugged his shoulders and inserted the plugs.

I dozed off briefly in the darkness, only to be awakened by more screaming. How someone could sleep through it, I didn't know? But I did off and on.

Daylight dawned, and the noise from outside died down. My mother's whimpering persisted here and there, but no screams.

All three of us jumped from a buzzing sound vibrating in my pocket. The screen lit up to display a dark-haired kid with glasses. It was Arty, our neighbor, and my BFF. Without thinking, I pushed talk and yanked the earplugs out.

"Are you still alive? Are your parents alive?" He demanded, his deep voice cracked with worry on the phone.

"Yes, what about yours?" I asked.

An explosion of air blew into the mic, reaching my ear. "I stayed at youth group. We're all fine. Can you check my parents' house?" He pleaded and his voice broke.

My heart squeezed as liquid fear pumped through my veins.

Then louder Arty asked, "Can you please look outside and see what my house looks like? Is it okay?"

It was daylight and 'they' were all gone, or at least I hoped. I opened the wardrobe door.

"Where are you going? Don't go out there." Mom cried, in a low voice her hands clawed at me, pulling me back. Her outburst came from the same place as my need to check did—fear. I couldn't sit there cowering in the closet.

"I'm going to take a peek out the window. Arty stayed at the church. He doesn't know what happened to his parents." I offer, while peeling her hand off my arm.

A ray of light cut across my father's face over his left eye. It was the muscle in his jaw that I saw first. It worked its way over the bone again and again.

"Hey, Arty, let me call you back," I replied, then let the phone slide down the side of my face as Arty rambled on.

"No, don't call me back! Keep me on the line. My parents aren't answering the phone. Please, I beg you." He yelled, choking on the last words.

I moved the cell back to my ear. "Okay, give me a minute," I said, and handed the phone to my dad, and then opened the door. I hopped out before anyone could say another word.

My heart pounded with every movement, and eyes searching every corner and shadow. The interior of the bedroom appeared untouched. I hadn't heard any loud crashing. I didn't think anyone came into our home. But adrenalin flooded my veins. What if I was wrong?

My mother grabbed my hand, silently pleading. I pulled her hand off.

"I have to use the bathroom. Stay in the closet," I said.

She pressed her lips closed and nodded her head as tears streamed down her face.

My mother wasn't as strong as Dad or me. She wasn't stupid, just softer, purer. She needed someone like Dad. She wouldn't make it on her own. It was something I'd learned about her a long time ago. I love her, I just can't rely on her.

When you're a kid, you can always tell which parent was the stronger of the two. Rarely were they both strong. These days everybody's parents were spineless. My dad was pretty well grounded though. He wrapped his free arm around her, and she leaned into it.

I headed for the closest window on the north side of the house. I didn't want to move the curtain or even be seen in the window. I pressed my body to the side of the frame.

My mother loved sheer curtains. She said they gave her a semblance of privacy while still letting in the light. During the day, you couldn't see anything. At night from the outside, you could see the outlines of anyone in the house. I'd stood outside several times, waiting to sneak back into the house. I always waited until the lights went out.

The northern window of the house faced the street. It looked like logs were strewn at all angles all the way to the end of the block and beyond. The day grew brighter, along with my realization that the logs were in fact bodies, and they weren't moving. The asphalt around them was spotted with dark circles of blood everywhere. There must've been fifteen or twenty bodies that I could see.

It looked like whoever these creatures were, they'd moved the bodies onto the streets and sidewalks. That was why the screaming had been so loud. They weren't people anymore. They were dead, every single one of them. They'd been our neighbors and friends.

A lump formed in my throat as the heat rose to my eyes. My already pounding heart tightened painfully. I dragged my eyes away, and then tiptoed over to the other side of the hall, pressing firmly against the southern window frame. I didn't see anyone alive, only more bodies.

Not far from our property line on the sidewalk lay Arty's mom. She was surrounded by a massive puddle of blood with a slash across her chest. Kneeling next to her was Arty's father, or what was left of him, slumped on his knees. A bloody stump remained where his head should've been.

I felt acid tickling my throat as it rose up to greet my tongue. I ran to the bathroom. A subtle sheen of sweat covered me as the contents of my gut spilled into the sink. Callused hands held my hair back.

"Okay, get it out. Get it all out." My father whispered, and smoothed my hair back from my brow.

I threw up the only thing left in my belly—golden bile. My stomach muscles clenched and unclenched. Standing over the sink with one hand on either side, I met my father's eyes in the mirror through my own watery eyes.

"How do I tell Arty?" I choked.

He ran his hand up and down my back. "You don't. That's my job, baby girl." Dad said, and went back to the bedroom.

I turned on the faucet, letting water flow into my hands. I splashed the water into my mouth and over my face.

I overheard my dad talking. "Arty, don't go home. It's not safe around here. Stay there. I know Doug and Lisa would've wanted you safe. No, they didn't... I'm sorry." Dad said, and anguish altered his voice.

He returned to the bathroom, and he thrust the phone under my chin. I pressed it to my ear.

"Did you see?" Arty asked. It was more a cry than a question.

Clearing my throat I responded, "Yeah, I saw them." The burning taste of bile still lingered in my mouth, stinging my nose hair.

"Was it quick?" His inquired, as his voice cracked with pain.

Tears pricked at my eyes again. "It was. It was really quick. I don't think they suffered." I offered, swallowing back the lump. I could never tell him about the screaming, crying, and whimpering.

"I want to see them." He replied.

I rushed on, "No, you don't. You absolutely do not want to see. I don't I'll think I'll ever get it out of my mind. Don't come. You stayed with the youth group. It was the smartest thing you could do at the time. I almost didn't make it home." My heart sped up, thinking about my mad dash.

"You think I'd be dead too?" He asked, then coughed.

"Yes, you'd be dead," I replied, swallowing to clear the lump that had lodged itself in my neck. "If it wasn't for my dad's smart thinking and me running like hell, I would be too." I finished. *Holy shit, Arty's parents are dead.*

The phone went dead. I didn't know if he hung up or not. Tears rolled down my face, and I felt a scream rising inside.

Dad came in and sat on the edge of the tub next to me. His warm arms encircled my shoulders. "It's okay to cry, baby, but keep your voice down. We don't know if they're still in the area." He whispered into my hair.

"What are they, Dad? Russians? Aliens? Terroristic, genetic mutants?" I asked.

"Someone called them Fae." He replied, then ran his hand up and down my arm as his chin cradled my head. His warm breath blew over the crown of my head, moving my hair.

What the hell are Fae? I wanted to cry and scream. Fear drives people. Fear was always overridden by survival. If anything was to happen, I had to survive. This wouldn't be the end of my story, not like Arty's parents lying in the street dead with Arty's dad missing his head.

All the electricity and water was still on. I would've thought if aliens were attacking, they would have sent an electromagnetic pulse to the local power plant. Or maybe poisoned our water system?

They didn't do any of those. What they did, it didn't make any sense. They appeared out of nowhere and dragged people out of their homes and into the street, all the while singing.

My father didn't want anything to hear us. He didn't turn on the television. I grabbed my earbuds for my phone out of my coat. I put one earbud in and handed the other to my father. It was a way for both of us to listen without bothering my mother. She wasn't interested anyway.

The anchorwoman's voice announced, "Today dawns a new day. We've been invaded by a foreign species. The question of whether we are alone has been answered. They call themselves Fae. Apparently, humanity has encountered them before. They are fairies—the Fae." She droned on.

Fairies. We'd been invaded by fairies. No one knew why they were here or what they wanted, but apparently, they couldn't handle daylight. They only operated at night.

The screen changed to the President. His face was gaunt. I didn't pay close attention to politics, but he looked like he'd aged ten years overnight. "For now, we are enacting a curfew, starting one hour before and one hour after dawn— nothing human moves. Wherever you are, stay there. If you have some means of protecting yourself, do so. City councils will create safe places where you can go, and your local police will provide protection. City councils will coordinate with the National Guard and the United States Army to protect as much of the civilian population as possible. We have recalled all armed servicemen overseas for the defense of our nation against this incursion. We don't have any other information at this time, thank you." The President announced. The screen changed to video footage from the night before.

I couldn't hold back anymore. "Fairies, Dad. We're being invaded by fairies? Don't fairies have wings and flitter around?" I scoffed.

"No, apparently they wielded swords and crossbows." He offered and took my hand interlacing his fingers with mine.

I shook my head. "You can come out of the cupboard, Mom. Apparently, the fairies won't be back until dark."

My eyes trailed down to the floor but stopped and landed on my father's holstered handgun. He always had a gun. It never bothered me. He'd taught me how to shoot.

Something the anchorwoman said, I found interesting. They couldn't stand the light. I thought fairies were supposed to be creatures of daylight. Apparently, the sun hurts them.

"Hey, Dad. The light hurts fairies. Tell me, don't humans have a flashlight that imitates sunlight?" I asked.

He scratched his chin, tilting his head to the side. "Yeah, the military issues them; it's a special kind of LED. They just recently became available to the public." He stopped talking and turned to look at me. "It's an excellent idea. A couple of weeks ago, Roger Epstein, down the street showed me, a few he has. Said he was taking them camping. Why don't I go and see if he still got them?" He replied and released my hand and stood up in one motion. He reached down and pulled me to my feet.

I knew what my dad meant. He wasn't going to borrow them. He thought Roger and his wife were dead. He was going to collect their supplies.

"What about the rest of the weapons?" I asked.

He shrugged his shoulders. We both proceeded to the stairs, but my mother let out a yelp.

"Please, George, please don't go down there." She cried.

"It's okay, Allison. They don't like daylight. We'll be fine. We need to get some food to shore up the house." His replied and his face softened, as did his voice. My mother needed a soft touch, and my father gave it to her.

All her crying had caused her makeup to run. My mother had the look of a raccoon. Fear bled through her every motion. She jumped at every squeak and every sound. I knew she was terrified. My father took her hand and gently led her down the stairs. I followed behind.

Everything in our house looked perfectly normal, except for the fact that there was a giant wooden bookshelf against the front door. My father had moved my mother's cabinet against the back door.

"I'm starving. Do you think you could make something for Sarah and I to eat?" Dad asked.

Humming erupted from my mom, and she nodded her head. She looked around, searching as if she'd never seen the kitchen before.

CHAPTER 3

He waved me over to his office, and I followed my father without a sound. Somewhere in the back of my mind, I still felt like the creatures were out there, roaming the streets and killing people. How anybody could ever have thought fairies were sweet wonderful creatures, I didn't know.

My father had a gun safe hidden behind one of the bookshelves in his study. I'd known about it since I was little when I pulled all the books off the shelf in front of it. He'd been mad at first. "You can never tell anyone, Sarah. Can you do that?" Dad ordered. At the time, I didn't understand why it would matter.

He spun the dial, putting in his little code, which even from a distance I could tell it was my birth date, not very imaginative. But when the safe swung open, that was when my eyes grew big. He had several assault rifles, about eight handguns of varying calibers, and a few long rifles. One of them looked like it might've been a 30-30 long gun. It must've been the one he taught me to shoot, when I was twelve. My father wasn't a survivalist, nor was he some kind of nut either. He'd gone to Afghanistan, and he was a retired veteran that liked having a few weapons around. He said they could come in handy. Knowing how to shoot a gun could mean the difference between living and dying. So he made me go to the gun range, and I learned to shoot. I was surprised he didn't also make me take some hand-to-hand combat classes and basic self-defense. He figured if you pick them off with a bullet, you wouldn't need to fight. He thought his little girl was never going to be in that kind of danger. America wasn't a dangerous country.

It wasn't like it was Africa or the Middle East with roaming bands of crazy people ready to hack you to death. There were gangs in America, but that was an inner-city problem; that wasn't something that happens out in the suburbs where we were.

He pulled out two sidearms, the first was a Smith & Wesson 22. It was a small caliber handgun that I'd used it before, with an ankle holster. He strapped it on me. Dad called it a lady gun.

It's really a pussy gun.

"That's your emergency backup. Don't touch it unless you have to. Most people aren't going to notice it. I don't think these creatures know that much about guns. They look like they're using weapons from the medieval era. Did you see the one wearing the golden breastplate?" His asked, his eyes were serious, but his lips quirked at the sides.

"Yeah, I did. Wasn't there one carrying a crossbow?" I offered, with a small smile.

He continued to strap a knife onto his belt, tying it down around his thigh. "Yes, you have a lot to worry about with a crossbow. From a distance, they can hurt you; maybe even kill you. They're not nearly as accurate as a gun, but a bullet or arrow in the right place will kill you just as dead." He said. Next, he handed me a 380.

It was a mini nine made by Khan. I'd never shot it before, but my hand recognized it. It felt familiar and was a good fit. My hands weren't big, but they weren't small. If you want to be proficient with a weapon, you need something that fits your hand; something that feels good. This one did. It melded with me.

Dad smiled and said, "Bought that one a couple of months ago to give it to you when you went away to college."

He pulled out a shoulder holster. It was brown leather with red scroll-work on it; small and dainty, apparently for me.

I wasn't one of those big fatty Mcfat-fats, but I wasn't a little pixie chick either. I was your average ordinary plain-Jane girl. I bought my clothes in the junior section of the store like the rest of the girls, hoping that my jeans were skinny enough and my hair was big enough—to fit in and not be noticed. I wasn't interested in being one of those flashy girls. You know, the ones who run around trying to be the most popular chick in school.

I wasn't a social outcast either, just dull normal. I keep saying normal. What I meant was middle-of-the-road average.

The holster under my arm was new and a little uncomfortable.

"Don't fidget so much, Sarah. You get used to it. It'll be uncomfortable for a little while, but then, it'll be like a second skin, and you won't notice it anymore until you need to use it." Both his hands settled on my hips. "I'm not saying I want you to sleep with it on, but I am saying I want you to keep it as close by as possible," he said, while crouching down to look into my eyes.

"Are you kidding me? Those things come out at night. Who the hell is sleeping at night ever again?" I retorted.

My father ducked his head as his forehead crinkled into a fatalistic look. I knew he wouldn't give up. My dad wasn't a quitter, but we were being invaded by fairies for god's sake.

I went and sat at the kitchen table, and put my earbuds back in. I started surfing the Internet for every website that had anything to do with fairies. They must've been having the type of traffic most websites could only dream of. I could only imagine how much money it was costing the advertisers. Every book on Amazon about fairies was suddenly a number one best seller. I betcha if I went to the library, I wouldn't find anything there either.

Most of what I read was flawed, filled with fairy pixie horse crap. Fairies had wings, fairies were mischievous, fairies could help save you, and they helped you find things or lose things or hide things. A lot of it sounded like bullshit made up by a bunch of people who wanted fairies to be nice, instead of the mean, cruel killers they were. I jumped ten feet in the air when I heard a knock at the back door. I was surprised how fast my gun made it to my hand, with the safety off. I guess all those times at the gun range were worth it. I hadn't had one single thought about that weapon before it was in my hand and ready to shoot something.

"Let me in! It's me, Arty." Arty's demanded through the door.

My father was already standing at the door. He gave me a solemn glance, and then slowly moved the cabinet. He didn't move it all the way—just enough so Arty could slip through.

"I came in through the back alley and kept to the shadows. I don't think anybody saw me." He offered, his chest rose and fell rapidly.

"The creatures don't go out during the day. Haven't you been watching the news?" I asked, as my hand found on his arm.

"No, my phone went dead. That's why my call ended. I left my charger at home, so no, I haven't seen the news." He retorted, then leaned over, placing both hands on his knees to catch his breath.

"I have a spare charger in the drawer over there. Throw your phone on it." I ordered.

Dread filled me. He was going to ask where his parents were. Then he'd want to see their bodies. Just the thought of seeing them again or even bringing up the image in my mind, it made me want to yak. Nobody should see their parents like that.

His pleading eyes shifted from his phone, to my father, to me. "Where are they?" he demanded.

"You don't want to go out there. The whole street is lined with all of our neighbors' bodies. I think the only reason we're alive is because they didn't think we were home." My dad responded. His words hit home to me how lucky we were.

"So, while my parents were dying you just huddled in the dark?" Arty yelled.

"Hardly. While your parents were dying, we huddled in a dark closet hoping to live so we could stand here and tell you that your parents are dead, and that you don't want to look at it. It was the most awful thing I've ever seen in my whole life." I yelled back, choking on the last few words. "Everybody on the street is dead, Arty. Don't you get it? Whatever you thought the world was yesterday, it's gone. This is the new world." I didn't know why I yelled at him. He didn't deserve that. He wanted to see parents' bodies.

I didn't want to go out there. I didn't want to hear him crying or hear the screaming that might erupt from him, or me, or my mother if she saw. I wasn't going to stop him, and he wouldn't have tried to stop me, if it were my parents.

"What? You think you know what's best for me? Spit on my face while you're at it." Arty bellowed, then turned around shoved the cabinet to the side and stormed out the back door. I moved to go after him, but my dad pulled me up short.

"Don't. Let him go. Whatever he's got to handle, he's got to do it on his own. You can be there to help him. He'll come back." Dad said.

"But nobody wants to see their parents that way," I replied.

He pulled me into a big hug, resting his chin on my head. "Everybody's got to grow up sometime. He turns eighteen next month. He's old enough to go to war, according to America's laws. His war started a little earlier than mine. You know, I was eighteen when I went off to Afghanistan. It'll either make a man out of him or break him. I think he might rise to the occasion. Let him come to his own conclusions. The real question is, how are you going to handle it?" he asked.

My dad was right. I couldn't be a crutch for everybody else or anybody else. I had to figure out how I was feeling and not worry so much about everybody else.

Mom finished making her semblance of breakfast. I put the food in my mouth, but the truth was I didn't taste it. I didn't appreciate it. One of those things where you're eating probably the best meal of your life and you have no idea what any of it tasted like or what it looked like. All I knew was it was a source of energy, which I needed.

My mother made fried eggs, hash browns, bacon, gravy, and biscuits. It was a big southern-style breakfast. But I didn't taste any of it.

Bacon, one of my most favorite foods in the whole world is bacon. Everybody loves bacon. I've concluded that anyone who doesn't like bacon must be a communist.

Arty came back and went straight to the bathroom. Gagging noises filled the house, which ended breakfast for me. He kept the door closed for a while, crying. He stopped when the faucet turned on, then he came out looking pale and pasty. "Can I stay with you guys?" he asked.

"Of course. You're always welcome here," I said before my parents could think.

"My dad had a watch. I was going to look for it. Would you come with me, George?" Arty sputtered.

My dad picked up his shotgun and a black thing lying on one of the kitchen counters, and tossed it to Arty.

"Dangerous world out there. I think maybe you should be wearing this. I'm not going anywhere out there without it. The sons of the evil know it's safe to come out of their holes." Dad said while he handed Arty a Kevlar vest.

My mother cried out. "Don't go out there." She reached her hand out and put her fingers to his lips and kissed him gently.

"It's okay. We're just going next door. Arty and I are going to pick up some supplies. We'll be right back." Dad replied softly.

My mother covered her mouth with her hand as big fat tears rolled down her cheek. I loved my mom, but sometimes she was such a waste.

I didn't want Dad to go either, but I wasn't going to cry about it.

"He's just gonna jump the fence between the yards and through the house." I rubbed my hand down her back. "It's not even like he'll be on the street. That's what I've been doing for years." I offer.

My mother walked to the table in true automaton fashion, tidying up breakfast and packing everything away in containers. She sang as she went along. She placed it all precisely in the refrigerator and then mechanically washed every dish. Mom was a nervous cleaner. If she got uptight about something, you always knew by the house and the level of sparkling clean. She'd scrub every nook and cranny into a lather humming and singing all the while until her problem went away or just stopped bothering her.

When Dad was deployed to the Middle East, he was gone for a year. My mother cleaned constantly. She scrubbed holes where the stains were in my clothes. The house was awash with music and her voice.

I went to the side window and peeked through in time to see my dad leap over the fence. He cleared it. Dad was in pretty good shape. Arty had a harder time clearing it.

I didn't even know they returned until I heard drilling on the outside of the house. My father had hoisted up sheets of plywood, and they were drilling holes and then screwing them onto the exterior of the house. They covered every window on the lower floor. Then, brought over a metal frame for a screen door, one of those steel security doors like the one for Arty's back porch.

Dad leaned his head in the back door. "Hey, can you grab me some of those ceramic coated tap-cons I left in the junk drawer? I think there are six of them in there. I need them all." He asked.

"Sure. You want the blue ones, right?"

"Those are the ones." Dad yelled, over the drilling.

I pulled them out. He was right; there were six. I hate junk drawers. Everything's in there, but you could never find anything, without having to touch something dusty, dirty, grimy, or sticky to get to what you want.

I placed the tap-cons in his hands, and the drilling out back was joined by drilling out front. My father came inside and locked the exterior doors.

"Well, that's all the plywood I could find." He announced.

"I took the security doors off my house and put them on yours," Arty said. "Let's go back and start moving food and stuff." Arty's hair was disheveled and sweaty.

"While you're over there, grab any and all cash and jewelry; not because people are gonna steal it but because we might need it for trade. We have no idea if society is gonna break down or not," Dad informed us. He understood the breakdown of society. Gold has an intrinsic value, paper not so much.

I heard what sounded like a huge diesel truck. I dashed to look out the window, and it resembled a military vehicle. It wasn't driving around the bodies lying in the street but instead drove right over the top of them—cold, heartless bastards. The time said three o'clock in the afternoon. When the loudspeaker announced.

"Curfew starts at five o'clock. Do not be outside after five o'clock. Wherever you are, stay there. All looters will be shot on sight." The military vehicle continued down the street, repeating its message.

Wow, that was their public service announcement? Hey, stay in your house and if the Fae don't kill you, we will.

My mother made another meal, that I didn't pay attention to. My father and Arty had somehow managed to unload his parents' freezer and move the whole thing over to our house. They loaded it back up so when it came to supplies, we had two households' worth of food.

"By my estimates, we have about three months of food supplies." My dad scratched the back of his head while searching the kitchen with his eyes.

Something in the back of my mind told me it was going to be mighty long three months.

"We had better pray that's all we need. The grocery stores are empty by now." My mother hadn't spoken in hours. The sound of her voice jarred me.

Five o'clock curfew. The sun doesn't go down until ten. Twilight starts at nine; that leaves five hours of nothing to do. My dad turned on the television.

"CNN." Arty plopped down on the couch.

My father threw a glance over his shoulder at Arty and smiled.

"Sorry, we're Fox News network here. But I'll switch around to whatever channel has information. Don't worry about it. I'm sure we will hit it eventually."

Watching television was like watching a snuff film on replay over and over again. Videos of murders streamed from all over the world. My stomach rolled around. The last thing in the world I wanted to watch was death. As if I hadn't seen enough.

An anchorman read off the TelePrompter. "Authorities haven't been able to capture one of these creatures. Scientists have studied videos of the creatures and discovered the harmonic singing induces a hypnotic state, making humans highly susceptible. Wearing earplugs or headphones deadens the harmonics of the noise. It isn't perfect, but it can save the life of you or someone you love." His voice droned on but I wasn't listening anymore.

I tilted my head back, allowing a smile to spread smugly across my face. "See, Dad? Earplugs."

Arty went rigid next to me. The screen changed to a white-haired Fae, whose blade flashed while beheading a kneeling man. My hand found his, and I squeezed his fingers.

"Yeah, that was good problem-solving. The only thing keeping us alive is critical thinking." My father replied, and clicked through the channels, landing on the local news. It consisted of more of the same. The anchorwoman's words caught my attention.

"Dallas's inner-city hasn't been affected. The creatures continue to terrorize the rural and suburban areas." She informed us.

I found it hard to believe they didn't appear over the top of any city, or maybe that was their plan.

Maybe they knew more about our world than we realized. They didn't go into any major cities. No major metropolitan areas, only outlying suburbs, and small towns. Strategic?

But what frightened me wasn't the murders.

"Hundreds of teenagers and young adults are missing after last night's massacre. Many didn't come home. Last known locations were in and around suburban Dallas. Many of them young girls."

Social media photos and selfies flashed across the screen. A few beefy jocks, but mostly smiling pretty girls with pouty lips. There weren't any ho-hum girls. They were stunning, every single one. A parade of prom queens. One of the girls was a pageant winner with her sash.

Arty nudged me. "Guess it's a good thing you're not that pretty, hey?"

"At least I'm not an asshole, Arty." I retort and shove him.

My mother had gone into autopilot a while ago. "Sarah, language."

I wish she'd stay dazed. Why wake up to give me crap about cursing? The world's going to hell in a handbasket, and suddenly she complains about my verbiage. I tilted my head to the side and rolled my shoulders. It was my way of saying 'whatever', without being sassy to my mom.

"I think we need to talk about tomorrow." Arty scratched his chin.

"I think we should worry more about what's gonna happen tonight," I say, was I the only one worried about the dark, other than my mother?

"No. Tonight, the creatures will come back," Dad said. "They're going to try to take or kill whatever they can. Maybe you weren't paying attention to the news? They apparently took food and supplies. Didn't you see the hole they tore out of Walmart?"

"Wow, Walmart is so famous even fairies' shop there." I said. Arty and I both snickered, pushing each other.

"Now, anyone who wants to go looting knows that the suburbs have been hit hard, and most of the people are dead. They're going to come here looking to steal whatever they can. It puts the rest of us risk." Dad replies, then stands and stretches. "Stay here and protect your mother. The sun doesn't go down for another two hours. Arty and I are gonna go to a couple of houses down the street."

My mother yelped.

"Don't worry! We'll jump fences and stay off the streets. We're going to do our own form of farming." My dad says, then rubs his hands up and down my mother's biceps.

Her eyes were large and darting like she didn't know where to look. "They said they're shooting looters on sight. Do you want you to die?" My mother's blue eyes grew to the size of saucers. She bit her lip while twisting her fingers in her shirt.

"Don't worry Allison, I got my flak jacket on. I know how to get around. What's more, is the National Guard uses body shots. It's easier to hit than the head. It'd knock me down, but I'll get back up and be fine." Dad replied, and raised his hands to either side of her face and stroked her cheeks with his thumbs.

"So many things could go wrong. Don't leave me alone." Her fingers dug into his back. "Don't leave Sarah alone. We need you. You're more important to us than a bunch of crap at some neighbor's house." She demanded.

He kissed her temple and then released her.

"Maybe I should go alone," Arty interjected. "I mean, you're going down to Sorensen's house, right?"

My father nodded. Everybody knew Fred Sorensen was a safety nut. He called himself a 'Doomer'. It had become quite popular in the last ten to fifteen years. A lot of people started keeping reserve amounts of food or cash and beefing up their security by hoarding guns.

"Be careful, Dad. Doesn't Sorensen have some crazy security system at his place?" I ask, and crossed my arms.

"I'm pretty sure it's not active, seeing as how he and his wife are both dead on the lawn." The impact of my father's words hit Arty and I at the same time. Arty shrunk into himself.

Dad's face grew red and tight. He didn't mean to hurt Arty, but it was the truth. Fred Sorensen's security system hadn't been on, or we would've heard it.

Arty shook it off as he stood next to my dad. He grabbed his AR off the table.

"Next time you put your weapon down, son, keep it no more than six inches away from your hand." Dad gave him a steely stare. "Sleep with it. It's your best friend. Don't ever leave it on the table or across the room from you again. Understand?"

Arty's eyes grew large. He bobbed his head in understanding. They shuffled out the back door, and I locked the security screen. I peeked out the front door to watch my dad and Arty cross the street into the yard next door.

I didn't hear any gunshots or screaming, but the sun was still up. There would be plenty of time for that after it went down. I unplugged my phone and took out my emergency battery pack and plugged that into charge. The last thing in the world I wanted was to be caught with my phone dead as a doornail and unable to send out a text if I needed.

My dad has never been a party to sexism. He taught me everything, regardless of my sex— how to take apart a single-stroke lawnmower engine, change the oil, replace the rings, and all the filthy, grimy work. I really wasn't into it, but it was important. Girls should know enough about engines to fix one in desperate times.

I never thought there'd be desperate times. I'd drive my car to a mechanic, and Eureka, my oil was changed. But looking at all the corpses in the street and the birds settling over them, I wanted to toss my cookies. The bodies sat in the sun, all day baking. It brought the dogs out. A local dog tore at a body. Tomorrow, when the sun would come up, everything will start to stink.

"Maybe tomorrow we should use a truck or something to move the bodies off to the side?" My words hadn't been for anyone in particular. I didn't want to touch bodies or sit there on the street filled with dead, rotting corpses either. It didn't matter if they were neighbors or not. I didn't want Fred Sorensen and his wife to rot and turn into dog meat on my street.

My mother wrapped her arms around me and attempted to pull me away from the door. I didn't budge.

I stared out the window until I felt it was time to close the curtains. I spied my father and Arty coming down the street. They carried a big sheet of plywood. They came up on the front porch and screwed it over the window blocking out the last bit of sunlight.

At twilight, the sun was going down, and Dad came in the front door. Arty came through the back. I did my best to shove the bookshelf out of the way. They both had huge black duffel bags slung over their shoulders.

"Fred hadn't turned on the security system," Dad said through heavy breathing and rosy cheeks. "His front door was kicked in. Water for the bathtub was still on. It looked like his wife just walked away. I got all the cash I could but didn't get into the secret room. It's somewhere in that house. I don't know where it is."

"If you can't find it, that means the looters can't either," I said. "You've been in his house a hundred times. Plenty of time to go back and forth in daylight." My dad patted me on the shoulder.

He and Arty took their duffel bags upstairs. They both returned with rectangular shaped shoeboxes. Arty went out the back, and Dad out the front. I watched Dad pull at an invisible string from one side of the walkway to the other. They didn't put them on the house, but on the walk away to the house.

They made it back into the house in time for me to hear singing. My mother froze in place, but I had my earbuds in. I heard the tonal quality of the singing, but the rest was lost on me.

I raced around the house, turning everything off. I grabbed earplugs off the kitchen counter and shoved them in my father's ears and then Arty's. Afterward, I gave some to my mother.

The reason my father had drilled holes in all those pieces of plywood was to see out the window and, if necessary, shoot. I never stopped moving until I found myself standing next to my parents' northern bedroom window looking down at the street.

Five of the creatures walked around with weapons. Every now and again, they stabbed at a dead body. I guess they weren't sure they were dead. Maybe birds picking the flesh off of them wasn't enough of a clue.

Fred Sorensen always had vicious dogs, or at least I thought they were vicious, especially the Rottweiler named King. King was a monster of more than one hundred and fifty pounds of rippling muscle and tension. He drooled, and when King shook his head, the ropes of saliva would stretch and break off, flying in every direction.

King approached the lead Fae, with teeth bared. Deep down, I hoped the dog would jump on one of them and then tear them apart. Instead, the Fae's lips moved. King sat, and his tongue lolled out of his mouth. King nudged his head against the Fae's hand.

The Fae had tamed the beast, King, who had chased me down the street several times. I was always terrified King would catch me and tear me apart. He'd killed the neighbors'

Jack Russell by picking it up and shaking it until it snapped the poor dog's neck.

People complained about Sorensen's dog, but Fred's best friend was on the city council. Nothing would happen. No one would take the dog, and nobody wanted to file a lawsuit.

This was the suburbs. You can't file a complaint and sue your neighbor unless they're parking on your lawn. Apparently, public safety wasn't as important as who parks where and whether you planted the correct plant in your yard.

King sat like a puppy with its tongue hanging out of its mouth, wholly enslaved. *Unbelievable.*

My mother's eyes glazed over, catatonic. "He's here for me, and you." She wasn't making any sense.

I didn't think this was something she could deal with. I took her hand and led her to the wardrobe. I coaxed her inside and then closed the door. I left her with a little flashlight. She didn't even ask me to stay.

I crept down the stairs. My father was near the front window, spying out one of the kill holes. Arty was still at the back door. I had more gun experience than Arty, and yet for some reason, my dad thought it was okay to have Arty guarding and me, babysitting.

Maybe my job was more important. Everybody had a part to play.

I heard a knocking on the side of the house through my earbuds. I made out the flat quality of the song. The Fae wasn't singing; he whistled. And then in English, it sang as clear as day.

"Come out, come out, whoever you are, or I'll huff and I'll puff, till I blow your house down." The musical quality of his voice ran down my back like fingernails raking over a chalkboard. His quoting of nursery rhymes freaked me out.

"Sarah, get your mother and go into my office now," Dad whispered, but in my mind, it sounded like he was screaming.

I crept upstairs, and I grabbed my mother's hand. She pulled her arm back and shook her head. Her eyes were wide, and her pupils dilated with her breathing elevated.

"Dad says we have to go to the office. Do you know why?"

"I'm not leaving the house. He's coming for us."

I shook my head and felt my eyebrows cinch down. "There's no exit out of the office. There are just more guns in there." Ignoring the cryptic 'he' reference.

She refused. I tiptoed back downstairs to Dad. I pointed up shook my head while raising my shoulders. What was I supposed to do? She wasn't willing to go. I was afraid that at any moment she'd start screaming for no apparent reason.

My father grabbed Arty and pulled him away from the back door, herding us both into the office. He opened the closet, revealing the gun safe. Dad picked up one of the big black bags and slung it over Arty's shoulder. My father then opened the other one and pulled out a couple of harnesses and several boxes of ammo. He put them in a small backpack, slipping it on my back. He inserted several water bottles in the side pockets.

He turned me around with his hands on either side of my face.

"You're going to go through a tunnel. When you come out the other side, you're gonna be in the Vougher's backyard; it's a rain-drain cover. Doesn't look like anything. Once you to exit the tunnel, go into Mrs. Vougher's house and find a closet. Stay there. They think the neighborhood is clean, and we're the only ones left. As long as they think the house is empty, you'll be safe. I shouldn't have put the plywood up over our windows; it's a target. They realized we're here. It's my mistake. I'll stay here and get your mother."

He pulled on the handle of the safe. The entire safe swung to one side. I thought the safe was bolted to the floor. Instead of a floor below, a gaping hole with a ladder reached down into darkness. Dad handed me one of the LED lights he'd stolen from Fred Sorensen's house. He clipped an extra one to my belt and handed the other one Arty.

"Take care of my girl, Arthur," my dad said. "I'm trusting you with her. Whatever you do don't come back here." My father's earnest face met each of ours.

I shook my head. "No, Dad. You can't stay here."

"I'm not staying. I'll sneak upstairs and get your mother. You go on ahead. I'll join you in a little bit." He kissed my forehead and pushed me toward the inky black hole in the floor.

It was crazy. My father wasn't one of those prepper nutters, but apparently, my house had a secret tunnel.

I went first, one foot at a time, rung by rung. It resembled the layers of a terrarium, starting with the wood flooring from the house, then the cement slab, only to turn into rough CBS block. The beam from my flashlight cut through the darkness. It didn't reveal any creepy crawlies, but there were enough spiderwebs to have rivaled any haunted house I've ever seen. The tunnel wasn't deep, maybe ten feet down. The tunnel itself was only about five feet high, two feet wide, and big enough for a grown man, but he would have to crouch. Arty followed behind. He hunched, and it struck me that Arty was tall.

Arty was the kid next door, my best friend, the person I got in trouble with. Now, I was looking at him in the context of this tunnel. He was a big dude. That was probably why Dad had him standing at the back door and not me.

The light at the end of the tunnel wasn't a light at all; it was just less dark. We weren't far from our backyard to Mrs. Vougher's backyard. How had my father been able to dig this tunnel all the way under the alleyway and into Mrs. Vougher's backyard, and no one noticed? How did he get all the dirt out? Dad used to stay up late. Maybe this was what he was working on.

I felt a warm breath on my ear. It was Arty. "The end. We should listen and wait; see if anything's close by before exiting."

I nodded my head, which was silly because we were in the dark. It wasn't like he could even see me.

CHAPTER 4

The sound of rocks ground under their feet. They were close and speaking among themselves. I didn't understand what they were saying. It came across garbled and indistinct. We also were too deep in the ground.

Out of the corner of my eye, I saw a flash of light; it glinted off Arty's glasses. Anyone looking down here would see the light reflecting off our skin. Trailing my fingers along the cold and slimy CBS block wall, I reached up to feel the ceiling, only to encounter more cold and slimy texture. I crouched down and my fingers slid across the floor. It was gritty, plain, old dirt. I rubbed my hands in it.

I'd seen pictures of my father from Afghanistan. At the time I didn't recognize him. His entire face was covered in camouflage. It looked like a yellow and brown dirty mess. At the time, it was funny. Daddy was playing dress-up and trying to disguise himself. He'd been holding a big cigar between his teeth with a helmet under one arm. His buddies surrounded him. The only way I knew it was him was the hair.

I took the dirt from the floor and began rubbing it all over my face. I smeared it down my neck, over my shirt, and on to my arms. Recognition dawned on Arty's face, and he shoved his glasses in his pocket. He grabbed a handful of dirt to rub over his face.

The muffled noises in the distance faded away. The only thing left was the sound of a dog's sniffing. The neigh of a horse followed along with the clopping of hooves.

I glanced back into the black void behind me. The fear in my belly cinched into a tight ball. My father still hadn't come. He had to be here. My hands moistened, and I rubbed them on my pant legs. My eyes searched the darkness, willing my parents to appear. Come on, come on you have to make it.

We waited for what seemed like forever, but the lack of traffic around us wouldn't hold. Arty tapped me and pointed upward. It was quiet out. The tension in my belly said no, but my brain told me it wasn't safe. There was no going back to the house, but my parents were still there. We couldn't stay here in the open and exposed. What if somebody saw or heard us?

Arty moved his large frame up the ladder and gently pushed on the heavy iron grate. It swung open without a sound. Obviously, my father kept it oiled. He'd probably come out here today.

The rat-tat-tat of automatic weapons fire filled the air in the distance. Arty was out of the hole in a flash. Halfway up the ladder, Arty grabbed me by my backpack handle. He yanked me out of the hole. I hadn't realized he was strong enough to do that with the way he carried himself hunched over. He wears glasses for god's sake.

A lump took up residence in my throat. Everyone on our street was dead. My dad was the only one with an AR. Tears muddied my vision. Daddy, Mom.

Arty never released the backpack as he dragged me into the house. My feet stumbled and dragged. I saw my way through the tears burning their way down my face. Arty only let go to make sure the door didn't slam as we went through.

Mrs. Vougher was a widow. Her husband died a couple of years ago. Mom took me to the funeral. Mrs. Vougher wore her widow's weeds and carried around a hanky. Her hat sat back on her head with a little black mesh falling over her eyes. I felt sad as her husband had planted a flower garden every year.

The garden was long gone now. There hadn't been a flower garden in her backyard since he died. I did bring her flowers once. She accepted them kindly, but I didn't think she wanted them. I didn't see her plant it. She probably chucked it in the trash.

The back door led into the kitchen. The house had that old, dried out peppermint BenGay scent with a hint of rose. At a glance, the loneliness reached out to me—the drainboard with one plate, one cup, and one saucer. She probably used the same utensils every day. Why take everything out or put it away? It was a three-bedroom house, but clearly, only one room was used. Everything else was covered with a thin layer of forgot.

We didn't linger since the windows were right at ground level. Anyone walking by could look in and see us. Arty dragged me into the hallway. It was dog-legged with one window at the end, and a double-door closet in the middle. He yanked it open. Coats hung to one side, and a few shoeboxes underneath them. There was plenty of room for both of us. We hunkered down. The weight of my backpack pulled out my shoulders. I didn't want to take it off. What if we had to get up and run?

Arty's warm, moist breath filled my ear. "I don't think they're in the neighborhood anymore. We should be safe for tonight. Sleep in shifts. You go first."

I whispered in the lowest voice possible, "You must be kidding, right? Not that I don't trust you. I do. I just don't think I'll sleep. Didn't you hear that semi-auto gunfire? That could be my parents." He wrapped his arm around me.

I couldn't remember the last time Arty and I hugged. We became teenagers, and it kind of made things weird. Arty was like my brother and my best friend all rolled into one. We had played in the mud together as children.

My heart was still beating a wild animal's rage in my chest, but the shuttering of the chest behind me brought it all back. Hot tears leaked down my cheeks. My body pulled away from Arty's, only to be brought back. My ears strained, listening for more weapons fire. The longer the silence stretched, the larger the pit in my belly grew. They were dead, and we were alone.

Light from the streetlight peeked through the cracks in the closet doors, cutting across space. He whispered in my ear, "Sleep, Sarah. I promise I'll keep you safe." He sniffed and shuttered but never made a another sound. Arty's silent grieving silenced my own, we couldn't both fall apart.

Maybe they weren't dead. Maybe they fought them off. One AR sounds pretty much like another. Maybe it wasn't my dad's gun. I latched on to that, and I leaned back for the long night.

I messed up on the not sleeping thing. The last thing I remember was listening to the rhythm of Arty's heart beating. I didn't stay awake. It was my job, and I couldn't do it. Arty was still asleep, and it was still dark outside. Something woke me. Crap.

The rise and fall of my diaphragm slowed. I slowed my breathing, hoping to stop the pounding in my chest. Funny how whenever you're desperate to listen to something, every little thing sounds like it was on a megaphone.

I nudged my elbow into Arty's belly. He jumped slightly. I waved my hand in front of his face, but he didn't say anything.

There it was, the hiss of a cat. Mrs. Vougher had a cat. Why was it hissing? The hissing grew closer, along with scratching. A dog barked. It was in the house. My heart sped up, and all my muscles tensed. Next to me, Arty compressed all his muscles, like a spring ready to be freed. I heard clicking on the old hardwood floors, along with the sniffing and heavy breathing; it was indicative of a canine. The cat hissed, along with a low-throated yowl.

I heard one of them.

"Hey diddle, diddle, the cat and the fiddle, a cow jumped over the moon. The little dog laughed to see such fun, and the dish was killed with a spoon."

Why did they repeat fairytale nursery rhymes?

My hand wasn't big enough to cover my mouth and hold back the scream waiting there. My fingernails dug into the side of my face as the liquid fear filled my chest, lighting it on fire.

A low-throated growl vibrated down the hallway, followed by hissing and yowling. The sick sound of flesh colliding with the closet door came next, followed by the sharp fall of a body.

We flinched as Arty's hand pressed over mine on my lips. The footsteps retreated along with the clicking of dog nails on the linoleum floor in the kitchen. The back door clicked, and the screen door slammed shut behind them as laughter carried on outside.

"Wherever his daughter went, she has to be close."

"The priest said she hangs out with the boy who lives next door. We should take them both. He said the boy was strong."

I sucked in a breath. They were talking about us. Arty pressed his hand tight over my mouth.

"Did you check this house?"

Adrenaline worked like liquid fire, engulfing my limbs, Arty's arms tightened around my torso, forcing me to stay in place.

"Yes, nothing but one of those irritating felines. You know how I despise them."

"Don't let your hate for the animal life on the surface cloud your judgment. We are only here for one reason. Focus on the task at hand."

"Deston said, find the girl and move on to the next."

They want me. Why?

Their conversation continued, but they retreated. I could no longer make it out. I took a deep breath, and Arty moved his hand away from my mouth. His lips touched the sensitive outer edge of my ear.

"When the sun rises, we're out of here," Arty said. "We walk as far as we can for as long as we can."

I nodded my head. But what about my parents? He was right; we had to get out of this neighborhood. They were looking for us here, and someone at the church told them about us in hopes of saving themselves. People always sell each other out when the shit hits the fan.

The muscles in my body ached and groaned from being forced into a crouching position all night. When the time came to get up, I was going to be physically fucked.

The streetlights went out, and the color of the sun blazed its fiery oranges and reds across the sky. We were already out of the closet, and I was exhausted. I hadn't slept much the night before, and I didn't sleep last night. Now, Arty and I were going to walk god knows how far today.

Outside the closet, I looked down at our savior, Mrs. Vougher's dead cat. That thing kicked it so hard it killed him.

I choked on the pain in my chest. I went into Mrs. Vougher's bedroom and pulled out one of her many scarves. I wrapped it around the cat and put him in a shoebox.

"What are you doing?" Arty was impatient.

"If Mr. Wiggles hadn't been here, 'he' might've opened the closet door. You don't know, maybe this cat saved our lives. Mr. Wiggles didn't deserve to die because he was defending his house. The least we can do is give him a decent burial."

Arty didn't like Mr. Wiggles. He never liked cats. Always said they were backstabbing, two timers. I thought he was making it all up. Maybe he had an ax to grind? Based on an animation we saw as kids.

Out front, I scanned the street on both sides, looking for movement. It was only about 6:20 a.m. The likelihood that people were already out and in our neighborhood was pretty low.

There were more bodies on Mrs. Vougher's street. They were in front of almost every house, including hers. None of the bodies were of children. There weren't many kids in our neighborhood.

Wildflowers grew in Mrs. Vougher's front flower bed. They must've reseeded themselves after her husband had died. I set Mr. Wiggles down next to the flowers. He was probably the only one in the neighborhood to get a burial. Hot tears spilled down my face. I looked up at the carnage all over the road, sidewalk, and yards. Unshed tears burned in my eyes as they swallowed down the pressure in my throat.

"Should we go?" Arty's hand hung in the air, large and welcoming. I took it. For a moment, we could have been seven years old, walking to the park to play on the swings. Safe.

"I was thinking maybe we should head toward the city."

"Or check for my parents first." My reply was instant.

"The cities have more people to help keep us safe. Your dad said don't come back. I'm not going back, and neither are you." It's not like Arty to be bossy, and fresh tears welled in my eyes.

The world was pear-shaped. People didn't help each other.

"We need to find a town that looks like everybody in it is dead. Then we hide out in some building." His eyes scanned the other end of the street.

"And what if somebody else had the same idea?" I asked in a weak voice. He ran his fingers through his hair and released my hand.

I kicked at the dirt. My face turned to the fence in the backyard. I wanted to run across the grass and tear open my back door and...I didn't know what. What would Dad want me to do?

Live.

"I just think being in big city centers is a bad idea. My dad always said to stay away from the big cities. They'll run out of food fast, and people get violent." I crossed my arms holding my elbows.

He knew I was right. He just didn't want to go to some strange town. "All right, we'll go to Athens, but if I don't like it, I want to leave. It's a good idea to keep moving. Maybe we'll stay alive that way." He scratched the back of his neck and then looked around, letting both hands fall to his sides.

"I want to do one thing before we leave. I want to go to church. Somebody there ratted us out."

Arty nodded his head. The only people who knew I had been at home or even where I lived was the youth group. And the only reason they knew I was home was Arty.

There was no way they would've known I'd made it home. They could've assumed that I had been snatched up or killed. I could've been hiding anywhere. Arty called, and then Arty left. Someone there had to have ratted us out. The question was why?

We walked the few blocks to the church, past all the dead bodies. We should've taken the alleyways.

My answers came pretty quickly. Pastor Rollins' body knelt on the ground with an arrow through his chest, and the shaft was holding him up in a prone position. His white shirt had a dried blood color cascading down the front.

I hadn't eaten anything since the day before, but my diaphragm convulsed, and the acid bile clawed its way up my throat. I wanted to free the wrenching in my gut, but there was nothing. We hadn't bothered to eat any of Mrs. Vougher's food.

And there they were, or at least most of them.

Arty bit down on his knuckles as he tried to shove his fist down his throat.

"There's nothing you could've done. If you'd been here, you would be dead too." My face felt like a mask of fire, tears flowing like liquid magma. The ache in my throat spread down to my belly. I reached out for Arty's hand. He snatched it and dragged me into a tight hug.

"I know." His muffled whisper barely reached my ears.

I didn't want to bring myself to look Pastor Rollins over. His collar lay on the ground in front of him, and his shirt was torn open at the throat. Blood ran down from his eyes and his lips, and one of his eyes was swollen shut.

"I don't think our pastor would rat us out." Arty was always so kind and thought the best of people.

Arty released me, but we stayed close to each other.

"I don't think so either, but look, a couple of the kids are missing body parts. I think they did that to make him talk." The saliva pooled in my mouth again, giving me the swallows—the kind you get before you throw up.

Most of the kids were missing their hands, and they weren't close to their bodies. They'd bled to death. I whipped my head around searching, but the extremities weren't there. All the hands were gone.

All that pressure in my chest, I couldn't hold back any longer. I screamed.

All those kids, they were my friends. None of us were religious. My youth group wasn't about God and praying. We met every week to hang out; it was fun. The church was our safe hang out.

If I'd left earlier, I would've been home with Mom and Dad. I couldn't warn them. Would we be alive? But if I'd stayed here with the youth group, I still wouldn't be alive.

How did I get so lucky?

"Camille's gone. So is Nina. And Brad." Arty's tone told me what he thought. He hated Camille.

"Maybe they got away; maybe they left like you did." I moved to go inside, but I changed my mind. The fae had called them all out.

"No, Nina wouldn't have gone home. Her parents are out of town. Camille's dating Brad, and his car is still here.

They should be here. Brad wouldn't leave without his car." Arty waved his arms around, desperate for an answer.

It dawned on me; they must've taken them. "All those missing kids, I think they're taking them. They were looking for us, right?"

"Did you see all those kids on the news? Every single one of them was gorgeous, a jock superstar, strong and good-looking. Why do you think they're looking for us?"

Arty was strong, and when he wasn't wearing his glasses and hunching over, he was good-looking. Had he better coordination, I'm sure he'd be a jock. That wasn't how he saw himself.

"I'm not one of the beautiful people. I'm just boring old me." I shrugged my shoulders.

"You really are thick, Sarah. You probably gotta be one of the most beautiful girls in the entire school, and you're nice, which makes you pretty special. How do you think I've been friends with you for so many years? You're cool and smoking hot, and now you're wondering why they are looking for you? I'm sure Pastor Rollins told them where all the kids in the neighborhood live to save the few that were lying on the ground, missing their hands. And if I knew

Camille, she probably told them who was pretty and who wasn't. She is a self-centered harpy who would say anything to save her own skin."

I didn't think I was pretty. Arty was mistaken and need new eyeglasses. What he said about Camille was true. She was a snob and totally stuck-up. She'd always been a bitch to me, except when we were at youth group and she became a real person.

"Brad's car is still here, and they are not. Maybe his keys are still here." Arty wanted to drive Brad's car. It was a classic 1978 Camaro, drove fast, and had terrible gas mileage. I thought it made a lot of noise.

"Actually, I think we might be better off with Pastor Rollins' Jeep. If Brad's not here, neither are his keys." I said.

What he was suggesting made my stomach roll. Someone would have to go through his pocket where he kept his keys.

"Don't worry, I'll get the keys," Arty volunteered. "You don't have to do anything; it was my idea."

A lump formed in my throat and saliva filled my mouth. Arty knelt down on the ground in front of Pastor Rollins' dead body. He touched the front pockets on either side. The one on the left had what he wanted.

I watched Arty trying to work his hands into the pocket, but Pastor Rollins was small. Arty has big hands. There was no way he was going to get his hands inside. He looked up at me, and his eyebrows creased in frustration.

"Sorry. I can't get them out." He pulled back, dusting his knees off, only to rub them in blood. He worked his hand across the fabric of his pants over and over; he was desperate to rub it off.

Tears rolled down my face. I could do this. Don't think about him like a person. It was a mannequin. If I took them from behind, I wouldn't see his face. It wouldn't matter so much. I'd reach in and grabbed the keys. Deep breath in through my mouth and out my nose.

I squatted down behind Pastor Rollins, and slowly I worked my hand into the pocket of his black polyester slacks. The body was cold, and I kept looking away, trying to focus on the buildings across the street. His body was stiff. I wiggled my fingers around in the pocket, but it was empty. I removed my hand and took a deep breath. I started again on the other side.

No matter where my eyes landed, it was another dead body or severed limb. Nothing I did would take my mind off digging in a dead guy's pocket.

My fingers encountered a metallic object with etching, the key. I clasped it between my thumb and my index finger and pulled it out.

Just as the keys freed from his pocket, his body fell over on its side. He held shape like a stone statue. Lifeless and immovable.

I screamed and couldn't stop; it kept coming.

Arty was next to me with his arms around me. "It's okay. You did good. You got the keys. It's okay, you didn't hurt him." He whispered.

My breath came in gulps. "He's okay? I didn't hurt him?" The light breeze turned my hot tears into cold trails of water down my face.

"No, you didn't hurt him. Nothing can hurt him anymore. It's okay. Let's get the Jeep, and let's get out of here."

The rumbling of an engine broke the silence of our macabre death scene. We both dashed toward the parking lot and the hedge there. Cowering behind the hedge, I peeked through only to spy a big black Escalade with gold trim, slowly driving by. All of its windows were down, and they had guns peeking through the openings.

It was amazing how quickly and easily society broke down.

Arty tapped me on my shoulder and then pointed toward the black Jeep in the corner. We crouched behind every vehicle, moving slowly until we reached the Jeep. He opened the doors, and we both climbed in through the driver's side. We hunched down to wait for the Escalade to leave the area.

"Shit," Arty exclaimed.

"What's wrong?" I looked down at the steering wheel, pedals, and over all the dials before my eyes landed on the gear shifter.

"Stick. I can't drive stick." His shoulders slumped down. He was emasculated.

"You know, my dad said something about that couple years ago. He said 'kids these days don't know what's important.' " I smile at him and snickered.

"What are we gonna do? I don't I want to go back for more keys, do you?"

A ghoulish shiver gripped both of us.

"Don't worry. My dad taught me. I'll drive."

He exhaled a breath of relief, and we traded places. My left foot slowly released the clutch, putting us in reverse. The Jeep crept backwards, and I waited for the front end to clear the car next to us. When I pressed the clutch back in, I shifted into first gear and we took off.

CHAPTER 5

Driving down the street, I did my best to make sure I didn't look at what was on the road. I drove around the bodies, pretending they were logs, downed trees, or sticks left on the road—anything so I didn't think about the dead people lying in the street. It was working until we reached the grocery store.

It was a giant shopping plaza with a grocery store and other big box stores. Dad called them the McMansion stores. The parking lot was a bloodbath. Hundreds of bodies lay out like Lincoln Logs in front of the permanently blocked open doors. People had left their carts everywhere. Flies swarmed around the bodies, creating a loud, buzzing noise. I pulled my shirt up over my mouth to deaden the rancid, gagging stench. Arty reached over and turned off the AC and all the fans, and then he closed the vents. But the sickly-sweet scent of rotting flesh worked its way through the cracks. CJ Jeeps weren't known for being airtight. I pressed my foot down harder on the gas pedal. We didn't gain speed, but the RPMs shot through the roof. I pressed my left foot to the clutch and shifted gears, causing the Jeep to lurch forward.

We soon entered a commercial district. There weren't many people logs on the roads. I drove as fast down every street. It didn't matter if the light was red, green, or purple—I wasn't stopping.

Finally, Arty reached over and touched my arm. "It's okay, Sarah. Slow down. I think we're past the worst of it. Take this on-ramp to the highway. I don't see dead bodies on the road." Arty's hand grabbed hold of the holy-Jesus bar as I made a sharp turn, crossing two lanes of traffic to make the on-ramp.

Cars were on the shoulder on either side of the highway. When the Fae had come down out of the sky, they all pulled over? They made the drivers get out of their vehicles and…

Every Fae I'd seen was male. Didn't they have any girls? Was that why they were taking all the girls? I shook my head. It was too gross to think about.

I drove for about an hour. I worked my hands back and forth over the leather of the steering wheel. Driving was good. How we thought we could walk to Athens was a dumb idea. If you could drive, you should always drive. If you can't drive, then you walk. I looked at my shoes, and I realized what a moron I was. Little canvas shoes encased my feet. I might as well have not even been wearing shoes. I couldn't walk far in these, even if I wanted to; they didn't have arch support.

We should've gone back to my house. We could've looked for my parents. Then I wouldn't be driving down the road wearing the wrong shoes and hoping for the sign of a sporting goods store. One of the billboards on the side of the highway advertised for such a store. Even though I knew a plaza was probably going to be wall-to-wall, dead bodies, I couldn't walk anywhere in these shoes. We had to dump this cheap crap I was wearing.

"You sure you want to go in the store? I see you eyeballing that sporting goods store." I saw Arty gripping the door handle and whitening his knuckles.

"Yeah, see my shoes?" I slammed my left foot on the clutch and downshifted with my right, grinding a gear as I went.

"Yeah, I guess mine aren't in much better shape." Arty's tennis shoes were probably about a thousand years old. The rubber was peeling back in various directions. I thought he'd thrown them on to run out the house. Who pays attention to their shoes at the end of the world? Normally when we hung out, it didn't matter which pair he wore. Now it did.

I took a right turn at the end of the off-ramp and drove fifty yards down the road, heading toward the sporting goods sign. I slowed down to turn into the parking lot when Arty's hand landed on my forearm.

I noticed the vehicles had pulled up into a line in front of the store. Twenty men wearing saggy Chino pants and bandannas around their heads stood out front with guns—gang bangers. The store was clearly taken; there was no way we were getting in there for a pair of shoes. My heart shifted gears with the Jeep as I tore out of there. A bullet ricocheted off the back end.

But I had to have a pair of shoes. I wouldn't get far with what I had. My soles were too thin, and if my feet became wet, well, forget about it. Let's not even talk about foot rot.

"Arty, get on your phone. Look up the nearest biker store."

He gasped. "So you don't want to go to the sporting goods store because it's being guarded by a gang, but you think it might be a good idea to go to a biker store because that might not be guarded by a gang?" The sarcasm dripped from his voice. I didn't mind being mocked if I deserved it, and I did.

"All I know is this: you can walk a pretty good distance in a pair of biker boots. Most of them are steel-toed, and if you kick somebody with them, it's going to hurt like a motherfucker."

Arty shook his head and seemed to agree. "Turn left up here."

"That'll take us to a mall?" The muscles in my legs and arms tensed in anticipation. I ran through all the moves I'd need to do to shift gears and get the hell out of there in a hurry. I wasn't that great a driver, and this was the longest I'd ever been behind the wheel of a stick shift.

"Yes, there's a lot of stores at the mall. Something else they sell at the mall, shoes—lots and lots of shoes. Really good hiking, walking, and kicking the crap out of people shoes." Arty liked to make fun of me, but I didn't like to shop at the mall. It wasn't my favorite place.

"Yeah, that's assuming that the mall isn't guarded by armed guards too."

"Every major department store at the mall sells shoes. We just need to get into one of them."

I guess Arty was right. It'd be easier to sneak into one of the entrances of the major department stores and snag a couple of pairs of shoes. If we were lucky, the shoe department would be right next to the door.

We discovered the mall was guarded on one end. I stayed on the perimeter road, doing no more than eight to ten miles an hour. The perimeter road was lined with trees providing shade that we used for cover.

"Hey, have we got binoculars in that backpack?" I took my foot off the gas, allowing us to coast.

"I don't think so, maybe." He leaned over the center console to rummage through the backpacks. "Holy crap, your dad really was prepared. Was he a Boy Scout?" He snickered.

"No, he was an Eagle Scout." I snickered back.

Arty put the binoculars to his face, scanning the mall entrances. He extended his right hand, pointing off to the far left.

"Pull over there. By that bunch of cars near the door, and I don't see anybody around."

This end had cheaper stores like the stores no one wanted to shop at. I wove around the parked cars in the parking lot. Funny how we all seemed to park together in clusters near the doors. No one wants to park in no man's land and walk a thousand miles. I pulled in between a big black truck and a silver minivan. With no car parked in front of us, we could pull straight through for a quick getaway. Keeping low, we crept from one vehicle to the next. We made a quick dash to the door. Before Arty could reach for the handle, I pulled him back.

"Can we watch for a few minutes? There might be somebody inside." I felt the valves in my heart opening and closing, pumping blood to every vein. My eyes darted from the glass doorway to the shaded perimeter road. We were so exposed. I was terrified someone was going to drive by and see us.

But no one did. The store looked deserted so we snuck in. We wove our way around the clothing racks, stopping every few minutes to listen for footsteps or noises until we reached the shoe department.

Arty leaned over and whispered in my ear. "Are you kidding me, sandals? All they have is sandals? Huaraches aren't going to cut it for me, you can't walk anywhere in those."

I threw him a half smile as I surveyed the collection of strappy sandals and mule style wedges. I pointed to the exit of the store and the rest of the mall. We moved that direction, and I peeked out. It was deserted, and as luck would have it there was a high-end shoe store right across from the department store.

Taking a deep breath, I closed my eyes and counted to three. I scanned the hall and made a dash for it. I seized a pair of Timberland boots. They worked for me since they were easy to lace up and had good ankle support. They looked kind of like something my dad would've worn. Arty got a similar pair. I grabbed some stainless-steel water bottles so we could use them to warm food by throwing in the fire. Arty patted my back, and we headed out.

Working our way back through the department store to the door we'd come in, we crossed the outdoor section of the department store. I pulled a fleece jacket off the rack and tied it around my waist. Arty grabbed a pop-up tent and threw it over the shoulder. There were so many supplies that we could've used, but I didn't want to be weighed down.

We waited at the sides of the doors for signs of movement. When we saw nothing, we headed back to the Jeep. I did my best to make sure I wasn't looking around too much. While dead bodies littered the parking lot, but I was perplexed why the store had been empty. "Why did they all go outside?" My hands gripped the steering wheel.

"Maybe the Fae told them to?"

I think Arty was smarter than he let on. It made perfect sense why all the cars were parked on the side of the road and everyone was out in the street. They sang, and people walked out like zombies. They did whatever the music told them too. It was awful. How come it didn't work on me? I heard the Fae singing, and I stopped for a couple of seconds. But then I was like no big deal and suddenly I was able to run. Was I immune?

CHAPTER 6

I thought we escaped out of the mall situation pretty well. We had more supplies and good shoes. Now to head off into the wild blue yonder. I was pretty sure Arty and I were gonna be okay. As long as I didn't think about what happened to my parents or where they could be.

All we needed to do was find a good building to hunker down in, until the sun went down. It was only 2 p.m., and we had plenty of time to find a place.

Hindsight is 20/20. I should've realized that going on the main roads was stupid. I should've realized that eventually, someone from the mall would've spotted us leaving the area. But I was only seventeen. I wouldn't officially become an adult for a few months. How was I supposed to know? I wasn't checking my six. I didn't look behind me, and I should've looked behind me. I should've known. Arty should've looked behind us, but neither of us had done any of that.

We turned back on to the main thoroughfare heading toward the highway. It was a good plan, and it should've worked. All we needed to do was keep going toward the highway, right?

I looked in the rearview mirror. The sunlight glinted off of something in the road, but I ignored it. There were always little bits of trash left over from car accidents, and some of it was reflective. I rolled across something, and the wheel yanked to the right and left. The back into the Jeep fishtailed.

It was one of those police spike strips; the kind they throw down when they want to stop somebody who's driving too fast. They pretty much shred your tires. Usually, in the movies, the vehicle goes across a strip, and they swerve and flip up in the air. The car rolls over and over, and it seems like everybody inside the vehicle should die. But they're all just fine with a few bumps and bruises. They get out of the car, and they run from the cops.

That wasn't what happened; the movies were all bullshit. What happened was I didn't see the spike strip, and I drove right over it. Yeah, it shredded my tires. Blood thundered in my ears as I slammed my foot into the clutch and shifted gears. I was worried I'd lose control of the Jeep. My skin crawled with the screaming sound of metal.

"Oh, fuck, fuck!" Arty kept cursing over and over again.

I felt the squished rubber underneath the rims sliding us this way and that. I yanked the wheel to the left and then again to the right, trying to keep us in a straight line. My arms ached, and they shook as I gripped the wheel, white-knuckled. But then the vehicle righted itself suddenly, and all that rubber that was on the rims was gone. Instead, the metal rims ground as it slipped across the asphalt. There was no way to stop.

"Holy shit! Stop the Jeep!" Arty had one foot up on the dashboard, and his hand on the headrest of my seat.

"If we stop the Jeep now, whoever put that out there is probably going to kill us. Anyway, without any rubber, you don't have brakes. You can push all you want on those rims, but they're not going to stop. We'll slide down the road or grind or whatever it is until the momentum of the vehicle stops." I pumped the gas with my right foot, keeping us going without grinding the ground.

"Whoever put that spike strip down can have all this shit. I don't care."

I didn't stop, and I wasn't gonna stop. I didn't care what Arty said. Whoever shredded our tires wanted whatever it was they thought we had. Maybe the Jeep, maybe something else, or maybe me. Fear butterflied in my belly. "Pull up MapQuest, and tell me where the nearest neighborhood and take us there. We need to find another suburb."

Arty fingers worked across the screen of his phone. "If you can make a left turn without flipping the car, turn left and then left again two streets from now." His eyes never left the screen.

I did as instructed, and we were transported from the commercial district into a quiet sleepy suburb. All the dead log bodies were on the road again. I didn't want to, but I drove over them, slowing down with every bump. I couldn't swerve as I was trying to make sure that we were able to stop. Whoever was following us was gonna find us pretty quick. Between the screeching sound from the rims and the burn lines in the asphalt, we weren't hard to follow.

If we didn't stop soon, the sparks from the metal grinding on the ground would heat up the Jeep's gas tank and start a fire or better yet blow up.

There it was, what I was looking for: a four-wheel drive, Chevy pickup truck. My father would've approved. It was a dually with diesel, which meant we were more likely to find fuel for it. Most people go straight for the gasoline vehicles. They leave the diesel alone.

The Jeep slid to a stop about two houses away from the truck. I saw the owner's dead body lying in the yard. I looked at Arty, and I knew what had to be done. I had to do it.

"Start putting stuff in the truck. I'll get the keys." I swallowed the excess saliva that found its way into my mouth.

"Are you sure? I could do it. You don't have to do it. I could rip the pocket right off his pants."

I shook my head. I pictured Arty ripping the pocket open and causing the body to flop. I took a deep breath and swallowed. I walked over to the dead guy lying in the yard. The grass squished as I stepped on it. A giant puddle of blood had saturated all the grass around him. Now it was getting all over my brand-new shoes. I guess it had to happen sometime with all the dead people around. My shoes were bound to get blood on them eventually.

He looked like he'd been a nice man, clean-cut, and well-dressed. I didn't know what killed him, but it was clearly on the backside of his body. His lifeless eyes stared up at me, and he hadn't been touched by the birds or the dogs yet. He must've died last night.

My eyes darted away. I didn't want to look at him anymore. I reached into his right-hand pocket since most people are right-handed. There wasn't a key, but it was one of those fobs you set inside the car and it turns on. I pulled it out, pushing the button to unlock the doors.

"Great! Let's get out of here!" Arty was already in the driver's seat. An automatic—I didn't need to drive. I let out a relieved sigh as my nerves were totally shot. I didn't want to drive. I was scared if I pushed the gas pedal, it'd be to the floor nonstop until I didn't see another human, dead or alive, forever.

The truck roared to life as we headed out of the community in the other direction. I ran the Navigator on MapQuest.

"Still going to Athens?" Arty asked.

"If we can make it there without someone shredding our tires or trying to kill us, that's the plan." I looked down at my shoes, I'd got a little bit of blood on the tip of my boot. I opened the glove box, and there was a packet of baby wipes. I pulled one out to rub off the blood, but it didn't work. It was stained, but at least now it was brown instead of red. I tossed the baby wipe out the window.

"You did really good driving back there," Arty said. "I would've stopped, and we'd probably both be dead."

I nodded my head and stared at the road. It eventually entranced me, and I leaned my head over to sleep.

When I woke up, it was close to twilight. The truck was idling, and Arty stood on the side of the road, taking a whiz. He whipped his head this way and that. I guess he was trying to keep an eye out while peeing. I saw him redo his drawers and then jump back in the truck.

As he was about to touch the steering wheel, I shrieked. "You don't touch that! Wait a minute, I'll get you a baby wipe."

He stared at me sheepishly, holding his hands up as if he was a doctor getting ready to go into the operating room. I handed him a baby wipe. The last thing in the world I wanted was man pee on the steering wheel! What if I have to drive?

"Thanks. I didn't get pee on my hands." He flipped them over so I could see both sides.

"I know, but still the idea that there might be a little drop of urine on your hand and then you touch steering wheel—disgusting. Now please, wipe the door handle, inside and out."

"Well, they say germs are what kills you first. So let's stay safe for Sarah."

I punched him in the shoulder. "Where are we?"

"We're about fifteen miles outside of Athens. Sorry, I just couldn't hold it anymore. I had to pee. Anyway, you were sleeping, and there was nobody here. I haven't seen another house, or soul, for probably an hour."

"That's good. Maybe we can just pull up to the first house we see and move in."

"I was thinking about that. I think whatever house we go to, we need to make sure there are dead bodies in the front yard." I sat there and stared straight ahead. I had been feeling hungry until he said that.

"Any particular reason why you want to live like a necrophiliac?" I shrugged my shoulders in a grimace. "I don't want to." His hand was on my shoulder, but I shrugged it off.

"As long as there is a dead body in the front yard, the Fae will think they've already cleared the house. But if we bury them or move the bodies, they'll come looking again because they'll know somebody has been there. I don't want to live around a corpse either. I don't want to smell it, and I don't want anything to do with it, but we have to be smart."

He was right, as disgusting as it sounded and as much as I knew it was going to be awful. As long as everything looked untouched, whatever building we'd in we'd be safe, in theory.

Athens resembled a village after it had been struck down by a barbarian hoard. Human logs were all over the roads. The only street spared was Main Street. All the professional offices were closed by the time the Fae landed. The residents had gone home, and they were probably getting ready to go to bed like everyone else.

We crawled to the edge of town and then circled back around the outside. Arty spotted a cottage on the outskirts with one person in front—dead.

"That looks like a good one; quiet and off to the side." He averted his eyes from the human log, but it was all I could think about.

Everything about the town was quiet, tumbleweed perfect.

"Let me jump out, Arty. I'll go check it out and make sure it's safe. You drive around the block. If my gun goes off, obviously it's not safe and don't come back." I didn't feel brave, but I didn't want Arty to get hurt. Stopping the truck, even for us to trade places, could be catastrophic. It was a smart move, and we needed to be smart.

"Are you out of your mind? I'm not leaving you here. I promised your dad. He said to take care of you." Arty's bicep flexed as his hands gripped the steering wheel.

"Really? What are you like two seconds older than me? I know you told my dad you'd look out for me, but we need to work as a team and treat each other as equals. Otherwise, you're gonna get overworked, overtired, and we're both dead. For that, we need teamwork and strategy. Your part is to drive the truck around the block. If you don't hear a gunshot by the time you come back around, it means it's okay." I left out the part where we were fucked. No need to freak him out.

Before Arty could argue, I opened the door and practically jumped out of a moving truck.

Luckily, I landed on one foot but pitched forward. I managed to get my other foot underneath me, slowing my momentum. It wasn't very smart to jump out of a moving truck. Maybe I should've waited for Arty to slow down. If there was anybody hiding on this street, I was pretty sure they knew I was here. I didn't see any need to run around hiding and pretending.

I pulled my gun from my holster and flipped the safety off.

I approached the cottage from the side as if somebody could miss me. I was no ninja. I walked up, bold as brass. The front door was open, but the screen door was closed. The inside was relatively clean, and it didn't have any funny smells. The human log out front was a woman, and I guessed she lived alone. I didn't see any signs of a cat, a dog, or a man. The house consisted of two bedrooms and food in the fridge.

A fine place to hole up for now. The sun was going down, and we didn't have enough time to look for anything else. I stepped out the back door, whipping my head left and right. I had to be sure there was nobody around.

The rumble from the diesel engine cut off suddenly as Arty parked the truck down the road. He brought our supplies inside. I stared at him through the back screen door.

"Do you really think it's a good idea to put all our eggs in one basket? Maybe we should leave some stuff in the truck just in case we need to make a getaway? That way we're not totally screwed leave the camping stuff there."

He shrugged a shoulder.

"Yeah, I didn't really think about that. I'll take the camping stuff back. Good idea. What about all the weapons?" He gripped the AR-15 by the barrel tip.

Arty knew how to shoot a gun, but he didn't have a lot of respect for one. I made a mental checklist to get a medkit. Especially something with superglue—lots of superglue. I was certain Arty was going to accidentally shoot his foot off.

"I don't want to leave weapons in the vehicle. We can replace camping gear easily enough, but ammo and guns you can't anywhere. They are probably all guarded by a posse."

He nodded his head and dropped the big black duffel bag and my backpack. He double-timed the camping gear back to the truck. I heard the beep as he locked it up.

Arty pulled the screen door open and took four purposeful steps into the living room. He clipped the fob on my belt loop. I holstered my gun. The butterflies in my belly pulled me to hold on to it. But if it was in your hands and you jump, you're more likely to shoot someone on accident.

"I'm not leaving without you, and you're not leaving without me," Arty said. "It's just better you have the truck keys. This way I can't lose them, and I know you won't drive off without me." His eyebrows were squished together in seriousness, and his jaw set.

I smiled. "What makes you so sure that I won't drive off without you? You piss me off bad enough, I might leave your dumb ass here." We both burst out laughing. He knew I wouldn't drive off without him.

Who wants to face the Fairy apocalypse alone?

I slept most of the afternoon away in the truck so I wasn't tired. After the sun went down, it was ten o'clock when I heard something outside.

Arty grabbed his gun, and we both crouched down. We crept to a closet by the back stairs to the basement. I suppose we could've gone down, but if a fairy decided to search the house, I was sure the basement was the first place they'd look.

Truthfully, hiding in a closet doesn't give you a lot of safety either. Whoever it was that was running around, they didn't stay long. They took off, and everything quieted down. The rest of the evening was a lot of us jumping at strange noises from the house.

In the morning when the sun came up, I unfolded myself from the closet, as did Arty. I took the stairs, two by two, and flopped down on the closest bed to sleep. Arty was sleeping for a couple of hours when I woke up and it was closer to noon.

We made breakfast and turned on the television. Apparently, the Fae had struck all over the planet.

One of the commentators said, "If the Fae invaders keep this up, the extinction of the human race is a very real possibility."

The local news revealed a list of missing people, all kids mostly between the ages of sixteen and twenty-one, and the list had grown longer. It didn't cover just the suburbs. Some of these kids were missing from the city.

"Wealthy real estate developer Richard Dubois and his wife are desperate for any information on their daughter, Britney Dubois. There's a million dollar reward for help in locating her. Last known whereabouts were Heathrow Airport in London."

It was strange. I wondered how many kids were taken that nobody was looking for. The pictures scrolled across the screen like an unending parade of Miss Teen America contestants.

"The kids aren't missing," a woman said on the television. "I watched them, the Fairies, Fae, whatever they're called, put them on one of those round craft things and disappear." The woman was wide-eyed and disheveled. She had scratches and bruises on her arms and face.

"There you have it, folks. An eyewitness account of a Fairy abduction."

A few moments later, someone released an actual video. It was grainy like it'd been shot through a window screen in the dark. I watched with a dry mouth as the tall willowy creatures led some kids onto their platform. One of the creatures turned toward the camera and in the full light of streetlights, I got a clear vision of him. Large glowing blue eyes like sapphires, and white hair with pointed ears sticking up between his thick hair. His hair hung down on either side of his shoulders. Even with the blur of the camera, you could see how beautiful he was. With high cheekbones and full lips, he brandished a sword in one hand, and he held a girl's arm in the other. He'd been singing, and she wasn't struggling against him. She stood there limp like a rag doll. Her eyes were glazed over wide, and she'd do whatever he wanted.

The Fae carried on with that singsong fairytale music I heard, "Mary, Mary, quite contrary, how does your garden grow? With bluebells, and cockle shells, and skeletons all in a row." The tone was flat and lost on me.

I didn't understand the connection between the creepy nursery rhymes and the Fae. They didn't even sing them right.

"That wasn't Mary, Mary, quite contrary. I don't know what nursery rhyme that was." It made me so angry that I stamped my foot and got up and left the room

"It's okay if they can't quote nursery rhymes." Arty splayed his hands out and shrugged his shoulders.

"Really? Do you really think that's what the problem is?" I shook my head while tapping my foot on the floor. I took a couple of deep breaths to try to remove the heat from my chest.

"No, I know that's not the problem, but it's just some creepy Fae. They can sing misquoted nursery rhymes. You don't need to get angry about it?" He patted the couch seat next to him.

"I'm not angry about them misquoting nursery rhymes. It's just creepy. What's more, he's not misquoting. What if we've been misquoting?" I gasped my own revelation. Why would I say that?

Arty didn't reply. I splashed a bunch of water from the kitchen sink on my face.

"No way. I need to get out of this building. I'm sick of being stuck here all night. There's nobody in this town, and we haven't heard anything more than a squeak since we arrived. I want to go walk around. I'll be safe. I have my gun. If I have a problem, I'll call you." I took my phone out and shook it. Arty lowered his eyes and looked away. He didn't like the idea of me getting out of the house.

I wasn't trying to get away from him. It wasn't about him. I knew my parents were probably dead, and his parents were dead. Everybody we'd ever known was probably dead. And we were sitting there, hiding in a closet, night after night, and hoping that some Fae wouldn't kill us.

I freaked out when I thought about the nursery rhymes. That level of creepy didn't work for me.

I slugged on my pack, rubbing my left foot against my right for the bulk of my ankle holster. I reached inside my coat for the 380. I held it in my right hand, released the clip, double checked my bullet count, and slammed it home. I chambered one round. The weight of it in my holster under my arm comforted me. The feel of it in my hand kept the helplessness at bay.

Three blocks away was Main Street. The lack of bodies on the street lulled me. This old town was cute. The sidewalks were clean, and every tree had a little fence around the base. The streetlights resembled carriage lights from the heyday of the electric bulb. The traffic light in the middle of the street length flashed red for the four-way stop. The town felt like a magic bubble of normalcy. That all came to an end at the corner of Main and Juniper. The sickly, rotten smell of meat left out too long wafted from the doors of the corner diner. The patrons were all dead. Some of them had never even got up from their table. There were three in a row across the bar. I pulled my sleeve down over my hand, and I put it up over my nose and mouth. With streaming tears, I reached over and pulled the door shut.

The rest of the street held stores. I began humming my own little ditty, one I made up years ago. I helps me calm down and take my mind off my problems.

I crossed the street and picked one. I went inside and found they had a little bit of everything. A little junk, a little grocery, and a little hardware. It got my mind thinking, what was in the rest of the stores?

CHAPTER 7

It amazed me how many of the stores around were left open. People were gone, and everything was wide open. The only things locked were the offices. I did see a pharmacy, but the windows were smashed in. The druggies would've pilfered the dispensary for Oxycodone, Fentanyl, and Xanax; things like that. Picking my way through the store, I stepped between the glass shards on the dusty epoxied floor. A tumbled pile of red plastic shopping baskets lay on the floor along with real estate magazines and weekly shoppers flyers. I grabbed a basket and began picking items off the shelves. I stopped at the First Aid aisle and picked up a kit, along with a bottle of iodine and rubbing alcohol. The cotton balls lay across the floor alongside rolls of gaze.

A fire ax lay on the floor in front of the pharmacy counter. They'd used it to hack out the cabinets. The wind whistled around the cavernous store. Closing my eyes, I waited for god knows what. All I was met with was the darkened silence. I crawled through the opening. The druggies had strewn the bottles on the floor. Stepping over boxes and broken shards, I picked my way down every aisle. I grabbed bottles with the words ending in 'cillin'. The painkillers were gone. I was sure I could've taken more, but what about the next guy?

I guess running away from Arty was a dumb idea. I took a couple of deep breaths and headed back to the cottage. Arty was still inside, watching the television, but really watching the windows and watching for me. "Are you better, Sarah?" His wide eyes stared at me through his glasses. He nervously pushed them back on his nose.

"I guess. I mean sometimes you just need a couple of minutes alone to get your head straight, right?"

Arty nodded his head with his eyes wide. He'd never been much into privacy. As a child, he didn't have a problem barging into my house. Maybe it wasn't just me, and he was like that with everybody else? I never paid attention to how

Arty treated other people. He was my best friend. I didn't need to know more than that.

"I'm filthy, and I've been wearing the same clothes for three days," I announced. "I'm going upstairs to take a shower and change into something else."

He nodded and then went back to watching television. I knew that most guys, with the world going to hell in a handbasket, would've tried to make a move or something, but not Arty. I was surprised. Everybody could be headed for death, and most guys didn't want to die a virgin. Arty was definitely a virgin, and so was I. I wanted to wait. I didn't want to be one of those girls everybody at school slept with. I didn't want to be one of the girls who fall in love and never dates anybody else. I'd rather spend my whole life on the sidelines waiting rather than rushing myself. Arty was either a gentleman or oblivious, I wasn't sure which.

Shucking off my grimy clothes was a blessing really. I still had dirt on my face from the tunnel and blood on my shoe and probably elsewhere. I didn't want to look for it. A little hot water would clean it all away. I wanted to pretend for a little while that the world was a normal place.

I closed my eyes and imagined my mother downstairs making breakfast. But the hot water ran out, as did my fantasy. The previous homeowner hadn't heard of hot water on demand.

Judging from the clothes in the closet, nothing looked like it'd been made in the past decade, except for a pair of sweatpants. I grabbed them and put them on along with a T-shirt.

I mounted the stairs with my clothes under one arm and a terrycloth bathrobe over my shoulder.

"Arty, take off your clothes—" I said, causing his eyes to rise and his eyebrows to shoot up to the ceiling, "—and put on this bathrobe so I can wash your clothes."

"For a minute there, I thought you were asking me to take off all my clothes for...not that." He pulled his shirt over his head and threw it at me.

I started laughing. "If I ask you to take off all your clothes, I'll have a reason, trust me. Anyway, that's gross. You're like my brother."

He chuckled low. "You're not exactly my sister, but yeah, it'd be kind of weird. But thanks for thinking of me and washing my clothes."

I smiled at him as he left the room and headed into the bathroom to change. He was probably hopeful. Sorry to burst your bubble, Arty.

What came out of the bathroom was the funniest thing I'd ever seen. I couldn't stop laughing. The world was ending, and Arty was going to be caught dead in a fluffy pink bathrobe with polka-dotted, fluffy trim.

"Are you sure that's what you want to wear?" I crossed my arms to keep my belly from hurting.

"What, it's soft! Anyway, it's only until my clothes are dry. Then I'll be Arty the badass again." He shrugged his shoulders and strolled to the living room. He plopped on the couch, throwing his feet on the coffee table.

I threw our clothes into the washing machine—nothing fancy; just a quick wash to get the grime out. I'd apparently fallen a couple of times somewhere. The grass stains on my knees told me so. Arty's T-shirt had dirt on it from the tunnel. I sprayed that spot treatment crap on everything. After the water was already running over the clothes, it dawned on me that the room was missing something—a dryer. My eyes strayed out the back door and landed on it—a clothesline. Great. Maybe next door had a dryer.

My eyes darted to the horizon and with the sun in its place, we had maybe two hours tops.

"Arty, this cottage doesn't have a dryer. I have to take our clothes next door."

I saw him sneak a glance outside. "You sure you want to go with it getting so close to twilight? I'd feel much better if you didn't. How long do you think it'll take those clothes to dry?"

I looked at him and shook my head. "I don't know. We both have jeans. They always take longer like drying towels. But I'd rather have partially dry clothes I could potentially run away in, than be stuck wearing a pair of oversized sweatpants and you in a fluffy terrycloth bathrobe."

He looked at his digs. He put his hands in the front pockets and shrugged his shoulders. He sheepishly looked back up at me. "Maybe I should put my boots on, just in case I gotta run. I don't have to run out barefoot and in a pink bathrobe."

I gave him a half smile with a little snort. "Yeah, I think putting your shoes on might be a good idea. Those shoes were hard-fought."

The back door slammed behind me as I headed over to the house next door. I entered through the rear, and as luck would have it, it was the laundry room. The problem was, they line-dried too.

Really?

I ran through the yard, jumping the fence to the house next door. They had a dryer, thank god. I chucked everything in and turned it on. We need to get this done before... I had to be back. I sat next to the back door, keeping an eye out.

The day had been clear and bright, and I had noticed that in the evening these days it always seemed to turn misty. The lower the sun sank in the sky, the more of a heavy fog formed around the area. It was enough to cut visibility. I couldn't see more than a block or so. It was creepy with the idea that fairytale creatures were running around and out there killing people. Judging from the position of the sun, I guessed there were only ten minutes left. My clothes had dried for only thirty minutes, but I couldn't wait any longer. I opened the dryer and pulled out the clothes. I shoved them in the bag and headed to the cottage.

I ran at breakneck speed with the duffel bag on my back bouncing around with every step, which threw my rhythm off. That was when it dawned on me—I hadn't brought a gun.

I'd taken off my ankle holster for the shower. I'd left both my guns in the bathroom upstairs in the cottage. Stupid, stupid, stupid. I put on a fresh burst of speed, approaching the second fence. Timing my steps just right, I leaped.

"Jack be nimble, Jack be quick, Jack jumped over the candlestick. Hey, diddle, diddle, the cat and the fiddle, the cow jumped over the moon."

Aww fuck, it had to be one of them with their stupid nursery rhymes.

In slow motion, I watched in horror as the leg of my saggy sweatpants hooked on the top of the chain-link fence. Gravity worked against me, and I slammed face first into the ground. I rolled over and pulled at my leg several times, hoping it would dislodge itself. I was stuck.

With a pounding heart, I pushed off the ground with both hands, slipping to the side in the mud to stand on my free leg. My fingers worked at the fabric, but out of nowhere two violet eyes with pointy ears and white hair peered into my face.

"Hello, pretty girl. I've been looking for you." He gave me a devilish smile with his full lips and a deep-throated laughed.

My heart clench as my mouth open to scream.

Arty screamed instead. "Run, Sarah! Just run! Don't worry about me." He hadn't even fired a shot. They knew right where we were. They had to have known.

The Fae didn't bother to unhook my sweatpants from the chain-link fence. He grabbed my arms and pulled me along. The tearing sound of fabric followed me.

"Oh, you ruined your frock. How sad for you."

All I could do was glare at him through the mud on the side of my face.

Why, oh, why did I take a shower? Here I am three hours later, filthy again. I should've stayed in my dirty clothes. Then I would've had my gun, and I could've shot this Fae right through the eye.

"Nothing to say? Cat got your tongue?" He had a firm grip on my arm, but he wasn't trying to hurt me. Though his words irritated me, they had a singsong quality.

"No, the cat hasn't got my tongue. I'm being stolen away by a pixie."

He stopped dead in his tracks and straightened slowly. He turned his head to the side, giving me a side view of his face. One violet eye pierced me. "If you truly knew what a pixie was, you'd never call me one. They are flesh eaters disguised as flowers."

I felt a chill run down my back. Something about the way he said it, I had no desire whatsoever to meet a pixie, ever.

He dragged me out toward the street between the human logs lying there. One of their rafts hovered above the surface of the street.

There were two monsters on the raft, and they really were monsters. They had two legs but one arm each. One eye dominated the center of their foreheads, like a weird Cyclops.

They were covered in bulbous, weeping boils. Their mahogany colored skin stretched tight over bulging muscles with sharp shining teeth filling their gaping maws. I shivered. Were they going rip me apart?

I dug my feet into the ground, pushing at the arm that held me.

"Let me go! No, don't take me! I won't go with you."

He turned around and sang to me, but it didn't do anything. I kept kicking him and digging my feet into the grass until we reached the street. My feet dragged across the asphalt, and he raised an eyebrow

"Bind her, she's a resistor." He turned and glanced at me with his evil, violet eyes. "Meet the Fomorians." He opened his hand, sweeping his arm as if to encompass the raft and its occupants.

I assumed he was referring to the hideous creatures that took my arms as he thrust me at them. I stumbled and almost hit the edge of the raft.

The creatures' hands were slimy and cold. It was gross like being touched by a wet washcloth. I cringed away, but with one holding me, the other bound me, turning my body over and wrapping me like a spider does a fly. They laid me on my side on the raft.

There's no way I'm getting away.

I heard the musical singing in the background and watched as Arty turned into a mindless zombie. He climbed up onto the raft and sat next to me. He stared through me like nobody was home. A whimper escaped my lips, I guess he forgot to put his earplugs back in; too busy watching television.

We were so close. If only we'd waited a little bit longer and been a little more careful. I was such a fool.

"We must go to the other towns and sweep them for challengers. Once we're done and the sun begins to rise, we will head home with our prizes." The violet-eyed Fae sang something, and we moved.

The raft was round, and the floor of it was lined with flagstones. It appeared to have mushrooms around the outer edge. I lay there with my face planted into the floor. One of the Fomorians creatures leaned over, his eye staring directly into one of mine.

"Would you like to sit?" His face was blank of emotions.

"If it means I'll get a better look at you so I can figure out how to kill you, yes." My heart raced with my bravado.

A dry huffing sound escaped his lips. "He, he, he. You will never be strong enough to kill one of us, silly human. You resistor, you're defective."

I didn't want to start arguing with them. I could see that it would be useless. Who argues with a half-wit? He was probably hoping to bait me into an argument. What if he hurt Arty because of it?

I gritted my teeth as one of the Fomorians grabbed my shoulder, yanking me up. I sat on my butt with bent knees. I couldn't wrap my arms around myself. I leaned my head on my kneecaps and looked over at Arty, willing him to wake up so we could get away.

They were gonna kill us, I was pretty sure of it. I could tell by the way they talked to me that we were nothing more than cattle with no value whatsoever. There had to be another reason for taking us. If we didn't have a use, they'd kill us like everybody else.

They hopscotched us to what must've been fifteen different towns as they gathered up other zombie-like pretty girls and strong boys. It was all they wanted. I didn't see them kill anybody, thank goodness. At last, the sun's fiery fingers reached out toward me. I stared at it, hoping with all my heart that they'd leave Arty and I behind.

"Take a good look, Sarah. It's probably the last time you'll see it." The Fae's words pricked at my eyes, and my lips quivered. "Say goodbye to your world."

Was he right?

He sang a beautifully haunting song. It wasn't just musical notes; he sang of his home and flowers I'd never heard of. About love and loss, battles, about his queen and her beauty. Most of all, the magic of the Fae and how Tuatha Dé Danann ruled the world. His final line.

"Take us home to the hallowed hills." As his voice reached the crescendo, there was a loud pop. My vision twisted, and we disappeared from our world, only to reappear somewhere else.

We were surrounded by greens, yellows, oranges, and purples, all the vibrant colors of the rainbow. They glowed like Day-Glo at a rave with everybody waving around glow sticks. It was everywhere, the plants, and the trees. The markings on the Fae were like he had a glow-in-the-dark tattoo that only showed up in black light. His eyes glowed. They were still purple, but his irises were white and his hair was illuminated around his face.

"Welcome to the land of the Fae, Sarah."

My eyes ate up the sights surrounding me. Plants covered the cavernous landscape. Butterflies and dragonflies flittered everywhere painted in neon colors and lite by a black light. The hallowed hills of Fae were an illuminated, psychedelic rave.

CHAPTER 8

A Fomorian picked me up by the ropes that were wrapped around my waist carrying me like a purse. It was all I could do to keep my feet from dragging on the ground. Animals. Unbelievable, just being next to them was torture. They smelled like a cross between rotting flesh and wet mucus. It was enough to make me want to hurl. The only time I ever smelled anything like that was when I went into the garage after the power had been out for three days. The freezer meat had rotted. It was awful.

The monsters were covered in a thin film of slime, and with every step my body banged against the slimy, mahogany monster. The rest of the captives weren't treated like me. The Fairy whistled something, and the kids stood in unison. It was Stepford Wives creepy. The Fomorian walked for a long time, and I got tired of holding my feet up. I let my feet drag on the ground while my brand-new shoes scraped ruts behind me. Maybe whatever the equivalent of soil they had here would rub the blood spot off the tips. I needed to save my energy. At the other end of this, I'd get a chance to get away.

We approached some kind of shed or barn. I'd always lived in the suburbs. Dad took me camping, but it wasn't like we spent much time in the country. So far, the most time I'd spend in the country was the two days at best.

The purple-eyed Fae whistled something, and the boys, along with Arty in his pink bathrobe, filed into the stable. Tears brimmed in my eyes; it was all my fault. Other guys were there too, standing or sitting. All of them looked lost and clueless.

I struggled against my bonds to no avail.

"Arty! God damn it, Arty." My voice rose in panic. The ropes rubbed my skin as raw as my voice from screaming. My violet-eyed captor never gave me a glance. My body shook, muscles trembling. Why did I think he'd wake up? Arty was a follower, not a leader. But he'd never turn on me. I kicked my legs in protest.

"Stop kicking me, stupid human." The Fomorian dropped me on the muddy ground. The clean side of my face squished into the ground. I turned my head spitting out the earthy goop, only to mash it into my hair. I whimpered.

Why? Why did I bother to bathe? If I'd stayed in my clothes, Arty and I would still be hiding in a closet, safe.

The girls were separated, and some were sent off with a different Fae. The drop-dead gorgeous supermodels, and there were quite a few of them, were taken along with me. I couldn't understand. I didn't belong with the supermodels. I was some dorky, average girl next door who tripped over her own feet. I craned my neck around to watch the barn shrink in the distance with Arty inside. My throat ached with the crushing knowledge that I was alone and so was Arty. I kicked at the Fomorian carrying me. He slapped my butt.

"Don't touch me, you monster! Don't ever touch me!" My tear-filled words sounded weak and feeble.

I clenched my jaw, locking my cries inside and pushing the pain to the side.

You can't win. I will.

I took one last look over the ground we'd covered, blinking the moisture from my eyes, and I drank in every detail from the trail.

I will find my way back. I need to find my way back.

We crested a hill, and a giant, medieval fairytale castle dominated the landscape. Similar to the Schloesses they have in Germany along the Rhine and on the edge of the Black Forest. It also carried Tudor qualities, along with Renaissance styles. It was kind of a mishmash of all of them with lots of towers, some of which were thin and petite with beautiful fairytale like tops and others that were square and imposing with the long crossed windows. They were the kind my mom said they used to shoot arrows out of. The castle was surrounded by a massive outer wall. The whole thing would be cute if it wasn't glowing in dark, Fae light. The light of Fae shot through the arched doorway and around stones. They gleamed with black opalescence, almost like the skin of the Fae themselves. Maybe they held magic? Okay, that'd be stupid. We all knew that magic wasn't real. Fairytales weren't real, except for the fairy standing in front of me, that is.

The closer we got to the castle, the more impending doom permeated the atmosphere. If I went inside, I'd never come out again. I didn't know how I was going to get out of this. I was tied up with a rope and trussed like a pig.

Arty stayed behind in the barn. The rope around my chest felt tight. It was squeezing me, it had to be. The ache in my chest was too great to be normal. I wanted to kick and scream and get all these ropes off. I wanted to run back to Arty. The lump in my throat made breathing unbearable. How was I going to do this alone? I didn't know if I could. Arty's vacant eyes and slack mouth danced before me in my mind's eye. They had him, they took him away from me. I took another shuddering breath. It wasn't enough, it would never be enough. I couldn't breath thinking about Arty. I was alone, just me.

They're gone, they're all gone. First Arty's parents, then mine, now Arty. I clenched my fists. The Fae can't win, they can't.

The closer we got to the castle, the more I made out the details of the embattlements. I saw other Fomorians walking the wall. Every now and again, something would glisten in their hands, some kind of weapon. Everybody here seemed to be lost in the medieval times or in some kind of fairytale story with Fae and a bad case of D&D.

I turned my head and craned my neck to get a better look at "it". The Fomorian's face looked unintelligent, but looks don't gauge intelligence. After all, anyone who took a look at Stephen Hawkins might not have assumed he was a genius. But this creature had a look of determination on his face as if it understood what its duty was, and that it was going to perform it. The question was why they worked for the Fae? Why wouldn't they just take care of themselves? After all, they're strong enough, and they didn't react to the Fae songs.

The feeling of terror I'd been carrying around in my belly faded away as the sameness of the Fairy kingdom all continued on only to reach a gate. It was on a drawbridge, and there was a moat around this castle.

I kind of laughed to myself. The purple-eyed Fae a shot me a look.

"Little girl, I wouldn't start laughing without a reason. People inside this building don't take kindly to being mocked." Whatever momentary mirth I'd been feeling, evaporated.

The portico was massive with heavy spikes on the tips. They glimmered as if razor sharp. But this was all fake and they were defended by Fomorians. Who would come here and overrun their castle? Humanity didn't know how to get here.

Were they at war with each other? That was silly. Why would there be a war between the Fae when they made war on us?

I shook my head. I was sure I'd have plenty of time to ponder these deep thoughts of Fae politics later after they dumped me in some kind of dungeon and left me there to rot. Right now, I needed to keep my eyes open and pay attention to where I was. Perhaps I'd figure a way out of here—hopefully. Thinking would get me killed, but it might also save my life.

I was dragged into some massive room. Everything about this castle was oversized. The Fae I'd seen were taller than the average human, but it was silly. I mean who needed a ceiling that was fifty feet high. There were curved stairways that led off either direction from the main entrance. The room wasn't sealed from the outside. It was open to the air, but the temperature was pleasant. I wasn't cold nor hot; I just was. The room didn't have any doors, and I didn't see doors anywhere. Every opening was arched with interesting filigree painted or etched into the walls. I guess if it didn't get cold, what would you need windows and doors for? The walls themselves looked like they were covered by some kind of painted ivy morning glory. Variegated greens and flowers covered everything. The wood looked as if it had grown out of the ground and been perfectly shaped into whatever form they wanted it to be. None of it looked like it was actually carved. It looked like it had grown that way. I wanted to use one of my hands to reach out and touch some of the woodwork, to see if it was real. I could tell the difference between a plant that was still growing and the wood that has been cut, carved, and was clearly dead. They had a different feel to them, almost as if I could sense the energy has disappeared.

The creature carrying me didn't stop in the foyer but turned left. The girls followed him. We continued on into a large room. The ceilings were every bit as high, if not higher. I noticed there was a minstrel's gallery on the back wall of the room.

Fear gripped me. There were Fae everywhere. Every one of them looked as if they'd walked out of a child's fairytale book. Their bodies and hair draped with flowery green variegated ribbons in all kinds of natural colors. Nothing here was Day-Glo, except their faces. Their skin glowed with an opalescent and then was painted over with glow-in-the-dark paint, giving them swirly designs. Some of them almost looked as if they had tribal tattoos painted on their faces. I turned my head, only to encounter an ocean of entrancing beauty.

The creature stopped in the middle of the room to remove my bonds. The purple-eyed Fae waited a few steps in front of me. As soon as my bonds were released, I fell to the floor. I scrambled back up to my feet. Then he spoke. "These are the new recruits from which to choose." He waved his hands toward the other girls. Fae, male and female, approached the group and chose one, leading them off by their hands. They were gentle, almost as if dealing with children. Considering the girls' reactions, they were childlike—wide-eyed with wonder vacant of understanding, and yet trusting as a toddler.

He turned his violet eyes on me, staring me down. He pulled me by my forearm. "Now, you must choose your own master."

I blinked at him, and of course me, I couldn't keep my mouth shut. "Choose a master? Why should I? Nah, I'll be my own master, thanks." I twisted my arm to free it, but he held firm.

His jaw locked down, and he ground his teeth together.

"Choose. You can resist, therefore no one can choose you. You must choose for yourself." I didn't get it. So, if I was capable of resisting their music, they couldn't choose me. I had to choose someone. It didn't make any sense.

"I don't choose to be enslaved to anyone. I'd rather die than be one of your slaves." I put my hands over my mouth after I realized what I'd said.

He reached behind his back, and with one fell swoop he pulled his sword out and pressed it to my neck. I felt the cold blade a breadth away from slicing me open. The crowd erupted.

"If you only wish for death, I can provide it for you, but if you wish to live and become something more than a stupid human, you will choose." His eyes lost the angry, benevolent look that he'd been carrying. They softened and opened wider as his eyebrows came down. He was pleading with me to choose.

If I didn't choose, he'd be forced to kill me, and he didn't want to do it. I could tell.

Out of the corner of my eye, I glanced around the room. They were all beautiful, yet evil, violent murderers; even if they weren't wielding the swords and crossbows themselves.

They knew what was going on. They were complicit and guilty, all of them.

"It doesn't matter who I choose. I'll be a slave one way or another."

He said they'd be my master. I suppose one master was as good as the next when you were a prisoner. I closed my eyes and waved my hand around, pirouetting in position. I pointed my index finger, and I opened my eyes.

"That will be my new master. Since it doesn't matter who it is, I want it to be him."

I had chosen a man seated on a small platform.

The room erupted with murmuring. The Fae gracefully stood, lowering his hand slowly. The noise disappeared. He strode across the room to me. Eyes locked on my every move, and he wanted a better look at me. I examined him in return.

He stared me down, unblinking. I matched his gaze, allowing his green eyes, surrounded with dark lashes, to bore into me.

"Take her. Get her dressed and fed, and then bring her to me tomorrow." Hands gripped my arms and dragged me off in a different direction and under an arched doorway. I turned to continue looking at him, but he stared after me as they dragged me away.

He returned to his seat, and the murmuring filled the hall again. My arm was held by a pink-haired Fae. Her pointy ears shot into the sky as her celadon eyes, surrounded by pink eyelashes, stared me down.

"You are a brave girl. I was told humans are weak and cowardly. But I guess there's always an exception to the rule, isn't there?" She whistled as she walked and cocked her head to the side.

I didn't respond. I didn't know how to respond. They'd said take her, as in me, but not to the dungeon that I was expecting.

CHAPTER 9

The walls in the corridor were carved in lifelike flowers and leaves. The pink-haired Fae pulled me along past arched doorways, leading to other rooms and even longer corridors. After a dizzying amount of turns and halls, we came to an arched stairwell. It wound its way up with the wedged steps following the curve in the tower wall. I lost count of the steps after 362. Instead, I began counting archways. Lack of sleep, along with the adrenaline streaming through my veins, made my muscles shake with the effort. I was ready to sit down for a break when we came to the seventh archway. She pushed me through. I stumbled over the uneven stonework, landing on my hands and knees.

The stairwell continued up, turning away and out of sight from the tower wall. I couldn't imagine how many floors there were or the daily walk up and down all of them. No wonder the Fae were thin. Who could gain weight running up and down the stairs all the time?

With their ability to control things with sound and music, I would've thought they'd like to have an elevator just to whistle them to the next floor.

The dim, narrow hallway branched off, but this was the main thoroughfare for the floor. We came to the end and made a 90° turn. I stopped counting doors. The place was massive. Did all the Fae live here?

Finally, I faced a set of double doors. My pink friend opened one side and led me in. She closed the door behind us. Her voice rose in song, and the latch caught inside the door. She'd locked us in.

It wasn't just a room. It was a suite with a large bed, alongside a sitting area adjoined by a small desk and a large wardrobe.

Everything about the place looked medieval so I figured the bathroom would too like the toilet being nothing more than a hole in the wall with your business sliding out the side of the building, or maybe a chamber pot I could throw out my window.

That could be fun, even from seven stories up.

Thank god none of these ideas were accurate. It was a modern-style bathroom with interior plumbing and some kind of bathtub look-alike. It had spigots for hot and cold, along with a vine-looking shower wand. Why were they so antiquated about some things and high-tech about others? In the medieval world, indoor plumbing was like futuristic sci-fi stuff.

Pinky turned one of the spigots on, and steam rose.

The only things curiously missing from the suite, were mirrors. There were neither mirrors or anything shiny. The glass in the windows resembled crystal. I went and gazed out into the dim world now part of my life. There were globes floating up in the sky, some too far away to make out what they were. The light was dim, not bright and warm like the sun. The words of the purple-eyed Fae rang in my mind—my last look, the sun I'd never see it again.

Was this what they told prisoners as they let them across the Bridge of Sighs in Venice before they locked them in the dungeon, imprisoning them forever? They sighed because it was their last vision of freedom. Only one person ever escaped from that prison, and he had to crawl through tunnels of shit to get out.

How much shit will I have to go through to get out of here? If I get out of here.

"Your bath is ready; you must be clean. His Grace wouldn't be happy if he knew I hadn't fulfilled my duties in their entirety." Pinky twitched her nose and wiggled her ears.

"His Grace?" I pulled myself away from the window and its dizzying height.

"Yes, your master." She crossed her arms while tapping a foot.

"Don't you mean slave owner? That is what I am here, isn't it?" Though these would've been the nicest digs a slave had ever seen, being imprisoned still makes you a prisoner or a slave one way or another. My feet found their way back to the bathroom.

"You're not a slave, nor a prisoner." Her eyes hardened as she bit down with her jaw.

"Yeah, I'm not a prisoner. That's why you locked the door?" I waved my hand at the door and gazed back out the window.

Her pink eyelashes fluttered down demurely at the floor. I wasn't buying it. I knew the Fae were tricksters. I'd read enough before they stole me away to know they played games. It was what they did best. All the stories said they lived forever. No wonder they get bored and fucked with humans.

"If I hadn't locked the door, would you not be trying to leave?" She nodded toward the tub dismissively.

"Where would I go? How would I get out of here? This place is a maze."

She briskly turned and headed to the tub. She expected me to follow her as if I was some kind of child like the rest of the humans with their toddler version of life. A life with their free will stripped away. I did follow, though. I was filthy, and it felt disgusting. I had dirt all over me. I probably looked like a monster myself. Being surrounded by all these beautiful creatures, the least I could do was try to look my best. They already thought I was some stupid, ugly human.

She took up sentinel at the bathroom door, hovering.

"Um, are you gonna stand there?" Biting my lip, I tried to run my fingers through my hair only to run into a tangle.

Her jaw set, and she crossed her arms. She expected me to undress right in front of her. I wasn't in the habit of showing off my all-together's. But she didn't look away, didn't blanch, nor did she smile. She tightened, her muscles waiting.

I turned away and pulled the grimy shirt over my head. I picked out the knot in the drawstring, allowing the sweatpants to sink to the floor.

Hard to believe not long ago, I was clean. Being clean was overrated. It lost me Arty.

A divine scent wafted up from the water. I didn't know if it was an oil or some kind of fairy bath bomb. It dredged up visions of vanilla ice cream, chocolate chip cookies, and sleep all rolled into one. There was a touch of lavender in the background. Come to think of it, the lavender scent was everywhere.

I entered the water, and she sang something. Whatever she sang, it wasn't for me. It was tonal—notes, no words. But it did something to the water—a subtle change in the temperature. The water didn't move, but somehow it was massaging my muscles, easing every tension in my body. I submerged my head, wetting my hair and face. The warm water filled my ears, blocking out the sounds from this foreign world. For a minute, I pretended I was home in my bathtub, taking a regular bath and at any moment my mother would knock on the door, telling me it was time to get out because dinner was ready.

A knot formed in my throat, and heat hit my eyelids.

I closed my eyes and allowed the warm water to envelop me, floating me away to that dream world.

From far away through the water, I heard her voice. "Sarah, it's time."

I opened my eyes to the reality of the Fae world.

Pinky had taken up a position by the tub. I would ask her name, but what did it matter; she was just another one of my oppressors.

My life is over. I've been abducted by fairies. It sounded so absurd.

She poured something on my head and worked it into my hair, all the while singing a low, soothing song. I wasn't sure if it was meant to affect me, but it didn't. I enjoyed the tonal quality of the melody played against the harmony, painting a beautiful image. Somehow, every knot in my hair fell out without a brush.

A nifty trick. I wish I knew that one.

"What were you just singing?"

"Oh, the song of washing. If you sing, everything easily comes clean. Your face is no longer covered in soil, and your skin should be nice and soft. We Fae pride ourselves on being the fair folk. The only way to truly be fair is to be clean."

I reached back and ran my fingers through my hair. It was wet but gloriously soft like I'd come from a hair salon. It was still a dull dark brown. There was nothing special about my hair, and there was nothing special about me other than my lack of reaction to their music.

"What's your name?" I didn't know why I asked since I'd told myself it didn't matter. But manners win out.

"My name is Lyra. I am named after Lyra, the fourth queen." Pride swelled in her voice.

"You mean the Fairy Queen?" I shifted in the tub, causing water to slosh over the edge.

"Yes, the fourth queen Lyra of Fae," Lyra said, stating the title as if repeating a line she'd learned for a play.

"I thought the fairy queen's name was Danu or Mab; something like that?" It was a stupid question. Everything humanity knew about Fae was wrong. The fact they didn't have wings should've told me that.

"Fae queens have had both of those names. Danu first, Mab was third." Her voice took on the bored quality of one who'd repeated a lesson too many times. She heaved a deep sigh.

"What happened to them? I thought the fair folk lived forever." Did they kill their queens? Now, I was interested.

"Many of the Fae live forever. Sometimes they become sad or bored with their lives, and they'll sing the song of forgetfulness to start a new one and become someone else. The queens can't do that. Queens live as they are until they don't. They don't die; they simply fade away." Her voice trailed away with her words.

I did feel the power of her loss along with the loss of her voice.

"You mean they disappear, like become invisible?" My breathing shuttered.

"That is a story for another time. For now, you simply need to be clean and to eat. Then you rest and prepare yourself for the morning. You will be presented to His Grace and must look your best, such as is possible for humans."

I loved the little dig, implying that humans were automatically uglier than anything Fae.

There was no point in arguing with her. Lyra had her own ideas, and seeing as she'd seen me naked, I guess she was allowed to make whatever opinions she wanted.

I climbed out of the bath, and she wrapped me in some kind of sheet. In the main part of the suite, she sat me down at the vanity, the vanity with no mirror, and brushed my hair until it was dry. Lyra offered me some form of a nightgown, which looked like a see-through dress. Creepy. I wanted to put my panties back on, but she had taken everything while I was in the tub.

She probably threw them on the fire. Thanks, Lyra.

She didn't offer me underclothing so see-through nightgown it was. A tray of food sat on the bed.

"When you're finished eating, put your tray off to the side and then go to sleep. Someone will come in the morning." She turned to leave and snapped the door closed behind her. I heard the lock sent home.

I sat in the room, looking at the four walls. Was this supposed to be the rest of my life? Stuck inside of some kind of twisted fairyland? If the Fae could get out, I should be able to do it as well. There had to be a way. The stories said at one time they lived on the surface. But then they were beaten and told that their share of the land was underground.

Sounds like a lot of the stories we'd been told may have only been half true.

They went underground. Was that where I was? Maybe we moved from the surface to a cave. Could I dig my way out?

I let out a dry laugh. I'd be digging for the next thousand years. I couldn't even see the ceiling of this place. That was it! These must be the Hollow Hills of Ireland? But I'd been in Texas for god's sake. How do you get from Texas to Ireland?

You can't dig a tunnel from Texas to Ireland. You'd run into the mantle or the core and then melt yourself in two thousand million degrees, or Kelvin, however hot it was down there.

They took us down here somehow using music. Everything they did was a song, laced with a nursery rhythm.

But I can't sing.

I froze with my hand halfway to my mouth. The grape I held between my fingers was damp and cool to the touch.

I'd never tried to sing. One of those things you didn't think about until you do. Everybody sings in the shower and in the car driving alone. Sometimes you sing with your best friend although Arty wasn't much into singing around people.

My throat tightened. Arty couldn't sing at all. He was so off-key that it was hysterical. I think a dog started howling once. An idea formed. Arty and I, we could get out of here. But only together.

I mused about all these things and slid deeper under the covers. Before I knew it, my eyes grew heavy and I fell asleep.

CHAPTER 10

I peeled my eyes back. A bright light shone through the window. For a minute, I thought it was the sun. "Waky, waky, eggs and baky."

God, their rhyming grates on my nerves.

"I'm awake."

"Good morning, Sarah. How did you sleep?" The voice wasn't familiar. This Fae had green hair. What was with the weird colored hair? Don't they have normal hair? They were supposed to be creatures of nature, but they didn't look it. From what I'd learned in the last week, they were nothing like any of the stories.

"Good morning, I guess." I allowed the sarcasm to color my voice; it was the best I could do before coffee.

"I'm here to dress and prepare you to meet His Grace. I hope you'll be compliant." Her lips curved back into a smile. All the while, her eyes never wavered from mine.

I gave her my fake smile with mocking bright eyes.

"Oh yes, I'll be very compliant."

Her eyelashes fluttered open and closed with every move. Her eyes grew wider with wonder and happiness. It was an act. No one could get that happy over compliance. I hate fairies.

"I'm glad. I can't wait. It's going to be very exciting. He'll introduce you to the entire court." She clasped her hands together.

Apparently, fairies were unaware of sarcasm when I said I was ready and I'd be compliant. What I really meant was, "Go fuck yourself!" Reminds me of a joke I heard once.

Three rich ladies were all having tea and talking about their lives. The first one says when I got married, my husband bought me a brand-new house and a brand-new car.

The other ladies said, "That's nice."

The second lady said, "When my husband and I got married, he took me on a European tour to go see the world and he bought me a new car and a new house."

The other ladies all said, "That's nice."

The last lady takes her turn. "When my husband and I got married, he sent me to a finishing school to learn how to say 'that's nice' instead of bullshit."

Every time I heard that joke in my mind, I laughed. I say "that's nice" at those times when you can't say "bullshit."

The fairy twittered on for a couple of minutes about something, I wasn't listening. I didn't really care. I was to be introduced to the whole court. Yeah, my new path. How exciting. They'd whisper things like how plain she is, look at how human she is. Everybody wants to be paraded in front of a bunch of freaky fairies. For all I knew they were going to make me wear see-through clothes. How lovely. Let's allow everybody to see my altogether. I'm all for that, what about you?

"Haven't you been listening? I need you to sit down in the tub so I can wash your hair." Her brows were drawn together in frustration. She waved her arm to the bathroom door.

"Why do you need to wash my hair again? It was just washed last night. I haven't been anywhere or done anything. I haven't even touched it. It isn't possible to get dirty in bed, is it?"

The sarcasm flew over her head, or she ignored it.

"Fae prize beauty above all else, and part of being beautiful is being clean. If you're not clean, you'll be viewed as an animal or beast. Do you want to be treated like a beast? I can show you how we treat our beasts." And just like that, she went from fluffy, cotton candy to bitch in two seconds. Unbelievable.

Her entire countenance darkened. Her eyes went from being the light kelly green to hot pink, almost fuchsia, dead and flat. How did fairies do that? One minute be sweet, kind, and helpful, but the next minute a raging lunatic?

I cringed back into my shell. I was being too forward. Not smart. Dad said to get the lay of the land before you jump in. I was jumping in and had no idea what they did to torture people here. A vision of the carnage at the church filled my mind. None of them could resist. What if they figured out some way to do that to me? Maybe my ability to resist their song was a momentary thing. What if I had a cold and that was why I couldn't hear them properly? But then, as soon as my cold clears out and my ears clear up, I'm screwed.

Meekly, I placed one foot in front of the other, leading to the bathroom. I took my seat in the tub.

Last night, I'd been so tired that I hadn't taken a look at the tub itself. Everything here was made out of wood. The tub had grown out of the floor, and similar to a Banyan tree the corded vines squished together to make a big, wooden bathtub held up from the roots. The faucet wasn't metal, but it glowed like gold with a sparkling, crystal appearance. It shot rainbows and purple-colored stars. It glistened and dazzled my eyes. The edge of the tub had scrolled flowers sculpted down to the very roots. They formed the leaves and petals of morning glory flowers.

What was the deal with the morning glory? Why do elves like morning glory? She hadn't bothered to put anything in the water, it was just regular water. There was no sense of peace or calm. The heavenly scent of last night was vacant.

The moment I submerged, I knew she hadn't done anything to it, and the desire to linger wasn't there. I wanted to get it over with as quickly as possible. I sat up, and she sang the cleansing song. I wasn't paying attention. I should've been paying attention. I couldn't focus. Having someone wash and run their fingers through tangle free hair was soothing.

"You may exit the basin and go sit at the vanity chair." Her words weren't unkind. Matter of fact and to the point? Yes.

Again, a tray of food appeared, though I hadn't heard the door. Funnily enough, a bolt of clean white gauzy fabric was draped across the bed.

"Oh, lovely. I love working with spider's silk."

My entire body shuttered. I hated spiders. Oh god, I hated spiders. The only thing worse than spiders, was running through a spider web and getting your hair caught in it. Then the creepy feeling of their little feet crawling all over you. The hair on my body stood as a shiver ran over my flesh. "Please, I don't want to wear a spider's silk. Please don't put some kind of creepy spiderweb on me. The last thing in the world I want is anything to do with spiders." I crossed my arms over my chest and took a step back.

"You're thinking of surface spiders. This is not the same thing. These are Fae spiders. They are much larger, and their silk is more like surface silk." Her hands went to her hips as she cocked one hip to the side. "Anyway, they haven't given me very much. You won't be wearing that much of it."

Oh, they're larger; that makes it all better.

I shook my head, but she nodded back.

"I won't let it touch your skin, but you need this for appearances. Fae need to see you as one of them." Her voice had taken on the tonal quality, soothing and pacifying me.

Lay of the land, Sarah. So long as it doesn't touch my skin, I shouldn't freak out about it.

"The Fae aren't worried about modesty and personal physical privacy. But I would really prefer to not have my nipples exposed if you don't mind. When you dress me, could you give me some panties and a bra, maybe?"

She smiled at me. It was neither evil nor was it a kind one. She was placating me.

"Do not worry. We will not be displaying all of your assets today. Today, we are simply presenting you to His

Grace and his court." She opened her arms as the display of theatrics.

"Whatever that means." I crossed and uncrossed my arms, unsure of what I needed to do.

She ignored my smart remark and droned on about court etiquette. Something about not talking, no speaking until spoken to, and smile all the time. I translated that as to never let them see you sweat, and when you sit down, no slouching. Don't pick your teeth, don't pick your nose, don't pick your ears, and as a matter of fact, don't touch your face all, or hair. I cut in, "So in other words, stand stock-still like a statue and plaster a fake smile on my face. Is that what you need me to do?"

Her eyes brightened and grew wide as a giant smile crossed her beautiful face.

"Precisely. You have it perfectly. You need do nothing more than stand upright with good posture, keeping your shoulders back, and smile continuously. Don't stare at anyone too long, and don't fidget with your hands. You may keep them nicely at your side, or if that is too much for you, clasp them together in front of you as if you were holding a ball." She demonstrated using her own hands.

As if I was holding a ball?

She set the food down in front of me. "You need to eat now before I put your clothes on. You will not be able to eat again until after the presentation."

"Why would my clothes cause me to be incapable of eating?" My eyebrows pinched in confusion.

"I simply do not wish you to spoil them, and I know how messy you humans are." She waved her hands at me, encouraging me to eat.

Humans are messy…

Everything on my tray resembled some kind of fruit or vegetable. It clearly came from a plant. If you asked me what kingdom, phylum, genus, or family, good luck with that one. I couldn't identify these plants if it cost me my life, and in this case, it could very well. How was I supposed to know whether these plants were even safe for human consumption?

"Is this poisonous to humans?" I cocked an eyebrow as I held it up with a fork.

"If you die under my care, they will strip me naked in front of the entire court and slowly cut off every limb, inch by inch, until there's nothing left of me and I am dead.

Fairies heal quickly so they'll take their time at it to make it hurt. You are His Grace's prize. You die under my watch, I die. Do you still believe I would poison you?" Her words were devoid of emotion and matter of fact.

I shook my head and shuttered past the idea of having every appendage on my body cut away. It was almost as bad as the medieval drawing and quartering.

I ate my meal, and it was quite delicious. Most of it resembled a type of tropical fruit. There was a flower that tasted suspiciously like broccoli although it didn't look anything like it. I understood that broccoli was a flower and you were supposed to eat it before blooms, but this was clearly a flower, a very large flower. It resembled an orchid with a thick broccoli-like stock. When I put it in my mouth, I wasn't expecting some kind of normal taste like broccoli. The only thing that would've made the "broccoli" tastier was cheese or balsamic vinegar. I noticed that my plate was suspiciously vacant of starch of any kind. No bread, no rice, no wheat, or no potatoes—nothing. I'd heard carbohydrates make you fat. Of course, with all the blather on television these days about what's good for you and what's not, who knew what to believe? I wasn't skinny, but I wasn't fat. According to all the medical indexes, I was completely normal for my height and age. I kept saying that, which was why I couldn't understand why I was sitting there.

As soon as I finished, she whistled, and the tray disappeared like magic.

"Good. Now stand in the center of the room on top of the square pedestal."

I'd thought it was a footrest, but in fact, it was some form of a pedestal.

She took some kind of white cloth and wiped my face off as if I was a toddler. It was invasive. What is it with elves or fairies, whatever, having no concept of personal space?

The top of the pedestal gave me a better view of my Fae companion. She was divine, absolutely breathtakingly beautiful. She could've walked out of any one of the Deviant artists' pictures that I'd seen online. Every feature on her face was perfectly sculpted, softened by a smile or made fierce by a scowl. Her eyes were almond shaped, tilting up at the sides. They were large and a beautiful kelly green kind, as gentle as the hills in Ireland. But when she'd been angry and they had turned fuchsia and flat, I shuddered to think of it.

"Are you cold?" Her green eyes perked with concern.

Why would I be cold? It isn't like I'm standing in the middle of the room naked.

"No, I shivered for a moment but I'm not cold." The last thing in the world I wanted was for this Fae to know she crept me out.

She picked up bolts of fabric, laying them on the bed. She spread them out and cut several sheets approximately three yards long. I did the math in my head because I was bored. Nine feet each.

I was only 5'5". Why would she need nine feet of fabric?

Then she picked a basket up the floor and set it on the bed. She began pulling out ropes and leaves in various shades. All of it looked as if it came from the forest. I even saw a pinecone. She sang, and the fabric lifted in the air, lacing and knitting itself. It floated over to me, partially wrapping around my torso to cover one entire shoulder and both my breasts, draping diagonally down and around to my hip to the back. The second piece did the same thing, only instead of reaching to my shoulder, it only went just above my breast. It was in a line top. It wrapped around to the opposite side, draping behind and covering all the backside of my body but leaving the front side below my hips exposed. She sang a few more notes, and a smaller piece of fabric I hadn't noticed floated out and proceeded to knit itself onto the lower half of the dress, creating flounces and ruffles. When her song stopped, I was standing there in an opalescent silk dress like I had never witnessed before. Creased and pleated to perfection.

I wondered what all those designers in Paris and Milan would've thought if they'd seen what I was wearing.

She walked around me, nodding. She tilted her head to the side, examining every stitch, none of which she'd done herself. She whistled something, and one of the berries from the basket rose into the air. It began to draw on the fabric, creating swirling designs in a deep purple. When it finished, I noticed that as the designs reached the floor, they gradually became darker. They went from a light lilac down through to a deep purple at the bottom. She whistled again, one of the leaves rose and slowly it drew golden colors all over the dress, mostly in the front underskirt area. Swirls and designs scrolled whimsically before curling, Finally, the leaf disappeared. Next, she whistled for the rope, only it wasn't a rope. It had transformed into some kind of corded trim. It attached all over the bodice, and it went around to the back.

The entire bodice tightened, cinching me in and pushing every breath out of my lungs. My head turned to look behind me.

"Yes, that's much better gives you the lift your breasts need."

What, I'm seventeen? Who has saggy breasts at seventeen?

I stood there barefoot in the exquisite creation. She strolled back around and pinched my skin before singing a few shrill notes. It looked like she sprayed me with fairy dust, and sparkles landed all over my skin, giving me that opalescent look that all the Fae have.

"Is this how you make your skin sparkle?" I scoffed at the simplicity of it.

"No, we naturally sparkle. This is so you sparkle. Fae like shiny things."

That's not creepy. Did she just call me a thing?

She grabbed two twigs, tossing both into the air, and whistled. Both floated toward my feet, and she lifted each leg in turn. One of the twigs wrapped around my foot, creating some kind of slipper. When I set my foot back down, there was a noticeable heel; the highest I'd ever walked on. I wasn't even sure I could walk in it. She lifted my other foot to repeat the process. When I placed my right foot back on the pedestal, I stood noticeably two to three inches taller.

"I'm never gonna be able to walk in this. I'll fall down. I don't wear high heels." I let my hands extend to the side in case I needed to grab something.

"You will never fall down in these shoes. They will not allow you." She smiled and clasped her hands together in excitement.

"Well, now there's something that humanity could really use—a pair of high heels you can never fall down in." Why the heck can't the Fae share technology? I could think of five girls in my high school that would die for a pair of shoes like that... Or would've died for a pair of shoes like that. They're probably all dead now.

My eyes drifted to the window.

The realization hit me hard. For a moment there, I was behaving as if everything was normal and they were all still alive. I closed my mouth and gazed off out the crystal window, breathing through my nose. My eyes burned, and the side of my nose curled up in a snarl. She reached out to touch me, and I cringed away from her.

CHAPTER 11

"You do not have to fear me. I will not hurt you. You're far too important." Her eyes bored into me while her fingers fidgeted with the various creases in the fabric of my dress.

"Important. Yeah, right. Like all those other humans that were so important you killed them or turn them in the mental slaves." I locked my jaw down, clamping my teeth shut. Why was I talking like that? For all I knew, they'd kill me for being a smartass.

"You may not understand our reasoning right now, but eventually you will see that we actually saved more than we killed." Her eyes darted away from me.

Saved more than we killed? What, by not killing them?

I didn't understand. They killed all those people, and they didn't give a second chance to any of them. Yet she's trying to justify it by saying they saved more than they killed.

That was like a rapist saying I only raped a few of them, but I saved the rest of you from my rapist tendencies. I looked away and tried to not cringe. I didn't want to be a coward. I didn't want her to think I was afraid of her, but I was afraid of her—of all of them. Clearly, there was something they wanted. Did they think I was their savior? I'm no Jesus Christ. If they were looking to be saved, they were looking to the wrong human.

Lavender sang, "Eeny, meeny, miny, moe, catch a Fae by its toe. If she hollers make her show, eeny, meeny, miny, moe."

A tingle started at my temple and moved back over my scalp. The hair on my head stood on end and then lay down. She took a few steps around me, nodding her head and rubbing her chin. She whistled, and my hair moved of its own accord, swooping up on the backsides. Something changed on the back of my head as my hair grew or changed.

I wished there was a mirror in here so I could see what the hell she was doing. I shifted on my heels. She could be making me look like Elvira.

But she was afraid for her life if something bad happened to me. I was assuming she didn't want to make me look like a fool. Of course, I didn't know what fairies found attractive.

After lots of moving, shifting all around, and making my scalp itch, she proclaimed perfection.

"Yes, I think that will do nicely. You look wonderful with black hair." She smiled wide and clapped her hands.

"Excuse me, I don't have black hair. It's brown; dull and boring brown, brown." I practically yelled.

She flinched back, and her eyes glazed over. She shook her head as a new sharpness filled her vision.

"What did you do to me?" Her brows pinched together.

Panic clenched at my chest, and my whole body shook with anger. "You changed my hair color without asking?" My voice rose with each word.

She cringed down on the ground as I leaned over to scream in her face.

"I am sorry, I didn't realize. I should've asked your permission. I only followed instructions." Her hand covered her head as she cowered on the floor.

"Of course you should ask my permission. Don't ever touch me again without asking my permission." By now, she wasn't just cringing in fear, she whimpered. I was hurting her.

"I am so sorry, I…I will never touch you again without your permission. I swear by Mab." Her chest was heaving as she knelt on the floor in front of me with her head and eyes downcast. Her hands were folded demurely in front of her.

"Why are you kneeling like that?"

"I'm sorry, I, you…you made me kneel like this." She didn't raise her head or moved a muscle.

What have I done?

"Don't be silly. Of course, I didn't make you kneel." My heart beat through my chest.

"But you did, my lady." Her voice came out small, barely a whisper.

"Why are you calling me 'my lady'?" My anger over my hair color bled away, only to be replaced by fear.

"You are clearly already of a higher status than I. I have not been showing you the proper respect. I will respect you from now on, I swear. I did not know." Every word from her mouth wavered, and her lips quivered.

What did she mean a different caste?

"I'm not of your status? I don't even know what you're referring to." My eyes darted around the room.

"I have mistaken myself." She trembled. Even her hair had changed to white with her fear. I could taste it in the air.

"I was only meant to reveal your true color. You forced me to kneel and told me never to touch you or change anything without your permission. I...am compelled to follow your orders."

Did I compel her? Is that what the Fae do? And if they find out I could do it too, what would happen then?

"You will tell no one of this. You will never speak a word of anything I just said or did." Think, what else? "Or anything I ever say or do in your presence. Do you understand me?" I ran my hand over my forehead.

She laid her head on the floor with her hands placed in front of her in full supplication. "As my lady commands, I will obey. I will not disobey you in deed, word, or action in any way. I will follow all your orders to my dying day, I swear."

"Oh, okay. Can you show me my hair? I want to see it in a mirror."

Her hands moved slowly as if she was fighting against something. Eventually, she waved her hand and sang a few notes. A mirror appeared over the top of the vanity. I crossed the room. Besides having an exquisite dress such as I never owned before, my hair was beautiful. I looked good with black hair, and it made my hazel eyes greener somehow.

I'd screamed and hurt her. How did that work?

"May I finish my lady's makeup?"

She had gone from being someone I was frightened of to a malleable creature, willing to fulfill my every whim. My stomch turned over at the thought I am no different then one of them. I might be able to do something with her, but should I? Maybe I could get her to bring Arty here and sneak us out. But how had this happened?

"Please, my lady. We must hurry. You are expected, and I must perform my duties to perfection before His Grace sees you." She lowered her head again.

I nodded my head and sat, the song familiar and yet far away. Every sound was a picture, not just on my face, but also inside my mind. The sound added highlights around my eyes, and my lips were plumped into bright red cherries. My lashes became dark black. I could picture every color, shade, and hue she applied. When I looked in the mirror, it was exactly as I'd imagine.

"Beautiful." The woman in the mirror resembled me, only her eyes were decidedly green. My hair had deep purple undertones along with dark green leaves.

"Thank you, my lady. My only desire is to please. If you are pleased, then I have succeeded in my mission." She grasped my hand. "By your leave, my lady, we must leave now. His Grace is expecting us. We must not keep him waiting."

CHAPTER 12

For some reason, in the back of my mind when she said I'd be presented to His Grace and his court, I thought perhaps it would be in a giant throne room. They certainly had me gussied up like I would be, but I wasn't taken to the throne room at all, nor was there even a throne where I was taken. Instead, many people were there when we arrived, and there were many chairs there that looked like they could've been the throne. The entire room, of course, wasn't sculpted. It had grown out of the forest with lots of ivy and morning glory, vining all over the place. There were also bluebells, and I even saw places where it looked like honeysuckle has grown, and it smelled of honeysuckle. The scent of spices permeated everything; it was an intoxicating mix of floral. Before we entered the room, my green-haired pixie stopped me.

"When we reach His Grace, you must curtsy and then wait to be recognized. Do not say thank you. The Fae do not thank anyone for anything ever."

"Really? The only words I'm not allowed to say, are 'thank you'?"

"Yes, I would not use your human curse words or the slang humans have adopted. It may confuse many of the Fae. They don't know what they are."

"And you do know what they are?"

"Yes and no. My lady, whatever you do, do not let them see that you are unsure of yourself. You must be confident. You must command the situation as best you can, while still showing acquiescence to His Grace. You show him deference only."

"Treat everybody else with disdain, but act like a kiss ass to the big guy. Got it."

After my first step, silence froze the room in that statuesque-like quality. Fae had the eerie ability to stand and stare at you, unblinking. It was creepy, and they all did it. A room filled with emotionless perfection and the chosen one sat upon the largest chair in the center, his Grace.

Of course, I had to choose the big wig because that was me; I always have to climb the highest mountain, ride the largest bike. If it was the biggest, the most troublesome, I had to have it or do it; that was me. I loved a challenge even if I didn't choose it.

His green eyes shone, and if you ask me, his white hair was perfect and pristine. And yes, he sat on his throne as if he'd been sculpted into it. It looked as if a tree had grown out of the ground solely to become his throne. It had branches that spread out behind him, creating a giant fan. He occupied it as if it'd been built for him, but there were extra pillows filling the space around him. It was obvious it'd been built for two; anyone with a keen enough eye could see that. He sat with his legs wide, and his hand lazily rested on the armrest, staring straight ahead. Nowhere was a crown on his head although he was clearly the king of this domain.

He refocused on me as did the statuesque Fae in the room. All eyes were glued to the scene and I was at the center of it. It wasn't that I didn't like being the center of attention; it didn't bother me. For the most part, I didn't care. It was just when you have hundreds of fairytale creatures staring at you, that was a little unnerving. I wasn't sure how it'd be for anybody else.

But every step could've been a step toward my death or my salvation. My green-haired lady stood in the doorway, trying to remain unobtrusive but still watching. Somehow I managed to compel her, and I didn't even ask her name.

Item number one: as soon as I'm done with this parade show, ask my green-haired Fae what her name is.

Item number two: I needed to ask His Grace what his name is. I wasn't running around calling him 'His Grace'. That was ridiculous. This wasn't the Middle Ages. I wasn't a princess, and I wasn't going to call him by a title; that'd be silly.

Item number three: demand from my green-haired Fae slave information on how to get the hell out of here. Scratch that, maybe that should be item number one.

I was letting my mind wander, and I needed to focus. Dad said that when he was at war, the only way to stay alive was to keep your head in the game. He did it, and he came home alive; I had to remember that. I needed to keep my head in the game. The game was life and death, and almost everybody else has died. I wanted to live. I needed to figure out what it was these people wanted for me so I could keep living.

When I reached a position just before the Fae, I stopped. His Grace nodded his head. "You have been treated well?"

"Other than being a prisoner, yes, I've been treated well."

"You're not a prisoner here. No one has imprisoned you."

"Perhaps we should define terms. I've been taken against my will and locked in a room. That's imprisonment. It's also called kidnapping or abduction. I don't know which word you would use for it. So yes, I've been imprisoned."

He raised an eyebrow and opened and closed his mouth dryly as his almond-shaped eyes looked from one direction to the other.

"You will no longer be locked in your room. You're free to roam the castle as you see fit. However, do not attempt to leave the grounds. This is for your own sake."

That was a step in the right direction. If I could run around the castle, it meant I could find a way out. There had to be more than one, and one of them had to be unguarded. I didn't say thank you. She said not to say thank you, so I nodded my head in acknowledgment. I saw that his ears perked up as the corners of his mouth rose slowly and then he stood up.

"Now, I shall adjourn. I wish to converse with my candidate in private." With an adjournment, I could almost hear a sigh of relaxation. They were happy he was leaving as if they'd been holding their breath and on their best behavior until Daddy left the room. Within a moment, my green-haired Fae slave was at my arm.

"You must follow him. I will lead you until we reach his private chamber."

"What is your name? What do they call you?"

"My name is Lavender. For my colors are purple, and many admired the flower at the time of my creation." Lavender, they named her after a flower. Wow, truly imaginative. I'm impressed.

I followed toward an exit behind the throne. There was always an exit behind the throne in every history book and fairytale story you'd ever read. The king always leaves from behind the throne, like they had some kind of hidden escape panel that you press a button and it pops open to run away. But here, it was a regular, old archway with no door. They didn't believe in privacy anywhere. Even the bathroom in my suite didn't have a door. I could see him ahead of us farther down the corridor, his long legs giving him a great stride. I couldn't keep up with him since I wasn't tall enough or fast enough.

Lavender stayed by my side, but she didn't push me or touch me. She did urge me on though. I saw him pull open an actual door and enter a room, closing the door behind him. When we reached it, I looked around. It was a singular door, arched at the top like everything else here was.

"Remember what I said, show him deference?" She sang something quickly, and a scent of flowers surrounded me; she perfumed me. She opened the door, and I entered. He was seated in a great ornate chair. His elbows rested on the armrests with his fingers steepled between them. A cold disdain flowed from him. I didn't see another chair so I stood in front of him.

"Do you have any idea why you're here?"

"Because the Fae are sick, sadistic bastards, and you like to kill adult humans while abducting their children?" I internally smirked at my twist of words.

"The truth couldn't be further from that."

"How so? You didn't murder all those people and abduct me?"

This has got to be good.

"Perception is everything. From your point of view, that is exactly what happened. From my point of view, we did something entirely different."

"Okay, I'm so glad that you have your own belief that it's okay to murder people. I can't make it all right in my own head; that doesn't work for me. What do you want from me, and why am I here all gussied up in this ridiculous outfit?"

"You're here to learn, that is all I ask of you. You have free range of the entire castle. You may even sleep whenever you wish. Every day at twilight you will come to my study, and you will take lessons."

"Lessons in what?"

"History. You will learn whatever I choose to teach you."

"And if I can't learn whatever it is you're choosing to teach me, will I be returned to my parents, my family?" I hesitated. "If they're still alive?"

"It's not possible. You can never return to the surface."

And there it was. Now I knew where I was—underground. "So, I am in the Hallowed Hills?"

He nodded his head, but he didn't smile and laugh; no other form of acknowledgment. I had correctly guessed where I was, just a simple curt, boring nod.

"If you know these are the Hallowed Hills, do you know why you cannot leave?"

"Because I ate the food?" Please don't let it be something so stupid.

"No, that's not why. That's another tale humans like to tell. Don't eat the food of the fairies or you'll be stuck in Fae. No, you cannot leave because you've already seen who we are, where we are, and what we are. We let you go back to the surface, you will simply rally the human army and begin to wage war, which is exactly what we're trying to avoid."

I laughed. "You're trying to avoid a war by starting a war, that you already started. You think humanity isn't eventually going to figure out where you are and try to stop you from killing and taking people?"

"At this point in time from what I've gathered, the surface inhabitants of this planet are still wandering around, trying to decide if we're fairies or aliens. They just can't decide which it is, so yes. I think they are not going to find us. Humanity doesn't have the technology to find us, and they simply don't know where to look."

"Arrogance is always the downfall of a great nation or leader, or really any man or woman. The Fae are arrogant. You think humanity won't find you? Then you've forgotten how truly ingenious and how much ingenuity we really have." I retort.

"I haven't ever forgotten. I remember when the first human was birthed. Humans are exactly what we made them to be," he returns.

His words sent icy fingers trailing down the back of my neck—"the way we made them."

I scoff. "You made us? I guess you think because you made us that you own us and have the right to kill us off anytime you choose? Assuming what you're saying is even true."

"I will not debate ancient history with someone who wasn't present to witness it. You will come to me, and you will learn whatever it is I wish to teach you, or you will not and it will be to your detriment. Now you are dismissed." He waved his hand as if I was some kind of servant being waved off.

"I'm dismissed? Just because I'm stuck here in your castle doesn't mean that you can treat me like one of your slaves or servants."

He was up and out of his chair and in my face in a flash. "You forget yourself, all of these things I have granted you, your freedom to move about and do whatever you wish, I can take them just as easily as I gave them. You forget who is in charge here, and it is not you, human."

I cringed back slightly, and I stopped myself. The last thing I wanted was this creature to think was I was afraid of him. I leaned forward. If I'm going out, I'm going out in style. My outfit was to die for, and today wouldn't be such a bad day to die.

"No, you forget yourself. You don't own me and never will. I will do whatever I want. This may be your castle, and I may be stuck in it but only because you decreed it so. Don't for one moment think that you can keep me here. I will free myself."

He leaned back and laughed. "You're welcome to try human. Many have tried to escape this castle, but very few ever succeeded. Even then, their success was short-lived. Everywhere you look, you're in the heart of the Hallowed Hills. There is no escape, no way for you to leave. You think the castle is holding you hostage? You are a human in the land of Fae, and you are incapable of freeing yourself, no matter what you do. I said I wouldn't treat you as a prisoner, and I won't. I don't have to. The very nature of who you are imprisons you, not me. Now go."

My heart beat faster, blood pumping through my veins. I wanted to reach out and slap his face. He was right, there was no way I could get out of the Hallowed Hills. I didn't know how I arrived here, and I had no idea how to leave. But if I had free reign to go wherever I wanted, that meant I could find those answers.

The door accidentally slammed behind me as I left the room. The sound reverberated down the hall, disturbing the leaves and flowers lining the walls. Strange.

Lavender stood in the hallway, and her eyes traveled down the hall in either direction, following the movement of the foliage.

"My lady, are you okay? Did you have crossed words?" Her eyebrows rose.

"It's irrelevant. Can we go back to my room and get me out of this getup? I prefer normal clothes, not dressed up like some kind of fairy doll."

Lavender turned to lead me back down to a different court.

I stopped and looked around. "No, take me back to the throne room. He said I could go wherever I wanted. I want to go back to the throne room." I straightened my shoulders, lifting my head, and focused my eyes on the end of the hall.

"My lady, the Fae are not known for their kindness. You may find many of the people are petty and jealous. Their vanity knows no bounds, and they will insult you because you're human. They find humans less attractive than fairies by default."

I turned and looked at Lavender. "Am I less attractive than the Fae?" as if it mattered. Being pretty won't get Arty back or me out of here, but deep down inside I did want to be pretty. To stand up to everyone armed with whatever I had and fight, if pretty is a weapon, I'll use it.

"The saying is beauty is in the eye of the beholder. What I behold, you are a beautiful human. You are truly attractive, even among your kind. Your youthful bloom is still fresh, but you have not reached the age of full, fierce attractiveness. You still carry the essence of naïveté, but it is very attractive and very alluring. Male Fae will flock to it, and female Fae, they will despise you for it."

I'd always been good at ignoring catty bitches at school. Those cliquey girls that always ran around thinking they were so beautiful. I despised them. Usually, a school only had three or four of them tops, but they all ran around together, dressing like drones and eyeballing you as if you were some kind of insect to be flicked way. Lavender's people were an entire culture of those girls. Ignoring their kind of abuse was actually pretty easy—you find a couple of other people you like and hang out with them. In this case, there would be no one cool to hang out with; it'd just be me.

"Lavender, are you my lady-in-waiting or my maid? What is your position to me?" I stopped dead in my tracks.

Lay of the land, Sarah.

"I am your companion, and I am to wait upon you." She squeezed her hands nervously in front of me.

"If you're my companion, then I can take you anywhere I go, right?"

"Yes, I am to accompany you everywhere outside your room."

"Excellent. Let's go to the party. I want to see the competition." I dug my fingers into my hand to raise my heart rate.

"If that is your desire." She nodded her head and waved her arm in the general direction we'd come from. Just as we passed under the arch to the court, I heard an office door open. I turned slightly to get an unobtrusive look back down the corridor. There, he was staring after me with brows drawn together. He clenched his jaw and turn the other way.

"This room is called a receiving room. It's kind of like a throne room, only smaller. It's where the leader of a court meets new people on a more intimate level."

Which was silly because every room was massive. Not exactly what I'd considered intimate. What does a real throne room look like an affair of state? Did they even do affairs of state?

We didn't reenter from behind the throne. Lavender said that would've been considered presumptuous. Instead, she took me back around to enter from a hidden side door. It wasn't hidden, but there was a panel over it, making it look invisible from the room itself. People could slip in and out without being rude. She said usually the seneschal was the only one who used the door but as their seneschal was away on other diplomatic matters, it didn't matter if we used his door.

"Who or what is a seneschal?" I asked.

"The seneschal handles the affairs of His Grace's domain on his behalf."

I tilted my head to the side. "What, like an executive assistant?"

Lavender blinked and started again. "I don't understand that title. It's a secretary and a steward together. He is the voice for His Grace."

"Okay, so who is this glorified secretary?" I snickered.

"It's His Grace's younger brother."

My smile died on my face.

"Their mother was lucky enough to earn several children. In the Fae culture, children are prizes awarded for service to the Queen. There aren't many, so our numbers remain relatively consistent. The Queen maintains control with a feudal system. You are born into your position, but you do not have to stay there. You can work your way into a higher status by distinguishing yourself in some manner. I was created to be in the lower serving class. Now I'm a step below Merchant class because of my way with clothing and makeup. His Grace engaged me to care for you. My services are rather sought-after." Her lips curved into a satisfied smile.

I was amazed. Lavender was actually nice. She wasn't some cruel, mean creature. However, before she thought I was of a higher status, she was extremely haughty, as if I wasn't deserving of her services. It was interesting. The moment I was able to dominate her or compel her, whatever it was that I did, her entire demeanor changed. She became helpful as if by my rising, she rose as well.

A rising tide lifts all boats.

If I became more popular, she would gain status by the mere fact that she's attached to me. I never thought much about how being around me might improve someone else's life. It gave new meaning to the statement, guilt by association. I'd never been friends with anybody who'd gotten into any real trouble, but I'd seen other kids and what it did to their lives.

Lavender isn't my friend; she was a means to an end.

My wide-eyed naïvety shown for the whole room to see, I couldn't help staring, but I wasn't staring at the people. It was the architecture and construction of the room that was beyond belief. When I thought of fairies and woodland-type magic, they were always associated with nature. They hid in plain sight, disguising themselves as a flower or tree. Judging by some of the Fae I'd seen, I could see how they would be mistaken for a flower or a tree, blending into the forest and practically disappearing before the human eye. Unless you know what you're looking for, you'd miss them entirely.

The whole room was a giant forest covered in vines and foliage. Not like one of those creepy glass trees that were made out of the semiprecious stones, but a real tree growing into the side of the wall with leaves and flowers. It could've been a Dogwood tree, displaying its beautiful pink flowers that fade to white, only none of the flowers were faded. They were all just vibrant, alive, and ever blooming.

"My lady, based upon your position within our society, you must stand toward the back of the room." Lavender opened her arms to the direction she expected me to walk.

"Oh, so I won't be standing near his snootiness?" I cocked a half-smile as I made my snide remark. I didn't care if I was only making myself laugh.

While humanity liked to splash out with colors using their clothing and maybe a little bit of makeup, the Fae took the idea of a rainbow of colors to a level I'd never witnessed before. It wasn't just about your makeup or your clothing; it was also about your hair, fingers, toes, and ears. They created a room filled with vain, strutting peacocks. Every single one of them was trying to outdo the other in some fashion.

One Fae had some kind of butterfly stuck inside her hair. The poor creature flittered around, desperate to be free of this monstrosity of a cage on top of her head. It was funny and disturbing all at the same time. They thought so little of the lower creatures that they'd use it as a hair prop. The Fae stood in the receiving room, looking around, but none of them spoke about anything of interest to me. Only shallow self-absorbed discussions about their latest hairdo, who was having an affair with whom, and whether His Grace should show favor to one lady over another.

When you watch television shows and movies about the high court in past histories of the world or about stories like King Henry VIII and Queen Elizabeth, you're told all of this stuff happened. As if there was a great deal of intrigue, and everyone was very silly about their clothing and about who was more popular with whom. You don't grasp the concept of how truly clinging and clawing those people were. But standing there listening, I understood why humans wanted monarchies. This was how humanity had been taught to behave. I was sure this wasn't a microcosm of Fae but a macrocosm of life.

I whispered into Lavender's ear, "What is His Grace's name?"

She leaned closer, her lips were barely a breath away from my ear. "Deston. He's one of the four princes of the realm."

My blood ran cold, that was the name of the Fae that had been looking for me.

It was funny. What a cliché. Girl gets kidnapped, and her new master is a prince or a duke or some such a noble person; it was ridiculous.

Yet, I managed to pick the most powerful person in the room. The story of my life. I always picked the biggest tree in the neighborhood to climb. I always had a knack for choosing the biggest, baddest, or worst of whatever. If none of the other kids in my school would do it because the jump was too high, too far, or too scary, I would. I didn't have a death wish or fear being called a coward, it was just the challenge. And here I was, standing in the reception room in the Fae realm.

Somehow being here, I was being challenged. It was the biggest challenge of my life. This wouldn't be about who could hold their breath the longest or climb the highest. This was life or death.

They'd taken hundreds and hundreds of beautiful girls, perhaps thousands for all I knew. What did he call me, a candidate? I was a candidate for something. That implied that I was going to compete for something. The big question was, what was the challenge and what was the prize?

Finally, I yawned.

"My lady, do not yawn in front of the other Fae. They will despise you for it; you must always act as if you are interested in or were amused by something. Boredom is despised in the land of Fae."

I leaned back toward her. "Then get me out of here before I fall asleep. These are the most boring people I've ever encountered in my life. I couldn't possibly spend another moment pretending they were the least bit interesting or amusing."

Lavender covered her mouth with her hand and giggled. A few of the other Fae turned their glowing eyes on us. One woman cocked her eyebrows and gave me the up and down. Another gave a dry laugh as she turned away as if she looked at me and found me wanting. Not that I really cared what she thought and she's just another evil Fae.

Lavender waved her hands in front of me to define which direction I should go, but I had to lead on. We headed out the same door we'd entered, and then we headed down several hallways until my eyes spied the dreaded steps. The last thing in the world I wanted to do was climb seven flights of a circular staircase.

"Isn't there some faster way to reach my quarters? I mean, honestly, seven stories? You can whistle my hair into a crazy design and change its color, but you can't find a way to get an elevator in here?" I huffed in irritation.

"My lady, the elevator is only for His Grace's personal, private use."

"Where are his quarters?"

"At the top of the highest tower of course, so he can survey all of his domain."

"Of course, because if I was a prince of the realm, I'd want my room at the top of a high tower too." I knew that sarcasm was lost on the Fae; they didn't get it. If I were to bust out and say half of what was bursting in my mind, she'd probably blink twice, look at me confused, and continue on licking her claws. The Fae were much like a cat, self-absorbed, constantly dreaming, and swishing their tails in irritation for no reason. They'd always be looking down their noses at you as if you were less than them. Yes, definitely catlike.

I mounted the stairs, dreading going up seven flights. I decided I'd start counting them. That way the next time I went down, I'd know when I was getting close to the bottom and when I went back up, I'd know how close I was to the top. Note to self, don't spend too much time partying or you might be too tired to make it up seven flights of stairs to your room. Halfway, I placed my hand against the stonewall, breathing hard.

"Could I request a room lower down?"

"No, my lady, the closer the room is to the ground floor, the lower your station. You're only on the seventh floor, which is very low."

"How many floors are in this monstrosity of a castle?"

"Thirty-two."

Well, no wonder everybody stayed in the receiving room as long as possible. They were putting off the dreaded, long walk back up to their quarters. God, I'd stay down there all day too if I had to walk up to the thirty-second floor. "So let me get this straight, the ground floor is predominantly public rooms for social functions, correct?" I sucked in another deep breath, hoping to regain my composure before starting off for the final round of stairs.

"Yes, the ground floor is for social functions with lots of public rooms and also for the army's training room. The second floor houses the entire army. The armory is in the far northern corner—the one closest to the front gate. The third floor is for scullery maids and chamber-pot maids, not that there are any more chamber pots, obviously. You've seen we've moved forward in technology. Now, we have lovely indoor plumbing, but we've only had it for about a thousand years. However, there are still ladies and gentlemen of that level, so that is the name we've given them. If you move up to the fourth and fifth floor, those are for personal valet and general serving people like myself. I'm on the fifth floor. The sixth floor is for visiting merchants and people of that station. You're on the seventh floor, so you are the lowest tier of the nobility."

"So you were haughty to me when you first showed up in my room because you thought I was a stupid human?"

"No, yes, humans were created by us. Therefore, you are a lower life form and should be subservient to us. I was insulted that His Grace had engaged my very expensive services for a lowly human, but now I see how wrong I truly was. He was quite right to engage my services for you; it is a great honor." She lowered her head and her eyes, clasping her hands in front of her.

Amazing how compelling someone could make them suddenly open up like an egg to show you everything. As we got back to my room, I wanted to lie down on the bed. There was no way anybody could get comfortable in a dress like this.

"Can you please strip this thing off of me somehow so I can take a nap?"

"Yes." She whistled, and the dress split itself in half. She continued whistling as it hung itself up on a hanger and into the wardrobe before the door shut itself, neatly and nicely put away. She sang a quick song, and my hair relaxed back into flat, boring straight hair. It was still black. It was okay. I'd seen the black, and it didn't look all that bad. I twisted it up and put it in a messy bun on top of my head.

"Oh, my lady, you cannot go out of this room looking like that."

I turned and looked at her. "Why not?"

"If you wish to be respected or earn the respect of anyone in the land of Fae, you must look polished. Appearances are extremely important to the fair folk. We pride ourselves on being fair, and your hair looks like you just woke up."

"Really? I was just getting comfortable. You know, relaxing."

"It will be fine as long as you stay in your room, but do not venture outside the door with your hair like that. Let me fix it for you."

I looked down. I was completely naked. It was really probably one of the most unnerving things about the Fae. Apparently, Fae didn't have any body issues, and modesty wasn't a thing for them. The entire time I'd been in the reception room and meeting people I didn't have any panties on, let alone a bra. Could you imagine if I'd walked through a dust pile? I'd have dust all up in my stuff. I didn't know any girl who wants dust in their stuff, do you?

"Lavender, would it be possible for you to whistle me up a pair of panties and maybe a bra?"

"Panties?" Her eyebrows shot up. She had no idea what I was talking about.

"Panties, pantalones, pantaloons, underwear, knickers, or boxers, I don't know. Something that covers, you know, the front part of my stuff and the back part of my butt. You know, it meets somewhere in the middle." I waved my hands around a bunch. "Pretty please, can I have a pair of panties?" She smiled as it dawned on her what I was talking about.

"This is something that only males wear, to protect their genitals."

"Only boys cover their junk?" I scoffed, well that's not sexist or anything.

"Traditionally, yes, only men wear panties, as you call them."

I snickered. "Girls wear panties, men wear underwear." She shook her head and gave me a searching look. Honestly, she didn't understand the difference between male and female underclothing.

"Well, can you make something like what men wear for me, only dainty and girly, maybe lacy? Pretty please?" I clasped my hands before me.

Her face darkened. "Fae don't say 'please', or thank you, ever." Then she smiled and whistled. In the blink of an eye, I had a sexy little pair of panties, similar to the ones that I had arrived in—a thong with lace around the band.

"What was the other thing you said you wanted? A bra?" Her ears perked up, and she cocked an eyebrow at me.

"Yeah, a bra, a brassiere, an over the shoulder boulder holder. You know, something to hold up the girls, make them look pretty and nice, keep them from bouncing in my face." I put my hand on my breasts and cupped them, trying to hold them up. I wasn't in the habit of feeling myself up in front of anyone while explaining clothing. Lavender didn't seem surprised about this request.

I would run away naked if that's what it took, but I would rather have panties and a bra when I catch up to Arty.

She nodded her head, tapping her finger on her lips. She pulled the different bolts of fabric out of the cupboard and began to sing. After a few moments, it didn't look like a bra to me. When she finished, it dawned on me what she made, which made perfect sense. I should've expected that was what she'd give me. I guess I was hoping for something a little more modern. After all, they had indoor plumbing while the brassiere had been around for a long time.

Instead, I was provided a corset, a full-on lace it up, cinch it tight, take a deep breath because you won't be breathing again corset.

"I was hoping for something a little less constricting."

"Yes, but this will keep your 'girls', as you say, from bouncing around, but will make them stand up nice and pretty. If you're referring to that thing you were wearing when you came with the metal pieces, I would not recommend it for the human breast, which sags over time."

Did she make a dig on human boobies, saggy human boobies? I guess the Fae breast never sags. They must be perfect and perky forever. Now, I really hated them.

Honestly, you live forever being immortal and have perky titties. I hated the Fae.

She whistled and it laced itself onto me and then cinched up tight. I squeaked, as every breath in my body was squeezed out, in a higher tone of voice than I had intended.

"Do you walk in this?"

"Oh, yes. Many of the Fae walk in them." She nodded her head, keeping her eyes on my undies, all the while patting and adjusting. I squirmed away from her intrusive touch. What was it with the Fae? Had they no concept of personal space?

"What about fighting? I mean you implied that you have wars down here. Do women fight in a corset?"

Her head pulled back as she cocked it to one side.

"Of course not. One wouldn't fight in a corset. You wear a breastplate." Of course, it was the most obvious thing in the world. Duh.

"Great. So what do you wear under the breastplate?"

"When female Fae go to war, we bind our breasts with spider silk to flatten them and keep them compressed against the body."

I felt the smirk on half my face. "Oh, my goodness. I think we need to discuss sports bras and how they could be advantageous to female Fae the world over."

"Can't you please just make me a bra exactly like the one I had?" I cried.

"But it's not good for your breasts." She waved it in the air in front of me.

"I don't care if it's not good for my breasts. I want to wear it. It makes me feel safe, please, please, please, may I have my brassiere?" I begged. She wouldn't give it to me, and like a petulant child, I lost my temper. "Lavender, give me my brassiere, please."

She complied, but her head hung as she cowered away for me.

"Did I just compel you again?" Bile rose in my throat. How do I stop this?

"Yes, my lady. I'm sorry. I did not mean to provoke you. I simply wish to help you." Once again, her head hung with eyes downcast.

I took a deep breath, trying to get control of myself. I wasn't being a very nice person. This wasn't me. I wasn't usually this big of a bitch. "Lavender, I'm sorry. I'm really, really, really, sorry. I'm not trying to hurt you, compel you, control you, dominate you, or whatever it is that I'm doing to you. How do we make this work? Can you make something similar to what I brought with me?"

She stepped back, looking down at the floor.

"You must never say sorry again. To me or anyone else. I will forget you said it. Yes, my lady, I think I can reproduce the bra." She whistled for a few moments and then began to sing a high, sweet song. The only reason why I was paying attention was to see if I could replicate the magic. Who knew that underclothing would be so difficult to attain in this underground world? Within a few moments, she created a beautiful brassiere. When I put it on, it did indeed hold up the girls. I was so happy I kissed her on the cheek.

"My lady, Fae do not touch one another."

"Are you kidding? You don't touch each other? How do you procreate if you don't touch?"

"Well, in matters of love, of course, we touch one another. But we don't touch each other in passing. Overt demonstrations of emotion are something only children display to adults."

I smiled at her. Just because they were emotionally repressed didn't mean I had to be, and I wasn't going to be.

"Can I see the mirror please?"

She whistled C, D, E to bring up the mirror. It appeared on the wall, and there I was, wearing my brand-new fairy panties with my brand-new fairy bra—they were beautiful. I mean really beautiful, probably the prettiest underwear I'd ever owned. Victoria could keep her secret; she had nothing on Fae undies.

As a lark, I whistle the same notes Lavender had, C, D, E, and the looking glass disappeared. "Ha," I exclaimed. My heart beat faster. I'd made the mirror disappear, oh my god. How did I know what notes to whistle? My eyes met the strangers in the mirror. It was me, but I didn't know the music. How did I know the notes?

I hated Fae. Everything about it had changed my world, including me.

"My lady, you made it disappear." Lavender gaped from me to the wall.

I whistled the same notes in a lower octave, and again the mirror reappeared.

The Fae claimed humans were less than them and they were better than us. I was quite capable of making the mirror appear and disappear. I didn't care how I did it. Next step, get out of here.

The wheels in my head started turning. If I could do the mirror, what else could I do? Deston said I had free run of the castle, but that didn't mean they wouldn't lock me in again. When Lavender left, I need to listen to how she locked the door.

She hadn't locked it when we came in; I paid attention to that. She will when she leaves. Free range of the castle or not, she was my babysitter.

"Is it possible you could whistle me up a pair of jeans? And a T-shirt?" I gave her a toothy smile.

"Jeans. Similar to the pants you were wearing when you came in?"

"No, those were sweatpants, and they're vile." I got a pen and paper and drew another picture, explaining they were blue and made out of heavy cotton denim, practically indestructible, unless of course, she took her scissors to them and then threw them in the wash.

She nodded her head and then using the fabric she already had available to her, she sang. They weren't jeans, but they were better than running around in a dress all day. She did whistle me up a shirt. She had no idea what a T-shirt was. The shirt resembled a sexy pirate blouse. It billowed everywhere with ties at the wrist and neck. I was dressed for a Renaissance fair. It was rather flattering even if it was mostly see-through.

I wanted to go for a walk and take in the gardens or any other portion of the castle. If I was going to find a way out, I needed to explore. But exhaustion weighed down on me, and I needed a nap.

"You should rest, my lady. I will go and seek out food for you. I'll also see if there are any other pressing matters for your time. I'll return later."

I waved her off and yawned as I climbed into bed. She exited and I darted over to the door to barely make out a few notes. They were a low A, D, F...I didn't get it all. I waited until she couldn't be standing there, and then I replicated what I'd heard through the door. Try as I might, the lock stayed firm. Better luck next time.

I laid down on the bed. I hadn't realized how much sleep I'd lost before coming here. Of course, going up and down seven flights of stairs was enough to wear any human out. Why did they walk up and down the stairs? Maybe some of them didn't.

No offense, if I was on the thirty-third or thirtieth floor I certainly wouldn't be walking up and down all the stairs. I also wouldn't be allowing the stairs to force me to stay downstairs all day. They had those floating raft things—why didn't they have floating stairwells? Or something like that? Maybe I'd need to figure out how to make stuff float first before I started reinventing the wheel.

That was my new plan. I needed to learn how to sing. I never really paid attention in music class. I didn't know how to play an instrument. I only knew notes because my mother played. She tried to teach me, but I really wasn't any good at it. I couldn't get my fingers to do all those things that my mother could. Trying to play the piano and make your fingers crawl across the keys like spiders, I couldn't play. My fingers wouldn't comply. Ugh, spiders...

It's not that I couldn't sing. I mean everybody could sing, but the question was, were you any good at it? I sang along with the radio, and I thought it sounded okay. Arty was always telling me I could sing. But then, Arty was my best friend, so his opinion couldn't be relied upon; he was biased.

I whistled again for the mirror. I wanted to see it appear on the wall, and then I whistled to make it disappear.

Okay, I'm not a child. I'm practicing.

I thought about the song that I'd heard her sing for my brassiere. I didn't know if I could replicate it, but it would be fun to try. Better to have a go and an extra bra, even if it was a little misshapen.

I opened the wardrobe and took out the fabric she'd used. I didn't want to use the wrong fabric. There were several of them in there.

I attempted to replicate her song, and the fabric floated in the air, folding and bending. What I made was kind of like a brassiere, but it was nowhere near as pretty, and certainly not as functional. Okay, actually it was lopsided. One cup was larger than the other, and whatever the clasping mechanism that she sang onto it, mine wasn't there. The straps on one side looked like sleeves, and the other side looked like a thin, spaghetti strap. It was the most misshapen bra of all time. It was ugly, and it certainly wasn't going to fit me, but I'd made one. The point was that I'd remembered enough of the song to make something that resembled a bra.

I could do this. The big question was what could I get Lavender to show me? I didn't want her to know what I was doing.

Just because I'd been able to compel her, didn't mean someone else couldn't as well. Maybe they could, I didn't know if my compulsion was strong enough to beat somebody else's. She said I compelled her. Every time I did, it was painful for her. Taking someone's will was painful.

Free will, that was exactly what Fae were doing to all the humans. They took Arty, they broke his free will, and they took it away from him. Maybe it was painful because it hurts your brain. All I knew was that it wasn't cool. I didn't want to do that. I'd rather she didn't know. If she didn't know, she couldn't tell anyone.

I placed the bolt of fabric back in the wardrobe. I placed the misshapen bra under my pillow. I wasn't sure whether that was going to keep it hidden. Obviously, I had to dump it somewhere. Where would you dump the ugliest bra of all time in hopes that no one noticed?

I fell asleep thinking about all the various things I'd need or want to do. The last thought before I closed my eyes was of my parents and Arty, but mostly Arty. I didn't want to think about my parents. Where they were, whether they were alive, or were they saved, or not. The gunshots still rang in my head. Was that my dad shooting them, or was dad shooting himself? Was it a Fae shooting Mom and Dad? That's silly, Fae didn't carry guns, but it didn't mean they couldn't.

CHAPTER 13

"My lady, you must rise and dress for dinner."

I lifted my head, rubbing my fist into my eyes. "For dinner? I haven't even eaten lunch."

"Yes, but you must prepare for dinner. We only have two hours."

Only two hours to get ready for dinner, are you kidding? I could get ready in ten minutes. "We must create something entirely new," she said.

"Well, I could show you how to make a strapless brassiere."

One of her eyebrows rose, and a smile spread across her face. "Yes, yes, I can see how that would happen. It's like a small corset." She whistled me up a strapless bra. There had to be specific components to a song, basics to build upon, like a pattern or a recipe. This sound would do this, and that sound would do something else. If I could learn the basics, I could build whatever I wanted, like making a cake or cleaning a gun. You must have all the components and put them together in the right combination for your gun to work.

I wasn't one for small talk. I really liked to get to the point rather than beating around the bush and making nice; nice wasn't my thing. But to learn answers to any of my questions, I needed to try a little finesse.

"Lavender, you sing beautifully, and obviously you use a song for everything. What is that all about?"

"It's part of the Fae life. All Fae are born with a beautiful voice. We can sing, whistle, or even make a pleasing rhythm." Her eyes glistened with love for her magic. "Music is in our lives; it is part of the natural world if you listen. Everything has its own rhythm, its own song. You must only be willing to listen for it."

"So, you sing, and the fabric tells you what it wants to be?" I held my breath.

She smiled, her eyes gazing down. She shook her head as if it was a simple concept that I should've understood.

"No! Everything has its own vibration, its own song. Or its own key. You have to find it and then manipulate it any way you wish. For example, fabric is always sung to in a major key. It's the nature of its design. We have fairies that are great artisans, and they do nothing but sing and weave. It is their one desire; they truly love it. Although we have a caste system, you might be mistaken in thinking that we are stuck. Advancement is always open to any Fae who wishes to try. You are not stuck wherever you began although you might be put lower than where you started. The Fae society isn't just about being feudal. Just because you start a scullery maid doesn't mean you couldn't become a duchess. Ability has more to do with Fae society than position."

It dawned on me that she'd started at the lowest of the low, but because of her talent, she managed to bring herself up. She'd been very haughty when she first came to my room, but she'd earned her position; she was proud of it.

"If all fabric is a major key, all you have to do is make a pleasing tune for it to create your heart's desire?" I asked.

"You can make the most pleasing tune in the world, but it doesn't mean your fabric will obey. You must coax it, like a cat you wish to pet. The only way to pull it to your will is to flatter it and, in your mind, picture what you want. Picture it precisely in its entirety, and you must see it from every angle all at once, along with its intended use."

Then, she sang into existence a dress of the sheerest chiffon it barely whispered over my shoulders, and it was in soft cornelian blue. Everything about it screamed femininity and desire. I whistled the mirror into existence and saw myself. It was my reflection, but it didn't look like me. I wasn't sure who it was. I could've been one of the Fae myself, but the only thing missing were two pointy ears.

My jet-black hair somehow dressed itself as she touched up my makeup. She truly was an artist, and I'd never been this pretty in my entire life.

I'd always run around with my boring brown hair, throwing on whatever eyeliner and lipstick I bought at the local drugstore. I didn't pay attention to all the little intricacies that make you beautiful. I didn't know who I was looking at, but she was beautiful—she was me.

"You truly are a special talent, Lavender. Thank..." I stopped. Can't say thank you.

She smiled, and her almond eyes fluttered.

"Don't worry, His Grace is paying handsomely for my talents. Although I have to say, you are probably one of the nicest Fae I've ever dressed."

I looked down at her. "You know I'm not. I'm human."

She winked. "I think you could fool anyone. The only thing that gives you away is your ears."

My hair was slicked back to ride high and full, with my eye makeup trailing off into my hairline. My ears were round, not pointed like hers.

She whispered, "If you wish, I could whistle them to a point. It would just be an illusion, but you would truly look like a Fae." Her almond eyes batted at me.

I found myself contemplating it. "No, I'm human. I'm not sure why I'm here or what you want from me, but I'm not one of the fair folk. No matter how much you dress me up and put pretty makeup on my face, I will always be a human."

Her eyes widened, and she lowered her head. My words had barely been whispered.

I didn't want to be a fairy. No matter how much she made me look like one. I wanted to go home, see my parents, hug Arty, and know all was right with the world.

I felt moisture building up in my eyes, and I didn't want to cry. I swallowed hard, pushing the big lump in my throat back down, to breathe around it.

"When I arrived here, I had a friend with me. His name is Arthur or Arty. They put him in a stable. Do you know where he is?" My voice shook.

Her eyes open and closed, flittering as she darted them away.

"He's probably still in the stable, learning his trade." She turned away from my desperate face.

"Learning his trade." I raised my eyebrows. "What do you mean learning his trade? He's a seventeen-year-old kid just like me." My voice rose.

"He is now a member of the Fae workforce. As it stands, he's part of the stables under the command of the Puca."

I felt my whole body shudder. "Who is Puca?"

"He is a terror. The truth is, every now and again he gets bored down here. He rides up to the surface, terrorizing humans for fun, and then chooses one, usually from an old Irish family. He prefers them because they are the hardest workers and the greatest fighters. He brings them back to become members of his stables. On the surface, the human is generally never seen again, and his family assumes he's dead. Sometimes he calls them out from their own home in the middle of the night. There is no way for your friend to get away from Puca."

My mouth went dry. Arty was big and strong, but he didn't lift weights or play sports. It wasn't like he couldn't. He was more of a bookworm, an egghead. It was one of the things I loved about him—his geeky nature.

"Is there any way I can bring him here?" A moist film formed on my hands at the idea that Arty was permanently a part of the Puca's stables.

"Highly unlikely. Puca does not give up his prizes easily. Nor does he like it when anyone meddles in his affairs. I don't think he would tolerate a human interfering."

There was the only way I was ever going to see Arty again—interference. For all I knew, he might enjoy taking care of horses. He always liked all the dogs in the neighborhood. I didn't care if he did like it; we were getting out of here. If music was the only way, so be it.

I whistled the mirror away but kept mentally chewing on what she'd said.

Everything has a vibration or its own song, some key. You had to listen for it and figure out what it liked and coax it into doing what you want.

The concept wasn't difficult, it made perfect sense, like getting a horse to go where you wanted, using the reins alone. If everything in the world had that same concept behind it, all I had to do was listen for the right key. That was what I was missing when I had tried to open the door last night; I was using blunt force.

I didn't get to think about it much longer because she made my shoes, and we were off.

CHAPTER 14

I stood at the top of the stairs while gazing down in horror. Seven flights. I'm gonna be sweaty by the time I reached the bottom. My foot pushed down on the first step.

"Sarah," a voice called out, deep and commanding.

I stopped mid-stride to glance over my shoulder. It was him, Deston. I lowered my hand and put my foot back down on the top riser before turning to face him.

"Yes, Your Grace." Lavender bobbed a curtsy, lowering her eyes. She placed one hand over the other in front of her.

"You'll ride down to the evening meal with me." He ignored Lavender, and she proceeded down the stairs.

He thrust his arm out, but I wasn't sure what he wanted me to do with it. I tentatively reached out, not sure where to place his arm. His hand rose underneath mine to lie perfectly on top of his. We turned down a different corridor to a set of intricately carved doors.

He sang something low and guttural, and the door opened to a boxy room. Thank god for an elevator! I breathed a sigh of relief.

"You have misgivings?" His head never turned to glance my way.

"No, I'm just thrilled to not walk down seven flights of stairs in my dinner finery." From the side, I glanced at his face. He had a smile.

"Yes, the stairs are rather tedious. Only the lower echelons use them. The lords don't." I took my hand down from his, and I turned to face him.

"Are you kidding me? So, all the servants have to walk up and down the stairs while the higher echelons do something else? What do they do?"

He laughed. "They don't have an elevator. They have floating platforms to take them directly to their rooms." His hand slipped with ease to his sides, hanging limp.

I put my hand on my hip and cocked it to one side. "So, if you're not a big wig riding a floating platform to your bedroom window, you get to trudge up and down the stairs. That's a real nice system you got going here. Why not put in a set of elevators for everyone? You wouldn't have to worry about all these floating platforms all over the place. There must be thousands of them. Do you really realize how inefficient that is?"

He crossed his arms over his chest as his green, bright eyes turned to the dark moss of a shadowy forest.

I put my hand over my mouth. I'd lectured him about how to run his castle.

Keep your mouth shut, Sarah.

"I'm sorry, this is your castle. I really shouldn't tell you how you run your life. I'm... I'll keep my opinions to myself."

His lips were pulled back in a smile, but his eyes told another story. "I know humans are impulsive; it's a part of your charm."

He hadn't told me to mind my own business. He extended his hand back out, expecting me to put my hand back on his. Was it some weird formal thing? Having never been around royalty or aristocrats of any kind, I wasn't sure how they behaved. I couldn't learn new rules for protocol if no one was willing to inform me.

I didn't feel the inertia of movement until the doors to our elevator opened. We were near the grand foyer. He led me off to a side section of the castle that I hadn't seen before.

His full lips curved into a blinding smile. "You may not enter with me. You are not of my station, and I will not elevate you."

I raised my eyebrows. Heat burned across my face. What?

"I didn't ask you to elevate me. I'll be happy to enter on my own. I'm used to being a girl, thinking and walking around without a man holding her hand." I snatched my hand away from his.

His smile faded into a blank face with hard, dark moss eyes.

I didn't need some stupid man escorting me to dinner. Although I was happy to not walk down seven flights stairs, his condescending attitude irritated me.

Don't look a gift horse in the mouth, Sarah.

I turned away from him and pulled in a deep breath. I entered the room with my chin high and with as much grace as I could possibly scrape together.

CHAPTER 15

The table had to be at least thirty feet long. It was ridiculous, but it wasn't a rectangle. It was an oval with a head seat that looked suspiciously like a throne. The other chairs mirrored each other, no station denoted. I didn't know where to sit.

"My lady." A servant motioned her arms that I should follow her, and she led me to almost the complete opposite from Deston's throne. Considering I was the lowest person on the totem pole here, that made perfect sense.

The table was vacant of decoration without even a place setting or cards. There were simply chairs and things that I thought were napkins folded to resemble a tree—a real honest-to-goodness tree with a woody base. It wasn't real. This was Fae; nothing here was real. Everything was beautiful and a lie, underneath it all was ugly. The reality was the same for Earth. From space, it was beautiful. Our world appeared peaceful, filled with life. A big blue and green glowing ball in the blackness. But the moment you arrived below the surface to the Fae, that was where the rot lived. They had pretty faces, but behind them hid ugliness.

No one sat in their seats, and Fae milled around the room in various states of crazy dress. I didn't know anyone so I perched near my chair.

Lavender hadn't even mentioned how you met someone, whether you we're allowed to introduce yourself or wait to be introduced. The only person I knew wasn't even in this room. I couldn't exactly wait for His Grace to introduce me. I didn't want to appear out of place. Not knowing what to do was more nerve-racking. Even if I had to stand on my head while holding a golf ball between my lips with a frog in my pocket, at least I'd know what to do—no matter how ridiculous.

The eyes of the female Fae were drawn back to me over and over, like a moth to a flame. I felt them assessing me from head-to-toe. The males also took their turn tearing me apart with their almond-shaped eyes. All had white hair with eyes every shade of the rainbow, some in soft pastels, others deep smoldering jewel tones, but the most frightening were the piercing neon shades. Cold yellows, frigid blues, and icy reds. I knew red was usually associated with warmth and fire, but only the Fae could make something hot, cold. Most of the clothing was predominantly see-through, revealing the swell of their breasts, and the curve of their buttocks. In some ways, the entire dinner party resembled a Renaissance Grecian fresco. With strips of fabric draped across body parts accidentally covering only the most important bits. The illusion was only disturbed by the sharp, pointy ears and the fierceness of their eyes. They had earrings, necklaces, and bracelets, made of several metals and semi-precious stones. Everything was shaped to resemble nature, a butterfly brooch, ant-shaped chain links, or spiderweb bracelets. Their fabric, like mine, was woven in an interesting all-natural way, resembling something that they'd plucked from the forest floor. Their lithe bodies and their long slender fingers moved with grace around each other, allowing the fabric of their clothing to wave and ripple behind them.

I schooled my face, making it resemble boredom. I was alone, and time dragged on me. Deston was the one who'd led me to the door. How long exactly was he going to wait before he decided to enter the room? Was everyone going to starve to death waiting for him to appear?

CHAPTER 16

My mouth went dry when I saw the purple-eyed Fae who'd brought me here. He was dressed in his finery, but no longer had flashes of light all over him. In the interior light, you couldn't see the Day-Glo markings on his face. But it was him, and I could tell the moment our eyes met. A smiled curled half of his face, and he made a beeline toward me.

"Well, Sarah, you clean up nice." Appreciation colored his voice.

He made my skin crawl. "No thanks to you," I mumbled.

He let out a deep chuckle. "If you only understood, you'd realize I have saved more lives than I've taken. How does it feel to be a candidate?"

"You know, you throw that word out there 'candidate' as if I understood what it meant, but I don't."

"I thought for sure His Grace would've immediately informed you what was expected. Well, no matter. I'm sure he'll get around to it. Judging by the competition, I'm not sure he should put in a lot of effort." He stood stock-still, arms resting at his sides.

My teeth ground. "What is that implying?"

"Well, there will be fierce competition. I'm not sure you're up to it." He didn't think I could win whatever it was, assuming I even wanted to win.

Get real, Sarah. You're super competitive. Of course you want to win. Whatever it is, you want to win. You want to do it, you want to be first. It's the highest mountain, and you must climb it.

"I don't know what your competition is for. Having a desire to win, compete, or even care, doesn't exist in my world." I didn't want him to see how his words had stung me.

"Well, as I say I'm not sure that you're going to really need to bother. I've seen the competition, and it's stiff." His face was blank as his eyes trailed around the room, examining each and every female in turn.

A thought struck me. "Is all of my competition human? All these girls? You know, people that you can't compel?"

He stopped staring at the crowd. A smile curved his face as his predator-like, purple eyes turned on me. I tilted my head back to meet them. He was at least a good six to seven inches taller than me. His eyes bored down on me. "Well now, that is an interesting question. Probably the first truly intelligent question you've asked me. No, you're the only waker. I've not heard rumor of any others."

So I was the only one that they couldn't compel. Sounds like I was already ahead of the game, whatever the game was, assuming the game wasn't doing whatever they tell you. For all I knew, they might've been treating humans like racehorses, and they wanted me to run and jump over hedges.

"So what exactly am I competing for in this competition that I've been thrust into?" I let my fingers dig into the back of my chair.

"Second most intelligent question. Only the greatest prize of all time ever on planet Earth. I can't tell you what it is, but once you know, you'll want it." He raised his chin as he spoke, allowing reverence to fill his voice. It added tonal quality to how he spoke as if he was trying to sway me.

"If you've seen all of my competition, am I to assume you've stopped making raids on the surface? You aren't killing any more humans or abducting any more children?" Please say you aren't killing anybody else.

"No, I've been ordered to continue the raids. We're not abducting any more females. We are indeed taking more males, only the young and strong." Once again, his eyes trailed away from me.

My stomach clenched. They were taking boys, guys like Arty. He called them raids, but they must've still been killing people—lots of people.

"You're still killing humans indiscriminately." My heart raced. The bile in my stomach churned over and over again. He was killing, and he was going to keep killing. It seemed ever since I was a little girl, there was always someone killing someone else. That was why my dad went to Afghanistan, to stop people from killing other people. But the truth was he'd been killing people. It was his job, and I knew it haunted him.

"I know from the untrained eye, you humans assume that what we're doing is evil or cruel or we're doing it indiscriminately. There is a reason for everything we do. Fae are not so shallow they would kill indiscriminately. If we were, we would've been doing it all along. We would've never gone away. Trust me when I say it brings me no joy or pleasure to kill. It is simply something I must do as Minister of War. I have no choice but to do as my liege demands or give up my position and leave in disgrace; that cannot be done." The sincerity in his words compelled me to believe him. I didn't really think he enjoyed killing anyone. For now, at least I knew what his position in the world was. Minister of War—his entire job was to wage war and prepare those for it.

"How am I supposed to refer to a minister in polite society, Mr. War? Do you actually Joust?" I allowed my grip on the back chair to ease. The blood flowed back into my fingers, turning my knuckles from white to pink. I'd always been good with the turn of phrase, making the mundane into something humorous.

He burst out laughing. "Yes, I do joust. I'm assuming by your queries that you're seeking my name. My name is Janice. I am a cousin to His Grace." Great, the psychopathic serial killers were all related; that was fabulous.

I extended my hand to him. "Nice to finally meet you, Janice. Thanks for abducting me. My life will never be the same." I put extra emphasis on 'never' as a lump formed in my throat.

"That fire, that instinct to immediately strike back, that is what will save you in this competition. You're very quick-witted, Sarah. You know I saw you when we first landed, when you ran away and slipped through my fingers. I didn't know where you went. I knew you were awake the moment I laid eyes on you. I hadn't stopped singing when you started running. I only managed to stop you for a moment. It was fascinating, thrilling even hunting you. I knew we had to have you." He moved closer to me, his eyes almost in perfect alignment with mine. Excitement laced his voice as his breath flowed toward me.

I wanted to throw up. Good hunting me, and he openly admitted it. He was thrilled by it. My mouth filled the saliva that I had to swallow back.

"I believe that if you do win this competition, it will be for the better of Fae and the world. If you lose, the world will be less bright without you in it." The violet of his eyes turned into a deep smoky amethyst, and when he said less bright, his voice deepened.

I snorted. Not a very feminine feature, but I did it sometimes when I inadvertently laughed. I put my hand over my face and pulled back.

"The world will be less bright without me in it?" I mocked his tone of voice. "You live underground; it's already less bright. How can having me in your world make it brighter?" I cocked an eyebrow at him.

"It's not always dark here, just lately." His brows knitted together, and his jaw locked down.

I felt like whenever I spoke to him, he was leaving something out—a super important piece of the puzzle.

One of the servants standing near the doors stabbed their staff into the floor, creating a tapping sound. All in the room went silent. Janice silently moved away to stand next to his own seat. I loosened my grip on the back of my own chair. As His Grace entered the room, I noticed that everyone bowed or curtsied so I did my best bob.

I didn't know how to curtsy. I'd seen maids on television give a little bounce up and down. That was what I did. I heard a giggle next to me. I didn't know all the intricacies of Fae social life or the rules of their courts. I'd always thought all those stories were made up. Now I was standing here in a real-life Fae court. I had no idea what to do. I was going to compete for the greatest prize of all time. Ridiculous. What could possibly be so important that it'd be the greatest prize of all time?

Deston took his seat at the table. Everyone followed suit as did I. Janice was seated close to his cousin. He wasn't just the Minister of War; he apparently was also the royal taster. He took a bite of everything from Deston's plate before he ate. Was it really that big of a deal that someone would poison him? Like I said, I didn't know anything about their politics, so for all I knew they could be trying to poison each other constantly, all day, every day.

Steam wafted from the plate of food in front of me, tickling my nose and causing my mouth to water. I picked up the two-tine fork allotted to me. I stabbed into something resembling meat, but as I pierced it, the texture was wrong. Still, the pressure in my stomach overrode my inclination to not eat it. I proceeded to raise it to my mouth.

Lavender's voice whispered in my ear.

"My lady, do not eat anything until I have tasted everything for you."

I froze with the forks, still midair, and then lowered it. As my appetite drained away, she took small bites with her own fork from every item on my plate and backed away. I looked around the table with wide eyes. Somebody here would poison me? Of course, they'll kill you.

I'd allowed myself to be lulled into a false sense of security with pretty clothes and makeup. Sitting at a nice civilized table wouldn't stop these evil creatures from killing me or anyone else they wanted to. They were bloodthirsty, no better than Attila the Hun.

I looked down at my plate and everything on it took on a sinister, unappetizing air. Another step in a long line of steps to kill me. Someone was willing to poison me to death.

The man next to me leaned over and whispered. "You should eat while you can. They will not allow you to have food sent to your room. If you do not eat, it will insult His Grace."

I nodded my head, trying to not display the emotions rolling through me. I took a few very small bites from every item on my plate. It all looked perfectly normal.

The food didn't taste bad. I was hungry, but it felt like sawdust in my mouth. Someone came and poured what resembled golden wine in my goblet. Lavender reached from behind and took a sip of it, putting it back quickly. After wiping the rim clean with a napkin. I took a small sip myself. I sat with my hands in my lap, staring straight ahead.

The room was beautifully sculpted with wood. Based on everything I learned from Lavender today, it was made with magic; they sang it into existence. Trees were sculpted exactly the way they sang it. Someone had to sit there for a long time with their very large voice to create this entire structure. I wondered how many thousands of trees had to die so this building could exist? Or were they really dead? I didn't remember stories of the Fae bringing people back to life. I did remember stories of them stealing the babies and leaving behind changelings. But every fairytale was either not true or different. What did that mean? My dad used to say there were "the known knowns and the unknown knowns." I didn't know what I didn't know. It was a smart way of saying I didn't know and I was blind.

My dinner companions broke me out of my revelry. "You should take a few more bites, you will need your strength for tomorrow." I turned slightly to inspect the man next to me.

His almond-shaped, daffodil-colored eyes gleamed, and his lips parted in anticipation. His long slender fingers gripped his fork.

I need my strength for tomorrow.

What was supposed to happen tomorrow? I ate a little more and then moved onto dinner rolls. Bread was filling. Probably the first carbs I'd seen since my arrival. My body ached for carbs. My greatest weakness was a tossup between bread and ice cream.

I raised the roll to my mouth and gazed around the table. Every face was sinister, every motion a potential threat. I couldn't help it. I looked around, and all I saw was another person trying to kill me. I had zero way to defend myself. I forced myself, sinking my teeth into the fluffy mass. The outer crust was thick and buttery, and I found myself savoring it.

They brought in the next course with some kind of salad. I loved salad. I was hungry, and it reminded me of a mesclun mix I had at a restaurant once with my parents. How was it that food kept bringing back memories of things I didn't want to think about it. I swallowed, looking at all those strange seaweed-looking greens. They clearly weren't the same, and yet at first glance I'd been fooled.

Next was dessert. Everyone got one but me. Okay, I didn't really want one. Lavender whispered in my ear, "Do not be offended, my lady. You're simply not allowed to have one because of the competition."

I sat in silence, watching everyone munch upon their sugary treats. It resembled a cross between Turkish delight and Jell-O colored squares, powdered on the outside. Each Fae ate them in their own fashion with fingers or using a fork. The forks resembled little pitchforks. I wondered if you could take out an eye with one? I pictured very creepily.

The woman next to me leaned in. "For a human, you're actually quite civilized. I'm surprised."

I turned and smiled at her. "For a Fae, you're not very civilized, and I'm not surprised."

The smile drained from her face as I smiled brightly at her.

"Yes, we Fae are rather a violent sort." She recovered quickly. For a moment, I thought she was going to stab me in the hand. She was holding the fork in such a way that it could've been a weapon, but I saw the light of it die in her eyes as I heard a voice drift over the table.

"Sarah, why don't you tell us all about yourself?" Deston inquired. My stomach rolled, and my belly filled with butterflies, food churning.

Why the hell would these people care anything about me? "I'm human. I will turn eighteen in two weeks. I've been abducted by sadistic psychotics, apparently for some form of competition of which I am unaware. If I had been left to my own devices, I would've been starting my senior year next month." I knew my words stung, and I wanted them to. From the corner of my eye, I saw Deston wiped the corners of his mouth with his napkin before slowly lowering it to the table.

"And do you have any hobbies, anything peculiar about you that would be interesting?" The female Fae next to me implored.

I didn't want to tell these people anything about me. Information was power. If they knew anything about me, it could be used against me. I looked at Deston, but his face was impassive. I looked over at Janice. His finger wagged as if to say no.

"No, there's nothing truly exciting about me. I like to read. My favorite pastime is watching football." The reading part was true, but the football was untrue. I hated it. I despised sitting in the house for hours on end on Sunday or Monday night. I would've much rather be out with my friends, actually participating in a sport versus watching someone else. It was a stupid pastime. Old men watched, dreaming of their glory days in high school when they had scored a touchdown and taken their team to the win.

The twittering of female Fae played in the background; that was a nice way of laughing at me.

"What is football?" Janice's query brought me back. I brightened. Now here was a subject that could really dig my teeth into. I had to sound as if I knew about football. My father liked to watch it sometimes.

Arty was a massive football fan; obsessed that was how I'd described him. I never heard the end of it. He was constantly going on and on. Arty played football, but wasn't any good at it. He realized he had two left feet. He wasn't physically talented like that.

"Oh, football is a truly American pastime," I said. "The game uses a leather, pigskin-covered ball. It's shaped like a pointy oval, and it has stitching on one side to help you grab it. You put your index finger at the point and your hand around the outer side, and you throw it to your buddy downfield. He catches it, and then he tries to run to a designated goal. You need to get there with the ball in your hands without falling down or letting the ball touch the ground. Then you get six points and go for a field goal by kicking." I was droning on word for word everything Arty told me. "Or run the ball back into the end zone for a two-point conversion. Most people just kick field goals."

The Fae females around the table looked bored; one yawned. How was it okay for her to yawn? Unbelievable. A male with orange highlights on his clothes and in his eyes leaned forward.

"These points, what you do with them? How do you gather more points?" His words rushed out.

"At the end of the game, the team with the most points wins." I smiled. His enthusiasm was contagious.

"So it's a competition?" Janice's voice cut through to the room, boring into me. The word competition echoed around the room.

I rolled my eyes. I got his point. "Yes. Aren't all sports a competition in some form or another?" I turned my head, leveling my eyes at the other end of the table.

Several males nodded their head. A female joined the discussion. "Sports are for men. Women do not participate."

"Well, that's just sexist, isn't it? If women want to participate in a sport, they should be allowed. Women don't generally play football, at least not in the NFL. That's the National Football League. But there are female football teams around the country. Women play, and it's very physical and requires a lot of strength and stamina that most women don't have. Ballplayers can get hurt pretty badly, and human women just generally don't like it."

Muttering ensued between male and female.

The man next to me spoke again, only this time he was whispering. "You'll find the females of the Fae are much the same. They don't like to be injured."

I thought that was his way of telling me to take a break.

"However, I would like to know what sports human women actually do play," the man asked. "Which sports you play that you find interesting or fun?"

Janice waved his finger again, this time up close to his mouth. He touched to his nose. He meant to keep it to myself.

"I don't really play sports. I like to watch football and walk." I figured they couldn't find anything wrong with walking. It was just walking. Lavender had said earlier that Fae walk, and several of the women gave simpering laughs.

"Do you walk to a place, or aimlessly?" The female next to covered her mouth with the back of her hand.

"Does it make a difference? Walking is walking. When you decided to come back up to the surface and start killing humans, did you to choose a specific place? Or did you just aimlessly go wherever?"

She laughed. "Well, that would be a question for the minister."

"Thank you, Sybil. You know as Minister of War, I never do anything without a plan. Of course, it was not an aimless choice to start murdering humans." His violet eyes hardened into a deep purple stone. His jaw muscle worked over the bone.

"Oh, so are you just being mindless killers, or do you have a plan for our genocide?" My heart sped up, and my grip tightened on my fork, whitening my knuckles. I stared down at the center of the table. I couldn't meet his eyes.

"Genocide implies we intended to kill all of the human race, or even a large swath of a specific population. We do not." His demeanor never changed.

"So you're just culling the weak? Genetically defective or perhaps you're indiscriminately thinning out the herd?"

Deston cut in. "I find this line of conversation boring. Thank you for your insights into humanity, Sarah. I'm sure you brought us all a little closer to our human neighbors. The meal is concluded. I will take my leave." A servant pulled the throne back as he rose.

He exited the room as many at the table twittered. Janice stood and headed to my end of the table. His eyes burned a hole in me, but I turned away.

His hand appeared in front of me. "You will accompany me, Sarah."

It sounded like an order, and I really didn't like orders. I turned and looked up at him. "Please?" I raised my eyebrows. At least if he said please, it wouldn't be an order.

He pursed his lips. Exasperation spread all over his face and shoulders, and his hands stiffened. "Please is not a word Fae use. Accompany me, now."

I leveled my gaze at the wall across from me. "And if I don't?"

He leaned in close, hot breath on my ear and neck, and he whispered, "This is not the place to make a show of defiance. I understand you don't want to be told what to do, but I'm not your enemy. There are enemies in this room. Come with me now."

I didn't want to take his hand. Lavender had pulled the chair back as I stood. I turned to her and nodded. My instinct was to say thank you, but the words died on my lips. Thank you, I didn't understand what their aversion was to it. Just another piece of the Fae puzzle.

His hand was still extended in front of me. My body was stiff and immovable.

Lavender whispered, "My lady."

I glance around. The room was quietly frozen, waiting to see what I'd do. I turned and walked out, I didn't take his hand. I wasn't going, and he couldn't order me about either. Was I a prisoner, a slave, or a person with free will stuck here? I could go wherever I wanted to. I didn't have to be escorted by him, a man who'd hacked up most of my neighbors and probably the same person who killed my youth group. I hadn't seen him carrying a bow and arrow, but somebody shot poor Pastor Rollins through the chest. Whether it was him or one of his cohorts, it didn't matter; he was in charge. It was his fault they were dead.

As soon as I was in the hallway, he grabbed my arm and yanked me into an alcove.

"You publicly shame me? You have no idea what you're doing or what's really going on here. This is a matter of life and death." His eyes bored into me. "Now I'm to take you to Deston. He needs to start training you. If you don't train, you will die." I felt his breath on my face, and my heart beat through my chest. I couldn't stop staring into his eyes. I couldn't breathe in enough air, the fire in my veins burned it off too quickly.

I hated him. He was Fae. Everything about them draws you in. They make you want their beauty. The coloring appeals to the eye. My lips parted, and his eyes darted to them. I tore my face away from him.

"You killed everyone I ever knew, and I don't even know if my parents are still alive. You probably killed them too." My index finger pushed into his chest. "If you didn't do it, you gave the order for it. If you think I care about publicly shaming you, you're wrong. I don't trust you, I hate you." The tears built up in my eyes. "You killed all my neighbors. Arty's parents—you cut off his father's head." I choked out the last words, unable to address my own fears over my parents.

He turned my face, forcing me to look at him. "You will understand one day. I didn't want to do any of this; it's my job. I must do what His Grace commands. You want to be angry at me, go right ahead—take your anger out on me."

His lips were inches from mine, but the warmth of his breath touched my lips. Deep purple eyes held mine hostage. He flashed from my eyes to my lips and back again. The hand holding my chin slid down my neck to my arm to caress my forearm.

"Remember for every war, you must have allies. And right now you have none. You think Lavender can help you?

She can make pretty clothes and paint your face, but she has no pull. Her ties are in the dressing rooms and the weaving halls. As long as she is engaged to dress you, she will remain loyal. You have no allies, and you need them. Let me say it very clearly, Sarah: this is a war, and if you want to win, you have to gather your forces." He stepped back, thrusting me away from him. My chest was heaving, and heart pounding. Hot tears fell down my cheeks, creating molten lava rivers down the side of my face. It was the fire in my chest I found most frightening.

He thrust his hand in front of me.

The only way to win is with allies. You can't fight by yourself; you need an army. I needed an army.

I placed my hand on top of his.

Lavender waited by the elevator doors, and she dabbed my tears away.

"My lady, Fae do not cry. Luckily all Fae makeup is waterproof."

I shot her a death stare. I am not Fae.

She whistled something, and I felt my face dry as the door to the elevator opened. Janice led me inside. It carried us up, up, and up. For all I knew, he might've been taking me to the highest tower to throw me off of it.

"You must sleep as much as possible tonight. I'm taking you to Deston, and then I will return you to your chambers." His breathing never wavered, like nothing happened.

I didn't want to talk, see, or touch Janice. I wanted him to go away. Instead, I pretended he wasn't there. Finally, the elevator came to a stop and opened. Janice snatched his hand away. I faced a foyer with stairs going up through archways and off to the side.

"Go to the left and down the hall. When you reach the end, you will be in His Grace's office. I will be here for you when you return."

I nodded curtly and headed down the corridor, my feet tapping on the stones. I reached the end. There were no doors, of course.

"Come inside." Deston invited me into a sitting room with two wingbacks in front of a green fire. It roared in its hearth and was pleasantly warm. He was already seated in one of the chairs with his legs stretched in front of him, resting on top of a heavily decorated footrest with clawed feet. His two feet poked up into the air. My gaze traveled from the footrest and up to the Fae sitting in the chair. His elbows rested on the arm rails with his hands clasped between. He indicated toward the chair adjacent to me.

"Study the fire with me." He never turned his head, keeping his eyes trained on the licking, green flames.

My eyes trailed over the wall and mantle, the folds of wood with twisting curves. The floor was dark gray, but I couldn't tell if it was wood or stone, or wood turned to stone? When I became bored, I stared into the green flames.

I didn't like fire. It was relaxing. It didn't just warm you. It soothes, reminding you that at one time it was the most powerful force in the human world. I needed to be alert and ready, not soothed into stupidity.

"I did not better prepare you for the meal. However, everyone has a right to meet the competition." He released a deep sigh. "I know right now you have no understanding of what I'm referring to, and by the rules we're not allowed to tell you; no one is. When it comes down to it, your job is to keep your mouth shut as much as possible and win this competition for me. Whoever wins will decide the fate of Fae and humanity. The world's a dangerous place, and you humans like to war amongst yourselves. Somewhere in the back of your mind, I'm sure humanity felt you were alone in the universe. The only intelligent life, or so you've been led to believe. Human authorities have known for a long time the Fae existed. They didn't bother to tell the rest of you. It's really not my problem. We had a truce with humanity. That truce has been broken. We broke it on purpose."

I gasped and turned to see his face.

"Don't allow yourself to obsess over the past, Sarah. Tomorrow is day one of the competition. If you win, you have my eternal thanks and devotion. Losing will cost your life. Now sit and stare at the fire, and relax. It might be your last chance." He never flinched.

"Will I be competing against other humans?" I took a deep breath and held it.

"Yes."

CHAPTER 17

Deston should have entered the Olympics in the statue category, he'd win a gold for sure. He was the Fae version of the thinking man, perhaps in marble instead of bronze. His eyes stared straight ahead into the hypnotic, green fire, unblinking.

"I'm a candidate for a competition. I don't know what the prize is, and you're supposed to prepare me for it without giving me an objective?"

"An objective, the prize at the end of the competition?" He lowered his hands to grip the armrest.

"Yes, what is it? What do I get out of this competition that I've been forced to join? What's in it for me?"

"You do realize how incredibly selfish you sound."

I snorted and rolled my eyes. Are you fucking kidding me? "I sound incredibly selfish? You abduct me, and now you're going to force me to compete in something where I very likely will die, and you're going to accuse me of being selfish." I was leaning forward fingers digging into the chair. "All because I want to know what my motivation other than survival is? What is it I'm actually going to get if I do survive? What is it, a life of the internal indentured servitude to the hollowed-out, selfish Fae, who are so shallow they can't even grasp the concept that abduction is wrong? Perhaps you shouldn't murder other races just because you think you're superior."

"That's an interesting concept coming from a human. Don't you slaughter animals and eat them? I don't know if you were paying attention to your food at dinner tonight, but we don't eat flesh; we're vegetarians."

Now I was really angry. "So that's your motive for moral superiority? We only eat plants, therefore we are better than you? We have the right to go and murder as many of you as we see fit. You use us for your own entertainment, and it ends in conflict? Bullshit! I call bullshit! I don't give a crap who you are, or what your position is in this world, you have no right to treat any sentient life form the way you're treating me." There, I'd said it.

He leaned forward in his chair, and I saw both of his hands gripping the armrests. "And how would humanity treat one of the Fae if they got a hold of us? Would they give us a nice bed to sleep in? Plenty of good vegetables to eat, nice clothes, and treat you to polite society?" I shrunk back into my chair.

He was right. If humanity had gotten a hold of a fairy, he would've disappeared into some Blackbag where scientists would run a bazillion cruel and unusual tests on it. Then they'd accidentally kill it and dissected it.

"I see your point. Yes, humanity wouldn't be cool, especially if the governments got involved. If it was just one human who met the Fae, just one, you would be fine. They might even help you keep your secret. They wouldn't force you to perform for their joy, or for their entertainment." I flicked an imaginary piece of dust from my dress.

His green eyes turned to black. "What you're about to participate in has nothing to do with entertainment and everything to do with the fate of every life on this planet. You need to understand what's at stake. It's not just Fae, it's not just human, it's life itself on planet Earth; that's what is at stake. That's the prize, that's what you get. Is that not a big enough prize for you?"

I slumped down. "Yeah, it's a big enough prize." Even for me, the world. It sounded silly and overinflated.

"I want you to think about my words. What is it that you need to do to win? Mentally, you need to prepare yourself. If you survive tomorrow, you will come here to my study every day. I will teach you Fae history. We remember history in song. I will tell you whatever it is that you need to know for the next day's competition."

My interest was peaked. I was allowed to train, and all I had to do was listen to Deston sing.

"What challenges do I face tomorrow?"

He looked away into the fire, putting his fingers up to his mouth. "I do not know. All challenges have been sealed until the morning of the challenge. I know what weapons you're allowed to bring with you into the arena. In the case of tomorrow, you're not allowed to bring anything—no one is. You go there with your wits and your wits alone. Are you ready for your first lesson?"

I get to face death with nothing, no weapons. Just myself and my brain. Great.

My brain ran a thousand miles an hour, and I stared off into the green inferno. How was singing the ancient history of Fae going to help me not die? At least it'd be a fairytale. I suppose it could be diverting.

The deep tenor of his voice reminded me of Enrique Caruso. My mother loved opera. She played it constantly in the house as she hummed and cleaned. She said the sadness always made her want to clean.

I didn't understand what he was singing about. Some woman who was beautiful and wonderful, the first Fae Queen. His voice soared with magical Acappella. The queen brought peace to her people and ended the wild abandon of war. She was the first to discover the rhythm of music. The songs were created by her, singing the world into existence. She created everything to be beautiful, from flowers to fawns. She grew her garden, and as the days went on, more flowers were created.

The only problem was when you created one thing of beauty, something ugly was also created, for all magic must have balance. In creating the Fae, she created the Fomorians as well. Ugly, mean, and strong. Where the Fae were weak, the Fomorians were strong. The Fae were cruel. But the

Fomorians were kind. The Fae were intelligent, and the Fomorians were simple-minded.

This queen had a wild Fae she loved. She chose him from amongst her people to balance her power and made him king.

She was meant to live for all time, until she started to fade and disappeared from this world. The magic was being drawn away from her, but no one knew why. She said a new queen would arise and that all must follow the new queen. A new queen did arrive. One of the princesses, she rose up. Her name was Jillian. She learned the magic music from the Queen and how to create life. In doing so, she took over all the Fae.

The old queen faded into the magical rhythm of life, leaving her wild king behind.

The new queen was not like her predecessor, and many wars ensued.

"That is enough for tonight, I will continue tomorrow," Deston concluded.

For a moment, I felt like I was seeing it with my own eyes, but I refocused on the green flames. I caught a flash of Deston's face out of the corner of my eye.

"Were you there? I mean, how old are you?"

"No, I am not one of the first. I was not there. I am old, but most of us are children amongst the first." He ran a finger across his lower lip, toying with it. He narrowed his eyes to stare at me.

"Are there any firsts left?" I shifted in my chair, my eyes darting back to the emerald flames.

"Yes, one of the other Princes is a first. You must watch out for him, he's dangerous. We are allies and must work together." His fingers trailed down his neck to wrap around a tendril of white hair.

"Don't give me the lecture on going to war and that I need allies or about how I can trust you. I got that lecture. Janice gave it to me. Just so you know, I don't trust any Fae. Not even one. There's only one person I trust, and you don't know who that is." I pressed my lips together, holding my secret close.

"You cannot trust Lavender."

I didn't move, only slowly taking a breath. "You really think I'm that stupid? Your Grace, I don't trust Lavender either"

He leaned forward with his finger steepled in front of him. "Are you referring to that boy you were captured with?"

I didn't say anything. Obviously, he already knew. I was captured with someone.

"Is that boy your, how do you humans call it, your boyfriend? Your beau? Your lover?"

My face stained with color. "No, no. Not at all."

He sat back in his chair with a half smile. "Good. I wouldn't want you to be distracted. Entanglements like that are bad. They can be used against him and you." Was there anything they wouldn't use against me?

"Am I free to go?"

"I want to sing one more song before you go. It's short."

I sat back in the chair, slouching down. I didn't care. I was ready to go. I wanted to go to my room and be left alone. I was tired of being surrounded by weird, creepy Fae.

I listened to the soaring words in his song. For a moment, I felt lost. I had to claw my way back to the surface. The music was entrancing and so was his voice. I swayed with it until I shook it off. He was trying to compel me with the music, to control me, but I didn't want him to think I knew so I sat there. Finally, the song ended. It was short, like one of those Irish ditties you always hear at pubs on St. Patty's Day. I didn't say anything. I waited for him to prompt me.

"You may go." He waved me away, dismissing me. Arrogant.

I really can't stand guys like that.

I got up meekly and walked down the corridor. Everything felt different. Janice was sitting in the room across the foyer from me. He stood and came to my side.

CHAPTER 18

"Did you enjoy your lesson?" Janice inquired.

I cocked an eyebrow at him. "Really? Was it supposed to be fun?"

His eyebrows wrinkled in the center as his purple eyes darted from the left to the right. "I thought you might enjoy the song of queens."

I shrugged. I had enjoyed it, but I didn't want him to know that.

Janice did not bother putting his hand out again; there was no one here. It was pretty telling of him, how he would treat me as long as people were watching. What did I expect? He killed indiscriminately.

I didn't want my parents' killer touching me. They could be alive. I'd only heard the sound of an AR shooting. If I'd stayed in the house, I'd be dead too or captured, and Arty would definitely be dead. I guess I should be thankful. At least this way, I had a chance and so did Arty.

They didn't want me to be a mindless slave. No, I was supposed to dance at the end of a string so they could watch me twist.

It was ridiculous, having sat at the dinner table, watching all of them stare at me while they talked about their superfluous bullshit. Humans are petty, malicious, and brutal, and yeah, we were barbaric; it was true. People still raped children, men still abused women, and women abused men; we weren't perfect. We had no moral superiority, and there was no moral upper hand. We'd invaded other countries, killing off the population. The only difference, we didn't know there was another race. Had we known it could have been a rallying point for humanity, something to bind us together into a single cause. I didn't care what Deston said. I didn't believe the governments knew about Fae. If we'd known of the Fae, we most assuredly would invade.

Great!

Now, I was rhyming as they did. Mostly Janice since I hadn't heard any of the other Fae's making their magic rhyme. I wondered if a rhyme would work for me? "Jack and

Jill went up the hill to fetch a pail of water. Jack fell down and broke his crown, and Jill came tumbling after." The hair on my arms stood as a chill ran down my back, stabbing my spine with pain. I covered my mouth with my hand, pressing in and wishing I could take it back.

He turned to me in the elevator. "You know what that rhyme is really about?" His arms were crossed.

"Yeah, it's about two kids who went to get water out of the well, and one fell down and hit his head because the hill was too steep. The two of them couldn't carry the pail of water together. The other one fell down too, but it doesn't say she hit her head though."

I mean it was pretty obvious it was just a nursery rhyme, a fairytale.

"That's not at all what it's about; it's a rhyme. It is a Fae tale, about two Fae who reached for more than they deserved. The bucket is the weight of their desire, and they desired power. Both climbed the hill to reach the stone throne the 'well' of knowledge. Only toward the top, Jack fell, and he hit his crown. He was knocked back down to his place. Jill, the girl, he attempted to put on the throne, she fell after. It's a failed attempt at a coup. That's what Jack and Jill were all about." Janice finished and turned away.

Well, that was something I didn't see coming. I had no idea that a fairytale or a Fae rhyme could possibly be the screen for a failed coup. That turned every fairytale on its head. Were all Fae tales a dark commentary on politics and societal nonsense? Humans turned it into a cute children's story about making kids work too hard, or at least that was what most people thought.

"Their names were Jack and Jill?" Those didn't sound Fae to me.

He turned his purple eyes on me. "Their names were Jacques and Jillian, and a long time ago, they did attempt to wrestle the crown away from Danu, but that is the history of wild. I'm sure Deston will be more than happy to sing it to you. What are your plans for tomorrow? You cannot take any weapons in the competition with you. You're only allowed the clothing you wear."

"I was really hoping I could wear a breastplate. Perhaps some kind of armor? Lavender said you had armor." My voice quivered, and the butterflies in my belly went wild.

This was real. They were going to make me fight for my life with nothing but the clothes on my back.

Who does that? Gladiators?

Janice chanced a glance at me, "she did? Fae, do have armor. I will talk to her tonight to discuss what you should wear. I will not allow you to compete without a way to defend yourself." He continued.

"I realize whatever I wear, it's not a fashion show. However, I want to wear jeans and a T-shirt, along with whatever armor you give me." I asked.

"You'll wear whatever I advise. It will keep you alive, and human clothing won't protect you." Janice replied.

I didn't appreciate the way that he mentally manhandled me, as if he knew better no matter what. He had the last word, and down here Fae were in charge. I was a nobody, a human for their public entertainment.

"Also, you will need to bind your breasts." He turned his head away from me.

I threw my head back and laughed. "Fae arrogance knows no bounds. You're telling me what to do with my boobs? I already know what to do with my boobs, thanks." I smirked.

In a flash, his lips breathed onto my face. His nose practically touched mine as his liquid purple eyes penetrated into mine. "I may not have a breast on my body, but I've fought more battles than any human alive. I can tell you how to stay alive, and you should listen. Male and female Fae fight and I know how to dress a female and her breasts." He retorted.

I knew my face must've been three shades of red. I felt the heat as blood coursed through my body.

He'd probably touched somebody's breasts. I was getting exactly what I deserved. Assuming he wouldn't know what to do with boobs simply because he didn't actually have them on his anatomy, I was stupid to think that.

He kept his face a breadth away from mine. His perfect skin turned pink, but he didn't blink. He was waiting for some kind of retort, but I couldn't muster one. My mouth was open and drying out. I ran my tongue along my lips. His eyes changed color, and they went from the light purple to deep, smoky amethyst as they followed my tongue. For a moment, I had the feeling that he might kiss me, and I wasn't completely repelled. How was I not repelled?

I stepped back and felt the wall behind me. "Bring me whatever you like. If I find it acceptable, I'll wear it."

He stepped forward. I was trapped between him and the wall. "You will wear what I bring you, because whatever I bring may keep you alive. Binding your breasts isn't just about keeping them under control. It's about providing yourself with a piece of fabric you can unwind from your body and use as a weapon or a rope or a sling. The fabric isn't just for clothing—anything can be a weapon." He stated.

I tried to laugh it off. I didn't like him getting up in my grill.

The elevator door opened. Janice stepped back, extending his hand in front of me. He expected me to somehow suddenly want to touch him right after he practically threatened me. I put my hand over his, but I didn't let our skin touch.

A strange perfume floated around in the elevator as he led me out. Fae always were intoxicating. I heard him sing the notes for the door before they closed. I rolled the tune over in my head several times to reproduce it later.

He didn't need to whistle my door open since it was already unlocked with Lavender inside. He waved her out the door with him for a few words.

I sat on the bed as my keepers discussed my care as if I was some kind of animal. Lavender returned and stripped off my finery. She put me in the bath and then to bed.

I couldn't decide which was more important: to think about Deston trying to sing me into some kind of stupor, or Janice constantly telling me how I needed to protect myself and defend myself. As if he gave a shit.

Both were overridden by a niggling in the back of my mind. Jack and Jill were Jacques and Jillian. They tried to lead a coup for the crown. Why would you put a well at the top of a hill and have it represent a crown? That didn't make sense to me. There had to be some deeper meaning to the Fae tale. They were trying to get to the well, but that wasn't what he called it. He said stone throne, and the bucket of water was the weight of their desire for power. They failed and were knocked back down into their rightful place but by whom?

Lavender twittered on about things at dinner, mostly about clothing and hair. It really was her thing. I tuned it out. When she left, I jumped up and hurried to the door. I was desperate to hear the notes again. There was one low note, a B-flat in the treble cleft. I waited a couple of minutes, singing the tune to myself, but I couldn't reach that deep of a B-flat.

Tomorrow was another day. My finger reached my teeth unbidden and I bit down on the nail, no, tomorrow isn't another day. I whistled for the mirror and looked at myself. I didn't look any different other than my hair color. I felt different. Before dinner to now, something was different. I couldn't put my finger on it. My eyes did look less brown, and my eyelashes were the blackest they'd ever been. Lavender had dyed all my hair. The black was so dark it carried a purple hue to it and shone like obsidian.

But there was something different, something intangible. I couldn't put my finger on what, but it was there.

I whistled the mirror away and climbed into bed. Whatever happened tomorrow, I definitely wanted to be awake for it.

CHAPTER 19

The Fae light dawned through the crystalline window, and Lavender bustled around my room. First, she brushed out my hair, and then she put it into the tightest, seven-strand braid ever.

"Would you like to see the braid?" Her hands never stopped moving over my hair and skin.

"Can you do that?" I held my breath, a new tune to learn.

She whistled, and the mirror appeared but only reflected the back of my head, which looked like a woven piece of fabric. My hair wouldn't come out any time soon. I had no idea what I was facing, but the last thing I wanted was my hair in my face.

She pulled out a sports bra. "I finished it last night. I think it's exactly what you were describing, and it will work perfectly for today." I was in heaven. The first Fae sports bra and she called it an activity brassier.

It fit perfectly. I didn't think the girls were going anywhere. My hands cupped both breasts.

"Now you don't have to bind your breasts and are able to run."

"No, Janice said go ahead and bind anyway. I'm allowed the clothes I wear. I can use the binding as a rope." I turned in the mirror, and my heart sped up at the thought that I might need a rope. Pulling air through my nose to calm my nerves, I breathed slow and deep.

She instantly saw the wisdom of his words much as I had. She pulled out a ten-inch-wide piece of fabric, and she wrapped it around my body, keeping one end loose to tie with.

"How long is this piece of fabric?" I asked. My breast compressed further with each layer adding weight.

"Four of your human yards. I think the equivalent of twelve human feet." Lavender had to be dizzy by now, running around and around.

Twelve feet might get me from one story to another. If I had to shimmy out a window, it could work.

She pulled out a pair of pants. They looked like a cross between yoga and Barbarella stretch pants. She presented me with a side-closure, quilted jacket. It didn't look like it would protect me. It had epaulets for god's sake. I was waiting for some 18th-century gentleman to jump out with a rapier and say, "en garde."

"This was the armor Janice instructed you to dress me in?"

Lavender smiled brightly. "Oh yes, it's a special type of armor, light and flexible. More conducive to movement, and much better than the breastplate."

I raised my eyebrows and crinkled my nose on one side. I didn't think it was an improvement on a breastplate other than the weight. Actually, I would've felt better wearing a breastplate, even if I lost mobility.

"I know. It doesn't look like much compared to a full breastplate, but keep in mind, looks are deceiving. This is Fae. It's made out of spider silk and woven with spun diamonds to create the hardest material. It will stop whatever weapon used to attack you, including a sword." I cringed away from her primping hands. She was talking about a sword attempting to chop off various extremities of my body or kill me. So yeah, the whole idea that it'd keep someone from hacking at me—real, fucking comforting.

"Attacking, that sounds lovely, I'm sure. It can stop the sword, but it won't stop the bruising, right?" Sometimes I thought Fae were complete morons. They didn't actually hear themselves when they spoke, but I knew that wasn't true because they loved to hear themselves speak, which was why they were always talking; they were full of themselves.

The weight of the entire outfit felt like nothing, and I was running around naked with a pair of tights. To top it all off, she handed me a helmet to match; it was ridiculous. I looked like I was wearing a padded hat. I ripped it off of my head.

"I'm not wearing this hat."

"My lady, take the helmet with you. I know it looks silly, but you are going into battle. Wouldn't you much rather look silly and live than be beautiful and die?"

I hate her. I snatched the padded hat and put it under my arm. I supposed if anyone was going to be hacking at me, my head would be the first place to aim for.

She led me to the stairs, and I cocked an eyebrow at her.

"Really, I have to walk down seven flights of stairs before I go to my death?"

I knew there wouldn't be a reprieve. No coffee or veggie breakfast, but seven flights of stairs along with my padded hat— the day was off to a brilliant start. Going downstairs wasn't as bad as going up. When you go down, your only hope was that you wouldn't trip and then end up rolling the rest of the way down. One thing I didn't enjoy about stairwells in a circle tower, they're corkscrews. Each stair was wedge-shaped. Footing was everything. One misstep and you'd be head over teakettle to the bottom of the tower. Fae didn't have these issues. Fae were surefooted, every move graceful and similar to a dance. I wasn't saying I wasn't graceful. I could dance, and I had a type of grace, but next to Fae I had two left feet. I liked climbing rocks, shooting guns, and field stripping my weapon. Not like other people who'd never taken a gun apart or didn't even understand the mechanics of how the weapon worked. I wish I had a gun.

All I knew was seven flights of stairs and no coffee so call me angry. That and I was desperately lonely. I wished my dad was here. He'd know what to say, even though I was going into the unknown. He'd gone to war for the United

States and into the unknown; he called it the sandpit. He said other than knowing that you're going to get a sunburn and sweat your balls off, you had no idea what was going to happen. You suck it up and make the best of it. I needed to do the same thing: suck it up and make the best of it, even though I didn't know what I was getting into.

We reached the bottom of the stairs and stepped out into the courtyard area.

"Where we going?" I asked.

"Janice instructed me to take you to the stables." She led me to a wooden structure. It appeared to have grown out of the side of a giant wall.

I was crestfallen. At least if she'd taken me to the other stables, I could've seen Arty. There was an honest to god carriage, a Cinderella look-alike, and it wasn't made with a pumpkin. It was painted midnight blue, and the wood curled and creating intricate scrollwork. The girl in me enjoyed it, but the tomboy in me said humpf.

Two pure white horses with fiery red eyes were harnessed to Cinderella's ride, my ride. The eyes of the stallions reminded me of the little white albino mice, the type used in laboratories. Janice dashed to open the carriage door and waved me inside. His magnetism affected the group of the gathered Fae. These Fae were heavily armed with crossbows, swords, and daggers, all wearing armor similar to mine.

My stomach flopped, eyeing all the weapons. My hands balled, digging my nails into my palms. I could barely feel the nails, they were too short.

Why did I bite them?

Other than the fabric compressing my breasts, I had no weapons, and now I couldn't even scratch someone eyes out. Adrenaline flooded my system, causing me to take deep breaths. Whatever it is, I can do this. I swear. Tears threatened, but I blinked them back. Save the crying for after, otherwise, I was wasting my energy.

I climbed into the coach followed by Janice, who shut the door and whistled the lock closed. I got it. It was the exact whistle Lavender had been using, and I'd heard it clearly. The notes played over in my mind, committing them to memory, G, F, G, B-flat, C. That was what I'd been missing and couldn't hear, that low C. I'd missed it, and that was why I couldn't unlock my own door. If I could reproduce the whistle, I could unlock whatever it was they'd put me in, freeing myself and maybe even Arty.

Janice cleared his throat.

"The seals were released this morning. The first trial will take place at a castle in Jacques' domain."

Big cold fingers trembled down my spine. "Jacques, you mean like the Jacques in the Jack and Jill story?"

"Yes, the exact same one."

"Is he one of the first? Deston mentioned there was a prince that was one of the first." I gulped. If Jacques was willing to attempt a coup to depose a queen, what would he do to a bunch of humans?

"You were paying attention. Yes, he's one of the first and probably the most powerful prince in the realm." His eyes darted over to me and back to the window.

"What's the challenge?" I held my breath.

"It's a challenge of his choosing, and it will be deadly. You're only allowed what you have on your back." His brows drew down over the bridge of his finely sculpted nose.

Only allowed to take what I had on my back and no weapons. I loved James Bond and Jackie Chan. Both were masters of fighting with what was around them.

Think, think… I got it.

"What's holding my hair in place?"

He shrugged his shoulders and glanced over at me like I was crazy.

"I have no idea, a leather thong I guess, why would it matter?" He tilted his head away from me.

"If there's some kind of pushpins in my hair, I could probably accomplish the same thing with long spikes and a leather strap or hair wire. If I take it all out, I could turn it into a garrote. That's a weapon, but in separate pieces, it's nothing."

His eyebrows reached the ceiling, and the color of his eyes turned into lilac as a smile spread across his face. "Well, aren't you a clever girl!" He knocked the ceiling of the carriage. It came to a jolting stop, and he lowered a window and waved a rider over.

"Get me two long, thin spikes and a long piece of wire." He measured about three feet. "Be quick about it."

The Fae on the horse turned around and spurred the beast hard on the belly, producing a squeal as he galloped off.

"My lord, should we keep going?" A voice traveled from another rider.

"No, we will wait here." He turned to me. "Killing someone with the garrote is not as easy as it sounds. You have to sneak up from behind and slip it over their head before they have any idea what you're about. It's twice as difficult for a human woman because you're not strong." He'd moved his hand to my arm.

I didn't want to kill anyone, a garrote or otherwise. A garrote wasn't the only thing you could make with metal spikes and wire.

My bravado took over with a smirk. "Don't you have some kind of song to make metal stronger that you can use on me?"

He touched his nose. "You have a clever mind. Yes, we do have such a song."

We waited for about half an hour for the rider to return. He handed the items through the window, and Janice held them in his hand.

I listened closely. Whatever magic he used would be important, and I had to remember it. If I could make an item stronger, I could survive. Maybe.

My eyes darted from the metal in Janice's hand to his face.

Assuming I could sing it, I knew that was the secret to getting out of here. I had to learn every song, anything to give me an edge. Janice was right. I needed allies. I needed Arty.

He began the song, and it carried the underlying current of a song I heard as a child.

Mary had a little lamb.

I didn't want him to catch me humming, so I tapped against my thigh and sang it in my head.

I turned away from him, and he took out the leather thong untying the base of my braid together. He rewrapped it with the wire, and then he inserted the two long spikes into my hair. I felt them scraping against my scalp as they slid in. It wasn't much, but something was better than nothing.

An hour passed until I spied on the horizon the spires of another castle. Of course, they all looked like a fairytale castle because they were. This was Jacques' domain.

"I'm here as an emissary for Deston. If I'm attacked, it is an act of war. However, having you attacked is not. Although you fall under Deston's protection as a candidate for the trials, you are provided no such protection under the law. No one within Deston's domain may attack you without reprisal. However, once we leave his domain, you're free game for anyone."

That was comforting. Within the castle and his lands, I was safe but the moment I stepped outside of it, everybody and their cousins were trying to kill me. Lawfully.

CHAPTER 20

In theory, if you'd seen one, you'd seen them all. Frankly, in the land of Fae, I was sure all the castles came from Cinderella or maybe Beauty and the Beast, or maybe even those old Hans Christian Andersen or Brothers Grimm fairytales. They were based on something and clearly, at least one of them was based on mad King Ludwig the II's castle Neuschwanstein. He must've been mad for a reason. Neuschwanstein was his response, a crazy castle he built in Bavaria, bankrupting his monarchy and his entire country between his obsession with the swan knight and all the castles he'd built.

Yeah, I thought I knew why he went crazy. Looking at this castle, I could bet he was here, and that explained why he didn't sleep in the same place for very long. He was probably terrified that they'd come back for him.

If I get out of here, I might never sleep again.

"This is the power seat in Jacques' domain. It's called Swan house."

My mother had shown me pictures of Neuschwanstein when I was little. She told me to never visit a castle, and that princes were evil and mean. None of them would ever save you, but most of all never to fall in love with a prince.

Swan house was a reflection of Neuschwanstein but with more towers. The extra towers were twisted with even more towers protruding from each other. They narrowed and widened without rhyme or reason. The scale was the real difference, and Swan house was four times the size.

"Jacques is a Prince in the Unseelie court." His eyes never left the window, vigilant to a fault.

"As opposed to the Seelie court?" I was being a smart ass. Sarcasm was my go to.

"Yes, you have been spending your time in Deston's domain. Now you will see how life is elsewhere." From a distance, the castle was fantastical and sweet. Something about Janice's words rang true that behind this fantastical beautiful tranquil setting lay a deep, dark secret terror.

"The Seelie are supposed to be the nice polite controlled proper ones? After murdering all those humans? Yeah, I see it. Absolutely. They're one hundred percent tame." The Unseelie were worse than the Seelie? Why, do they have entrails and heads on spikes?

Janice turned his face away, ignoring my jabs.

"Well, if Jacques is the one determining the test, what do you suppose he'll use?"

"He's only had three hours to construct or contrive whatever your test will be. Something he's already built and added to it. I have my suspicions, but until I see, I don't wish to alarm you too much. I'll give you as much information about it as I can."

Could I rely on this guy's information? Was he my ally? He proclaimed that I needed allies. I couldn't trust any of them. They were all Fae, intrinsically liars, manipulators, twisters, and murderers. Why would I listen to this guy?

Could I answer that question for myself? Was he worth listening to? He was loyal to his cousin. Did he have my best interests at heart? The prize was the world itself or something like that, the very destiny of human humanity, and Fae. They were my handlers, so what did that make them? Something in my gut told me that if I didn't watch what I was doing or how things worked out, I'd end up a puppet.

Okay, chill out, Sarah. You're jacking yourself up, and there's no reason to get all freaked out. Until you know what you're looking at, stop juicing yourself up.

There weren't any spiked heads on the wall. I didn't see any bodies or entrails hanging anywhere, but the butterflies in my stomach and the clenching in my chest wouldn't go away. Adrenaline seethed through my veins, and my legs kept fidgeting with my fingers drumming.

I hadn't even seen what the test was, and I was already pumped.

"Sarah, you need to breathe and calm yourself. The adrenaline flowing through your body is good, but you don't want to burn out too soon. You have no idea how long this test will take."

I looked from my hands to his hands and then to his face. He was a statue, cold. No matter what happened to me, it didn't matter to him. Or did it? My father's words rang in the back of my mind: in the real world, failure could very well mean death. If you're going to run the yellow light, you have to push the pedal all the way down. You must commit, and you must cross the intersection before the light turns red and traffic commences. If you falter, if you question your own resolve for even a split second, you won't make it through the intersection fast enough. You will be broadsided and likely die.

Whatever decision I made, I had to fully commit. I didn't have a choice on whether I participate in this event, but I did have a choice about whether I lived or died.

The fluttering in my belly slowed, and I pulled air in through my nose and pushed it out through my dry mouth.

The carriage pulled under the gatehouse, only to be directed around the inner courtyard.

"They're sending us to the gardens."

The entrance to the gardens was the mouth of a grotto, the walls of which were lined with faces. Some were open and screaming, and others were closed with gleaming eyes and vicious smiles. Everyone had a ghoulish display of malice. It was a short tunnel, and after you passed through, it opened up into a giant garden area. It'd been set up more like an arena with seating all around the outer edges of a hedge.

Janice began talking. "This entire garden is a maze, and it has been enchanted. The walls move about every five minutes, and there are all kinds of creatures roaming around. Many are vicious and deadly. There are too many to name them all, but that's not the part you should be worried about. In the very center of the garden is a round cylinder. It rises up and down continually, turning as it goes. In the center is where your prize will be. Getting onto the disk requires a trick, and I'm sure the only person here who knows it will be whoever Jacques' candidate is."

Note to self; watch out for Jacques' candidate.

"If you make it through the maze to the disk, don't be misled. The disk is massive, and it has its own maze on it. The entire garden is a labyrinth, and there are pitfalls everywhere."

Great. Just what I've always dreamed of—a labyrinth run by a Goblin King.

"There will be spikes with all kinds of poison. You need to watch out for lashing creepers. They're poisonous if they manage to wrap themselves around you, and they'll inject you with poison, paralyzing you while slowly eating your flesh. That is just one of the lovely things Jacques likes to keep in his garden."

Stay away from the nasty man-eating vine. Check.

My hands clasped and unclasped.

"When you reach the center disk, whatever your prize is, I'm sure it will be there. I'm not sure how you get out. Perhaps your garrote will help you, or perhaps not. I do not know." He sucked in and released air. He ran his hand over his face, allowing it to trail down a strand of long white hair.

Now that sounded exciting to go through a constantly moving labyrinth of deadly vines amongst other things.

The rocking of the carriage came to a stop. My heart sped up. Janice helped me down from the carriage, and I straightened for a better view, only to spy box hedges. If I didn't know any better, I would've assumed it was France. Near one of the water gardens, water tinkled and splashed. Water was a noise that soothed, but something told me that garden was deadly. Don't drink the water, don't eat the fruit.

He led me over to a corral filled with girls, the most beautiful girls I think I'd ever seen. Some with short pixie hair, others with long, gleaming tresses, and all were wearing armor similar to mine with their padded hats tucked under arms or on the ground around us. All were smothered in fear.

One of the girls had dirt under her fingernails. She wore jeans and a torn T-shirt. Everything about her screamed feral human. Her hair was tangled and filthy, and her eyes kept darting from the left to the right. There were thousands of girls black, white, Asian, Latin, Islanders; they'd stolen the best of humanity. We were all young.

Janice closed the gate on me, and I was corralled with them. I was one of them. My chest clenched, and moisture formed on my hands. I rubbed them across my belly to still the butterflies there.

The feral girl couldn't have been more than fifteen. I put my hand out and petted her hair. She darted away and curled up into a ball next to the gate. She'd probably survive better than the rest of them; they were too relaxed. Maybe they knew what we were facing. I was shaking and terrified, and I expected everybody else to be as well.

We were divided into four groups, and each was led to a different section of arched entryways shaped out of boxwood.

I was only surrounded by humanity, but I could feel it humming. When Lavender said every living thing had its own key, I hadn't been able to understand. Her close proximity interfered with my ability to hear the notes. I wasn't listening but standing amongst humans, because they weren't intrinsically involved with the music. I heard it vibrating, making my skin crawl and dance at the same time.

I reached out to the hedges, and I heard the sweetest C in the world. It was a middle C, a perfect C, and it wasn't a minor or major; it was all-natural. The type of C you only heard from a freshly tuned piano. Mother would sing it and play it. I didn't know how I knew all of this, but I did. It was a part of me, inside of me. It felt right, and I knew the boxwood would be a C. One of the girls with brown hair reached out and broke a few leaves off, and the vibration in the boxwood changed. It dipped down to a low C, natural but angry.

"I wouldn't do that again if I were you. Everything in Fae is alive, and you have no idea how it's gonna react to you attacking it." The words were out before I could take them back.

She cocked her eyebrow at me. "Well, egghead, did I really attack the bush? It's a bush, a plant. How do you attack a plant?" Her smug reply irritated me.

"I wouldn't be so sure. Not long ago, we thought fairies weren't real."

She laughed and flashed her hazel eyes. "Yeah, fairies exist, and they're trying to kill us. Stay out of my way, egghead." She put her finger on my chest and pushed me back. Her swagger was out of place with the rest of us.

I always liked to win. You didn't have to demoralize your opponent to win. It wasn't my style, and I didn't have to. I felt the anger in the boxwood, and it was gonna go after her first, I just knew it. She'd already sealed her own fate. It didn't matter who she was or what her story was. It was all over because she disrespected a boxwood bush. How pathetic was that?

"You should respect life. If you don't, they won't respect ours. That's why we're here. You should be better than them. Even a lowly boxwood bush deserves respect." My fingers ran over the leaves of the boxwood, and as I petted the plant, its volume grew and my words made it happy. Could a plant be happy? I got the distinct impression that it was pleased.

She threw her hair over her shoulder and glanced away, wiggling and weaving through the other candidates.

The feral girl looked up at me. "You really think the plants are alive like that?"

My eyes darted down at her voice. "Absolutely."

She tucked her head back down, keeping her hands balled in front of her. She stared off into the sea of legs standing around her. She'd phased out again, but her eyes darted around looking for danger. I thought she was a lot smarter than the rest of us. I still smelled the fear on her, or maybe it was me.

"Greetings, Fae. His Royal Grace, Jacques, welcomes you to his domain. As you can see, the candidates have been gathered. This is the best humanity can provide." The proclamation was followed by twittering of laughter around the arena. "Each and every one of our candidates was brought into the Hallowed Hills with a friend, lover, or someone from their family. Each of them will have to save whomever it is they were brought with. Anyone who doesn't reach the center of the maze to free their companion not only will they die, but their companion dies with them. Your lives are connected. Without you, someone you love will die. Your test is to see how much you truly love your friends and family. Because the only way to rescue them is with true love, and you cannot trick a Fae."

Arty, my heart filled my throat as I turned to the gate.

With that, a loud clanging filled the air, and the gates to the garden swung open.

That's it? No rules, no further information? Just simply go save someone you love? Bullshit.

The girls in my group filtered tenuously through the arched opening. I ran my hand along the box hedge, feeling the hum of its life.

"If you help me through the maze, I will bring you some fertilizer," I'd whispered into the bush.

Okay, it sounds a little crazy, talking to plants. I just offered it fertilizer. If bribing a plant helps me through the maze, then I'm absolutely willing to bring it something to eat. Hopefully, it doesn't eat humans but likes water.

"Are you talking to that bush?"

I turned and threw a look over my shoulder. "What difference does it make to you? Go save whomever it is you love."

"The girl I was captured with, I don't love her; I can't stand her. We were at school." She waved her hand around and cocked a hip to the side.

"Well, then you should love yourself enough to go and save her because your lives are tied together. Or didn't you hear that part?" I raised an eyebrow at her.

She put her finger up to her face, tapping her lip with her index finger. "I guess you're right." The shallow wench tossed her hair over her shoulder and trotted away. What is with all the self-absorbed abductees?

I ran my fingers through the tiny leaves as I passed under the arch. Passageways led off in five different directions like spokes on a wheel. I didn't know which way to go. Most of the girls picked randomly. I saw one of them do an eenie, meenie, miney, moe. As if you could actually control which one it landed on. I didn't know which way to go either. I placed my hand on the hedge trailing around the spokes, passing every corridor. I was hopeful somehow or another the plant would tell me where to go if I listened.

One of the corridors sounded sweeter, higher, and cleaner than the rest. It had to be the way. It was the only one that sounded different. That was the path I chose, my feral friend following behind. She too trailed her fingers along the bush until we came to a T.

I didn't want to acknowledge her or be responsible for her.

The left sounded sweeter than the right, so I turned in that direction. The screaming began far off in the distance. One high-pitched, shrill scream wrenched the air, only to be joined by another, and it didn't stop; it kept going. I moved faster, and the hedge led in the opposite direction. For me, that naturally said safe.

Off to the left, I heard another scream, but I couldn't see anyone. The hedges had to be at least fifteen to twenty feet high. They created a gloom. My feral friend still followed close behind. I began to hum a boring song, something I'd made up as a child. It was mindless and off-key, and everywhere I hummed my little ditty, a small hole appeared in the hedge.

The little leaves, holding themselves back on each other, created this little portal where you could see into the next row, almost as if I'd been telling the bushes to open up. I came to a three-way split. I could go straight ahead, right, or left. None of the three of the directions sounded better than the other. My feral friend sat at the T.

"Which way does the bush tell you to go?" she whispered it out.

"It doesn't. They're all the same. Even going back the way we came doesn't sound any better." My hands found my hips, and then I scratched the back of my neck. What the fuck do I do now?

"How do you know it's alive?" She tilted her head up, showing me one eye.

"Can't you? Don't you feel the vibration?"

She shook her head. "My mom used to sing to our plants. They always grew big and beautiful, and she said the plants liked it when you sing to them; it made them happy. You're the only person I've ever seen do it other than her." She wrapped her arms around her legs, pulling them tight.

I smiled down at her. "I feel pretty stupid singing to a plant."

She shook her head. "My mom never did. She said the plants knew, and she could feel it. I can't feel whatever she was talking about. But if singing to plants saves our lives, maybe we should do it." She gave me a tight-lipped smile.

She was right. Maybe we should do it. I had my song, and it created some kind of opening in the hedge. There was no north or south. You could look up at the sky, but with the dim gloom of glowing globes so far away, I could barely see if there was even a ceiling up there. I noticed that all around the garden area they had increased the light sources. Floating globes gave off illumination. I looked up to see that there was one following us.

It's more than light.

Time to commit. I chose the right. I couldn't tell where the center of the maze was, and I didn't know if the maze was round, rectangular, triangular, or an octagon. Janice left that little tidbit of information out when he was informing me of what I'd be facing. So I went to the right.

The bush screeched out a C-flat. It was bizarre like it was screaming at me. I stopped mid-step. After hearing the noise I didn't want to move. I stepped back into the T and turned for the middle, but the bush screeched again, hurting me. I stepped back.

The lanes moved, crashing together before altering the junction. Where the three lanes had been, they all disappeared and merged to form one and then divided into three new lanes.

I smiled down at my feral companion, and she returned a tight-lipped smiled.

"I bet if you sang right now, it would do something for you." She batted her eyes away and rocked back on her butt.

She was probably right. But I didn't know what to sing. The bush would save our lives if we'd gone down any of those corridors, or we might've been trapped or headed in the wrong direction. Maybe being nice to plants was smart. It didn't take me but a moment to realize which lane I needed.

I took the path to the right; that was my intended direction anyway. But this path led somewhere else. The C was sweet and natural, so I followed. It curved; we weren't going straight anymore. You could see the slight right angle of the hedges. Until the curved ended in nothing.

A dead end.

The C still rang sweet, and I hummed along with it.

It curved into nothing. There had to be a corridor on the other side, somewhere I could go. As I hummed, a hole opened to reveal a face. A girl's fawn brown eyes creased in pain met mine. Green trendles with sharp leaves wrapped around her neck and face, covering her eyes. She opened her mouth to scream, but her body stopped moving.

As soon as I stopped humming, the hole closed. I grabbed my companion's hand, running back the way we came.

I didn't want to hear the screams. We had to run from them, but they followed me. They came from my friend and I, but then they turned into whimpering. Slowly, the whimpering turned into nothing. Nothing meant death.

We made it back to the T, but it was different. The maze had changed again. I followed the C. My new friend didn't walk, so I dragged her. I didn't want to stop. My legs were shaking, and I'd dropped my padded hat somewhere; I didn't care. We stopped and leaned against the bush. A sweet C was still ringing in my ears. It vibrated on my skin all the way down the backside of my body. My chest heaved. Tears rolled down my face. The girl next to me cowered at my feet.

"Who was eating her?" Her voice came out a whisper, and she choked the words.

I shook my head. "A vine. She was eaten by a vine." My voice shook.

Janice had been right. The terror in that girl's brown eyes, I couldn't get it out of my head.

My feral friend's eyes darted around, searching for vines. I didn't see any, but that didn't mean they couldn't reach out through the bushes at any time and grab us. They could've been lurking out of sight beyond those small innocuous oval leaves hanging there.

I stood and straightened myself. My tears had created green streaks on the fabric. Apparently, the sadness caused me to change the color of my clothing. Now I looked like I'd been dragged across a grass field. The more I tried to wipe it away, the more the spot spread. It became a big blob of a mess over my belly.

CHAPTER 21

My head whipped to the left and to the right. I didn't have a lot of time to think about or cry over what happened. My heart was pounding in my chest, and my breath came in gasps and gulps. My hands clutched leaves, hoping that sweet C would come back to me. Maybe by humming, something would happen. But everything was frozen, scared, and trying to hide. It wasn't just the hedge that had gone quiet. Everything became deathly quiet.

When I first stood near the garden, I heard humming, the low keening of a song. Plants and creatures each with their own tune, all that humming was gone. In the silence, I could make out my own breathing and that of my friend.

"What's your name?" My eyes darted to the left and right as I pressed my back against the hedge again. Barely making out a vibration, I had to stick my hands in deep.

"My name is Zoe. If I don't get out of here, my sister's name is Olive. Try to help her, please."

"I'm Sarah."

I looked down at her, eyes wide with fear. She couldn't be more than fourteen or fifteen. I didn't want to speak, so I nodded, crushing my lips together. I shook my head vigorously. I turned my head back and forth, searching for what was different. What had changed? A crackling came from the background. Fire. We were in the middle of the garden, and there weren't any fires. What could've possibly sounded like a fire?

We weren't allowed to bring weapons. Nothing about the ground had changed. It appeared the same—brown marble stepping stones, hedged in by a regular box hedge with oval-shaped green leaves. No vines or flowers. Nothing, except for Zoe, who was cowering down by my ankles.

Off in the distance, the dry ground moved. Every now and again, there would be a spark as if somebody was rubbing fire rocks together or flicking a lighter without any fluid in the dark. The little sparks would rise and then crackle like fire, getting closer. The bush behind me shifted almost as if it'd pulled back so I could lean into it.

"Zoe, stand up. Stand up and get ready to run."

She shook her head at me, bringing her fingers up to her mouth and biting her nails.

"You want to live and save your sister? You die here and she dies wherever it is they have her. Our lives are tied together. Stand up and get ready to run when I say go." My insides quivered. God, I wish Arty was here.

Her lips trembled, eyes darting, as she glanced to the side. I grabbed her hand. Her entire body was nothing but shivers and trembling. Or maybe that was me, I didn't know.

I surveyed the other direction. My heart sank. It was coming from both directions. There's nowhere to go. I saw the fear in Zoe's eyes.

"We are never getting out of here, and it's all my fault," she moaned. "Olive's going to die, and she never even got to live." Her voice hitched at the end.

I reached in deeper to the bush. Instead of humming my little ditty, I sang it, letting the words come out loud. I wanted to power through whatever fear this bush had. It was afraid. Every plant was afraid of fire. Nobody wanted to burn.

The bush from the inside pulled back, and there was enough space for me to shove Zoe through. I yanked her arm to me and then thrust her into the opening and away from me.

"No, no, no! Don't let go of my hand! Please don't leave me alone." Her head was shaking. I was still singing, but it wasn't enough to keep it open. The opening collapsed. I tried to sing it open again, but I choked. The acrid smoke burned my throat.

I heard Zoe on the other side singing.

"Jack be nimble, Jack be quick, let Sarah jump over the candlestick. Jack be nimble, Jack be quick, let Sarah jump over the candlestick." She kept singing it, but nothing happened. She was singing out of tune. It wasn't going to work. Whatever it was that she wanted to happen, it had to be the right vibration, the right key.

I closed my eyes, and I listened as closely as I could. I didn't hear anything. I couldn't think of what Janice said or Lavender. The heat from the flames licked not far from me.

In the loudest voice I could muster, I sang, "Sarah is nimble, Sarah is quick, Sarah jumped over the box-hedge sticks." With the last word, my body propelled forward and pushed me to the other side of the hedge rising. I caught a quick glimpse of exactly what it was that we were also terrified of.

A little brown salamander made the fire. I was afraid of a lizard? I was scoffing to myself as I looked back and saw the salamanders reaching my padded helmet. The entire thing burst into flames, and they shot high into the air. Every lizard body that touched the fabric glowed bright red, like metal heated by a furnace or forge. Flames flew high, and I could feel the heat on my feet, just before I cleared the top of the hedge.

I heard a roar and screaming from somewhere. Frankly, I didn't care where. We'd gotten away from fire lizards, and that was all I needed to know. I landed, and Zoe let out a scream. I watched in horror as vines wrapped around her.

"Save me, Sarah! Make it stop!" She fell to the ground, and the wrapping began to squeeze her. I pulled the wire off the end of my braid. I wrapped one end around a spike and pulled the other spike out. With shaking hands, I wrapped the other end of the wire, creating my garrote. I slipped it around Zoe's body and down to the ground where the vines entered the soil. Zoe's fell over sideways and I murmured an apology.. I crisscrossed the wire and yanked to cut through all the vines, Zoe screaming bloody murder in the background. Her terror pierced my ears. Finally, I was able to not only choke the life out of the vines but cut it away from their lifeline. Zoe's eyes glassed over.

"I wish you could've saved me."

I put my hand to her face and began ripping the vines off. "No, no, no! Please don't die, Zoe. Please don't die! Please don't leave me alone in this maze. Stay with me! You have to stay with me for Olive. If you die, she dies. Fight it, whatever it is. You can do it! Janice said it just paralyzes you. It doesn't kill you." I slapped her face, pulling at the vines and ripping them away from her body. I saw where they cut through her clothing and into her skin. My face was wet with tears running down. After I got most of the vines off, she blinked. I slapped her face as hard as I could, and she coughed. I slapped her again, and her fingers moved. I raised my hand to slap her again.

"Please don't hit me again, Sarah."

I laughed and cried. I tilted my head back up to where the sky should've been and whooped. "Get up! We have to go."

"I can't make it. I can't stand up and walk alone."

I got up off of my knees and gripped both of her wrists. "You grab my wrist back in the middle. I'll pull you up. It's a climber's lock. It'll keep your hand from slipping off. If you can, we can make it together." My fingers tightened around her wrists, and I pulled and leaned back at the same time.

She was so small and slight, I lifted her up off the ground into a sitting position.

"Grab the wire next to you and hand it to me."

She released my wrist and grabbed the wire. She handed it up.

I wrapped my wire weapon around my waist, twisting the two spikes and locking them against each other.

There is no way in hell I was ever going to put that thing anywhere near my neck.

I opened my hands again, and she returned to our climber's lock. Bending her knees at the same time, she pushed up to her feet as I pulled. Soon, she was standing. Wobbly, but she was up on two feet.

There were little nicks and cuts all over her face and tears in her clothing. She gave me a tight-lipped smile, and blood oozed from a few of her wounds.

CHAPTER 22

I pulled Zoe's arm around my shoulders, securing it to me with one hand. I took my hand and wrapped it underneath her armpit. She was pretty light, so it wasn't a big strain to help her walk. She was one of those little pixie girls. I didn't know what a pixie looked like. "You need to do the best you can to try to walk. I don't know how long I can hold you up. We need to make it to the center."

"I'll try."

"Just remember that you're not doing it for me. You're doing it for Olive."

Out of the corner of my eye, a grim frown descended over her, and her eyes found the ground. I'd seen other siblings do stuff like that. As an only child, I didn't have anybody to look out for or take care of. My mother never had to say don't let somebody beat up on your brother. It was just me and then, of course, Arty. But I'd seen other kids with younger brothers and sisters fighting back to back. I was jealous of that. When you're an only child, you're always to blame if the lamp gets broken or for the spill on the floor. You can't blame it on the dog.

She held her head up a little higher and her back straighter.

We followed the sweet C. I glanced down at the awful vines, having severed them. They'd withered, turning brown, limp, and desiccated. They looked like they could've been lying in the hot sun for weeks. I guess fairies were swift about everything. Life and death.

The hedges curved. I was certain we'd gone in a circle, but I couldn't confirm it with no sun, nor any directional skills. We were heading in the right direction toward the sweet C, and it led us right to the exit of the labyrinth. Directly in front of me was a giant cylinder-shaped object moving and turning in a circle. It moved up and down at the same time like a spiraling piston. Janice's description had failed to mention the giant chasm between the edge of the main part of the maze where I was standing and the piston itself.

In the gaping chasm were more bushes. The sweet smell of gardenias wafted up, and white flowers bloomed surrounded by hunter green, waxy leaves. The perfumed air was heady with a drugging scent. If I had to guess, I would've said they were my mother's favorite, gardenias, But gardenias were massive, like three inches across and not like these piddly, star-shaped kiddy cutouts.

"They're only flowers. We can walk through. There's a ledge around the base, and we can climb up or maybe find a way to scale the side." Zoe really thought she could climb it, but I could tell by the way she was walking that she wasn't strong enough to climb anything.

I eased her down into a sitting position, keeping my eyes everywhere but her face. Her eyes searched my face and the surrounding area. A rustling off in the distance was followed by the appearance of another contender. She couldn't have been more than sixteen. Her cocoa skin and black hair shimmered under the light of Fae.

Zoe curled into her ball of protection, her arms wrapped tight around her folded legs, and she closed her eyes.

The black-haired girl wandered over to the edge of the leafy chasm. "Oh, beautiful flowers." Her high, sweet voice cut the tension in the air. She pushed a tendril of glossy black hair over her round human ear.

I stood at the edge of the chasm, searching for a way across, but I watched her every move.

She never glanced our way before plunging down into the chasm. The bushes reached her waist. The leaves rose into the air and came alive, and small green humanoid creatures with pointy ears and giant milky blue eyes swarmed as they grabbed her hair.

My hand slapped over my mouth.

A scream came from the girl's lips. The hive pulled at her clothes and glossy black hair. One jumped on her face to gnaw on her nose. I watched the blood spout from the sides of their little mouths. Their piranha-like teeth tore at her exposed skin. She dripped bloody screams, and they dragged her down into the perfumed moat.

I stumbled back, landing hard on my butt. A different section of bushes lifted up and flew over to their kill. Every hair on my body stood up as the horror struck me to my core. The gardenia bushes weren't pretty. They were Fae. There's nothing more dangerous than beauty? Sure, it was pretty. Right up until it kills you. Zoe scratched at my arms, whimpering. I placed my hand on the matted, grimy mess on her head. A hot trail of tears raced down my face. I clutched Zoe to me, holding her tight.

That poor dark-haired girl, she didn't look before she leaped. Her screams died out, becoming intermittent whimpers until nothing surrounded us but the garden and the thick scent of death. I whipped my head around. There was nowhere to go. The only way to the center was to somehow scale the side of the giant piston but not before crossing the moat of death. The top was edged in box hedges, a bushy wall hedging in trees and vines, some of which trailed down the sides. The gap was ten feet wide, too wide for me to jump.

I'd scrunched my eyes shut, waiting for the carnage to end.

Zoe's low, quaking voice informed me, "You can't go in there, Sarah. Those things will kill you."

"I know. But we have to find a way across."

The cylinder garden turned, rising up more than thirty feet and then lowering down to within ten feet of the ledge. The motion was hypnotizing, coupled with the low continuous sound of rock grinding on rock.

There were no trees in the chasm, no trellis, wall, or anything that you could take apart to use to build a bridge. Nothing. Why in god's name would anybody build this kind of giant garden of death?

Screams off in the distance somewhere reached us, but they were quickly silenced. Some turned long-winded and then muffled whimpers into nothing. Every one of those poor girls had been standing in the corral with us. I began unwinding the fabric over my breast.

Janice, he was right. You could use it, and I knew what I was going to do with it. I took the two spikes I'd used for the garrote and unwound the wire. I crossed the spikes and rewound the wire, crisscrossing over the center and creating an X. I wound it as tightly as I could, weaving the wire this way and that so it wouldn't shift. I tied one end of the silk to the X. My only hope was that it was long enough. I just needed it to hold long enough. I took the rest of the fabric and looped it loosely in one hand. I pulled out about four to five feet.

I looked down at Zoe. "I don't think you can follow me, but as long as you stay alive, I'll set Olive free for you, okay? They didn't say that you had to do it. They said your lives were tied together, and if they weren't freed, you'd both die.

There's a loophole to everything. I think that's the loophole, and if it isn't, it's better than nothing."

"No, I'll try to climb up after you. I think I can do it." She pushed up into a standing position, jutting her jaw out in determination.

"If you don't think that you can make it across that chasm and climb up after me, you'll only get Olive killed. Stay alive here. Staying alive keeps Olive alive." I placed my hand on her shoulder, and our eyes met. She nodded her head, tearing her eyes from mine.

I let the X hang down on one side, holding it back about three feet. Just as my father showed me, I started swinging it around in a circle. When it had enough momentum, I waited for the X to reach the right point in its revolution. It swung up behind me, and about the time it reached my shoulder, I let go.

I held onto the end, eyes glued to my makeshift grappling hook. It hit the cylinder wall and slid down. I yanked it back, breaking through the gardenia bushes and disturbing the creatures. They flew about, but for some reason, they didn't leave the chasm. Maybe they'd been trained to not, or it was Fae magic. All fairy magic had rules, and you only have to figure out where the loophole was.

Pulling air deep into my chest through my nose, I planted my feet shoulder-length apart. I rolled both shoulders and my neck. The blood pounding under my skin made my hands shaky, but I shook them out.

I wound my fabric up again, loosening three to four feet. I couldn't swing any more than that without dragging on the ground. I wound up again with the world's worst grappling hook of all time. I had to get it on the top of that cylinder, and I knew how I'd missed last time—my release. It was short by about a foot because I didn't wait until the cylinder was at its lowest. But this time I had the rhythm of it. The piston started slowly descending, and my hook rose. Just as it crested my shoulder, I released it. It hit the edge of the upper garden, going over the edge by two or three inches, only to drag back before it latched onto something. I jerked on the fabric, forcing it to dig into the box hedge. I wanted it to be secure.

The piston reached its lowest point, only to rise again while still holding the end of the fabric. It was too long. If I didn't do something quickly, I was going to be dragged into the chasm. I wrapped it around my hand three times. I jumped into the air and grabbed for a higher hold while pulling my legs up to my belly.

Aw, shit.

Limbs and leaves scratched my backside, raising a cloud of the pixie-like creatures. I pulled hard with my upper arm, loosening my grip on the lower hold to reach above. My body slammed into the side of the piston, and it rose higher and higher. The fabric dragged me across the ledge, twisting my arm in the process. My arm was fully extended above my head, pulling my feet up out of the bushes. A pixie dug his teeth into my shoes, but I nudged him off with my other toe. The pixie became angry and took another bite, but then it shook its head, realizing it wasn't going to be able to penetrate it. I took my other foot and kicked them off, and the pixie went careening back into the chasm. The pixies flew back to the bushes, and I must've passed out of their domain. They ceased to find me of any interest.

The moment my feet touched the supporting ledge, I realized I was already standing on my tiptoes. The piston was still rising, and my toes were soon touching nothing at all. I was being pulled up by my arm but turning at the same time. I was being pulled away from Zoe's location. Fear filled her eyes as she shifted her weight from one foot to the other.

"Stay alive, Zoe! I'll do my part, you do yours."

She nodded her head, chewing on a fingernail. There was no way I'd be able to get the fabric back to her.

I turned my body around in an effort to reach above and to give my shoulder relief. It was killing me. Slowly ever so slowly, the piston turned and began its downward motion. Eventually, my feet met the ledge again. My fabric rope loosened, and my left hand was able to reach well above my right. I grabbed the fabric and unwound my hand. I tied a loop and then tied the lower portion of the fabric around my waist, adding a rolling clove hitch to the end. The loop was big enough to put my foot in. Hopping along the ledge, I lifted my right foot and inserted the toe of my boot into the fabric loop. Pushing down with my foot, I pulled up. There wasn't time to do that trick again, the fabric was fully taught now.

Standing on one leg, I reached above my left hand and squeezed with all my might. I pulled as hard as I could, and I planted my left foot onto the wall.

Why hadn't I paid more attention to rock climbing? Dad said scaling a wall was important. Why didn't I listen? There was a reason why they taught it in the armed services as a part of basic training and everybody must pass it. Because you never know when climbing a wall might save your life. He made me do it, but I'd always had a terrible time with ropes and knots.

Rock climbing seemed like geometry and algebra—things you'd never use in real life.

It hadn't even occurred to me that I might not have had enough fabric to make it across the pixie chasm of death. My heart sped up.

The up-and-down motion continued until finally, I thought I would see Zoe again. But she wasn't standing there anymore; she'd moved.

CHAPTER 23

The muscles in my back ached, as did my arms and shoulders. Everything was creaky. I wasn't sure if I was going to be able to pull myself up even one more time. Zoe was definitely gone. Everything around the piston looked exactly the same. The hedges opening in shapes, it was an optical illusion, done on purpose to disorient you so you'd lose your way. That was the whole object of a maze.

But I told Zoe to stay there. I looked up at the rim, and it had to be a good ten to fifteen feet above my head. I was too far gone to give up. If I don't succeed one way or another, Arty and I would be dead.

Maybe I should've waited and watched for a while longer? I could've learned something.

It was easier to pull up when the piston was in its downward motion, like an extra boost from gravity. But as we were going down, at the point that it normally would've stopped, it didn't. It continued lower until my feet touched the ledge again. I removed my foot from its loop and untied the fabric around my waist. The piston continued down, so I pulled the slack back up and knotted it in several places above where I had reached previously. I took baby steps along the ledge. Following the edge at its lowest point I was within a couple of feet of the upper garden. I heaved myself, using my feet to find the knots I had tied and inching up the fabric fighting for purchase on the ledge. With one arm still wrapped around the silk fabric and the other poised over the top of the upper garden ledge, I pulled with all my might to the edge. Finally, close enough I hiked a leg up. There was a slight lip to the inside. My heel locked over it, and my quad strained along with my shoulders and arms as I rolled over the edge.

I had made it. Unbelievable.

I watched Zoe appear from the shadowy bushes. The upper garden was still receding down into its resting place until it was level with the pixie chasm. A bridge extended itself to the edge, and Zoe ran. Just as the piston of the garden began to rise, she jumped onto the edge. She wasn't that far away from where I stood.

I reeled up my fabric and pulled my grappling hook out of the bush. I wrapped it around my waist, affixing it to me with the X over my belly button. Some weapon would better than no weapon. I raised my arm and waved to Zoe. She waved back. I sprinted in her direction. My body came to a dead stop against some kind of invisible wall. I pounded my hands and kicked at it.

Zoe was on the other side. She gave me a tight-lipped smile.

"How did you figure it out?" I heaved a breath with both hands splayed out.

"Easy. Whoever owns this place had to be able to get to the other garden themselves. It turned like a clock goes around. You had to wait for the right moment for the cuckoo to come out and chirp." She wasn't just some stupid fifteen-year-old running around desperate to stay alive.

"You're brilliant, Zoe, but I don't think we can get through this wall. Got any ideas about that?"

"Can't you like sing it away or something? Isn't that what you've been doing?"

I thought about what she said, but it was an invisible wall. It didn't have a sound. There was no key or tune to it.

I shook my head. "No, I don't think so. I can't hear it."

We walked along the edge next to each other. I was thirsty and hungry, and I'd spent most of the day running. I was beginning to feel the drain. Nothing about this place was edible or livable or even really all that pretty. Gazing around, I saw trees but nothing like what I'd seen at Deston's castle. His gardens were magnificent, but this was boring and drab. So far I'd only seen three or four flowers, one of which harbored killer pixies.

"Zoe, when you were watching the upper garden, did you see any flowers other than the ones the pixies were living in?"

"No, I don't know what kind of garden this is, but it's not a flower garden." Her eyes still surveyed the area in a clockwork fashion.

With my back to the outer edge, I knew one way or another I'd find Arty. They said the prize was at the center. So as long as I kept walking in a straight line, I would find the center. Unless of course, this was an illogical garden and the center was off-center. The hope I had in my heart for the end of this game crashed and burned.

It was very possible that they wanted to be whimsical and decided the center wasn't the center. Like the golden ratio spiral, and it wasn't centered but off-centered. I guess I'd find out either it was the center or it wasn't.

I couldn't stop my eyes from shifting left and right, constantly searching around. With the invisible wall to one side, at least I knew nothing was coming from that side.

Zoe managed to get herself up there, so she wasn't stuck and completely helpless. There were trees and bushes but gone were the box hedges of the lower garden. They were replaced by small, sculpted topiaries shaped into flowers as if a Japanese man had come through and trimmed every single one.

I was waiting for Mr. Miyagi to jump out and tell me to wax on, wax off.

The hair on the back of my neck stood up, and all the bushes jumped to a crescendo. They hummed in the background, their sweet little songs, whatever they were. Someone came through and sang, shaping them. They morphed the song low, just out of reach and below my ability to hear. I felt the vibrations in my chest. Zoe wasn't affected.

The sound must've been imperceptible to Zoe. "Can you hear that?"

"No! Hear what?" I shook my head. There was no point in trying to explain it to her. You could hear it or you couldn't. The bushes moved, and they ceased to be flowers. They reshaped themselves.

Zoe squeaked. "The garden is changing. Did you see that?"

"Yeah, I think we need to move faster." I picked up my pace to a flat-out run. My chest heaved, lungs straining, as I pumped my arms back and forth. The bush in front of me took on a shape suspiciously like an octopus. My already adrenaline-soaked body filled with a new dose as I imagined a tentacle reaching out to me.

The eight limbs undulated as if it was on the seafloor. Octopi had eyes, but I had no idea where they were. They opened just as I passed it, brown, they were brown. The eye tracked me, and that was when I saw the wooden hooks and barbs grown into every tentacle. Octopi didn't just grab their prey with little suction cups and hold them in place. Oh no, they had little barbs next to their suction cups to hook into their prey. Sometimes they ripped out the barb to cause blood loss and weaken their prey or to tear their prey into smaller pieces to fit inside their mouths. I didn't see the mouth of this octopus, and I really didn't want to. I did see a giant arm swinging my way.

I ducked as it swiped past my head. I dipped out of reach, but I ran into the stupid invisible wall, crushing my shoulder and losing balance. I fell down. I couldn't roll to the side. I used a stick poking through the wall as leverage to stand back up and keep moving. I trailed one hand down the invisible barrier with my legs running. The octopus swiped again, missing me. I must've been out of range. By now, the garden was in full kill mode; it wasn't just an octopus. Other creatures from a ram, a lion, and several dogs were coming for me. A dog threw back its head and howled as it bared its white, woody teeth, licking its leafy tongue between its sharp canines. All of it was a green plant and very creepy. I saw how tightly packed the leaves were, creating the surface of the creature. The little leafy veins were in variegated colors. The leaves merged themselves together to create perfect skin, in some cases even mimicking raised veins and muscles. I wondered what it would be like to be digested by a plant? If I didn't keep my ass in gear, I'd find out pretty quickly.

Zoe yelped on her side of the wall. There was nothing I could do to help her.

The pièce de résistance of the garden was a mystical creature. A giant green leaf-covered dragon. I spied the head.

Maybe, it was just a head. But it reared up, exposing its chest and front claws. The woody tips gleamed in the light with their razor-sharp edge. Its long neck undulated as it pulled its head back and roared.

I would've rather dealt with one of those flying versions. It would've given me a minute to run away. It put one foot on the other side of the invisible wall and reared back, unfurling its massive wings. The dark green leafy skin stretched between the wooded skeleton. I heard a snap as it finished unfurling to reveal the little horns on the tips of the spiny edges. It leaned its head back and roared.

Please don't let it shoot fire. Please don't let it spew fire. Please don't let it spew fire.

I didn't think there was any way I could get around the dragon. It was connected to the garden ground at its belly. A massive umbilical cord attached to its belly button. I was able to move around relatively easy, but it was still anchored to one spot with only its wings and head capable of reaching out to me.

How am I going to get away from this thing while dodging snapping jaws and the hounds of hell?

I worked my way back and around, out of reach of the dragon. Its evil yellow eyes watched me, so I waved Zoe off in the opposite direction, hoping she'd walk around the evil dragon.

She stopped dead still and took a good long look at the dragon. She pulled something out of her shirt. I saw light flash off of it—a knife.

How the hell did she get a knife in here?

She ran dead straight for the belly of the beast. The closer she got to the dragon she crouched down and slid in like she was headed to home base. She reached the umbilical cord as the dragon turned its head under to snap at her. She hacked away at the base of the bush itself, the one thing attaching it to the ground. It morphed, growing smaller and smaller as there were fewer branches to connect it. Soon, there was nothing more than a baby wyvern. With no hind legs to hold it up, it beat its wings rapidly to stay in the air, balancing on the tip of its tail.

It opened its mouth and snapped at Zoe, pulling a chunk of hair and skin from her head, but it was too little too late. Zoe was already halfway through the last of the branches. It reared its head back to roar, but her knife sliced through the last of the fibers. It wilted with its wings held wide.

I jumped up and dashed to her side, dodging snapping jaws and growling mouths.

Blood poured from the wound in her scalp. She blinked blood from her eyes. I unwound a length of silk and took her knife to cut it. A high E issued from the fabric, raking over my ears.

Ignoring the pain that rang through my head, I wrapped the fabric around her head several times and tied it in a knot.

She resembled a trauma victim. She launched herself at me. "Thank you! You saved me."

I didn't know what she meant. She'd saved me. "We don't have time for this. Thank me when it's over."

With her arms wrapped around my neck, I stood, and we both continued to the center of this hellhole.

My eyes darted left and right, scanning for trouble. There had to be something more. It couldn't be over. In my gut, I knew there was more. Every rustle in the distance told me there was more.

CHAPTER 24

We pushed our way through to the last of the bushes, most of which were relatively inert. I heard notes coming off of one or two of them but nothing significant. I didn't get the feeling any of them were lying in wait to attack us. A bush resembling a pterodactyl, but it also looked like an Areca palm. It was bizarre with two long, spindly legs stuck into the ground, spreading palm fronds and shaping itself into the bird's long snout and its web-like wings. We skirted around it, waving the knife to ward it off.

This was the quiet before the storm, my gut kept telling me, like one of those horror movies where everything gets quiet before something jumps out and scares the shit out of you. Or just before the murderer decides to jump out and kill everyone. What were the words they used to describe it, eerily quiet?

Whatever was going to jump out, I wanted to be ready for it. I couldn't stop looking around. If I let my guard down, it was going to be there ready to jump or attack. There had to be something to set it off. I saw Zoe's hand kept reaching toward me, and then she would pull back like she wanted to hold on to my hand but was afraid.

"If you want to hold my hands, just go right ahead and do it. I don't think it's a good idea. I understand you're scared, but whatever comes, we need to have both hands available to fight it off."

"Who creates a garden to kill people?" Her voice pleaded with me.

"I don't know, it's a great question. What kind of sick, sadistic creature decides they're going to kill off someone in a garden? 'Hey, come over for a party. We'll go to the garden and kill some humans. It'll be fun, and bring a friend; it's BYOH.'"

"BYOH?"She asked.

"Yeah, you know, bring your own human." I snickered.

She snorted and covered her mouth with her free hand. "Bring your own human. That's funny. So the killers are already here, they just need to bring something to make them want to kill us?"

"Yeah, that's kind of the idea I was getting. They bring us here to kill us, yeah."

What was really obvious was that it was designed for someone to survive or maybe a few someones. The big question wasn't who survives, nor was the big question whether we survive. The question was why did they want us to survive? Why did they want anybody to survive? I mean, the running around killing us, this was some kind of contest, or the Fae said it was. Janice said there was a prize, something bigger and more important than humanity or fairy. Deston said it was the world. No one could offer someone else the world, so it was ridiculous. Maybe he said that to make me fight harder, to want to win more.

I shook my head.

Up ahead loomed a massive tree, one of those great old oaks or maples. The garden ended at the edge of a giant sinkhole. The tree sat in the center, suspended from a platform and linked with bridges. The roots of the tree trailed over the side, hanging down into the black void.

"What kind of tree is that?" Zoe asked. It was apparently a conversation to take my mind off the open, bottomless pit surrounding the tree and the narrow bridges leading to it.

"I think it's an oak. It looks like one that my grandmother had in her backyard."

"Yeah? Was hers over the top of a big hole too?" I asked.

"Yeah, no, it just looks like that." She replied.

Oak trees lived for hundreds of years, and this one looked like the first oak tree of all time. The massive gnarled branches twisted around on itself. Giant roots dug into the platform and curled around the bridges, clinging to one another in a twisted, woody vine.

It was easy to see the various humans surrounding the base. All had different colored hair and skin. I heard moaning from the direction we were headed.

A B-flat permeated the air. It was high and bright, and it rang from the direction of the tree, like the sound of a bow being pulled across the strings of a cello calling to me.

Zoe extended her hand, reaching out for it. She turned zombie-like with enchantment and walked to the edge of the pit skirting around to a bridge. I grabbed her hand, desperate to pull her back. She simply kept going, wrestling her wrist this way and that to free herself. I lost my grip, releasing her.

I wasn't entranced, and I didn't find the sound of the tree was entrancing at all. It sounded terrifying, but we weren't the Eloi and the Fae weren't the Morlocks, were they? Living underground, preying upon humanity, was that what was really going on here? It sounded like the bell that H. G. Wells described in his story. The one that rang the humans to their doom, leading them underground to be eaten and devoured by blue inhuman creatures that had once lived on the surface. How would Wells have warned us? What if it wasn't for some fun science fiction story about a time traveler? What if time travel was something he was describing to warn us in the future? The Fae had done it before, and they would do it again.

What if it had happened before? I saw the way she moved toward the tree, the way the other humans were enslaved as willing participants in their own death with little regard for themselves or anyone around them. They turned into mindless food or fodder. Maybe Wells got the food part wrong, but he hadn't gotten the fodder part wrong.

I wasn't sure how, but he realized there was a creature living underground, attempting to control us, dominate us, take us, and use us.

I followed behind Zoe, tentatively talking to her and hoping to snap her out of it.

The light globs hung in the air around the tree like marbles left where they may. They lingered under the bridges, revealing the flat surface holding the tree suspended above the bottomless pit.

The tree held all the prizes prisoners. They were stuck and incapable of freeing themselves. In their entranced state, the desire to free themselves was as vacant as their eyes. The roots of the tree had wrapped around their legs and driven through their hands, even wrapping around their torsos. It held them tight to the base.

There had been others, nothing left but a bloodstain. They'd been absorbed into the tree as if it lived on human blood and ate them. Bile rose to the back of my throat. The acid taste caused saliva to flood my mouth.

How do you free someone from a tree that absorbs them?

CHAPTER 25

H. G. Wells said in order to defeat the Morlocks, the Eloi destroyed their underground facilities, blowing them up to bury them alive. Few survived, and the only ones left, lived on the surface.

As this all ran through my mind, judging by the network of caves and the sheer volume of this massive cavern. They weren't just caverns. It was a whole other surface to the planet, an underground world. If I didn't know any better, I'd think that the Earth was hollow being down here. I'd never heard anything about a hollow earth, but if you tried to collapse what was down here, you'd destroy the surface in its entirety. H. G. Wells' resolution would never work.

Somehow there was a balance between the two, there had to be. Either we humans and Fae could both survive together, or we'd mutually assured each other's destruction. I didn't think humanity would survive.

H. G. Wells didn't have to worry about trees that sucked people dry of their blood.

Zoe approached the tree. I wanted to pull her back, but I was also fascinated to see what happened next.

She was entranced. How could you release someone when you didn't even have control of your own mind?

She stopped in front of a young girl, no more than eight. It had to be her sister, they had the same hair color and some of the same facial features. Both of their cheeks curved into a shy smile, and their eyes were vacant, but deep inside they recognized the other. Zoe stretched out and touched Olive. Her bonds fell away, and the tree freed Olive. It made no attempts to attack Zoe or her sister.

The Fae hadn't said how to get out of the garden. All they said was that we had to get to the center and free our friends. That was it. All we had to do was free our friends.

Nothing happened. Zoe freed her sister, but they were both still standing there in a zombie-like state.

I was a coward for standing off to the side, watching my friend and waiting to see what happened. She couldn't control herself, and I didn't want to take the time to tie her down to something that could kill her here.

I need more data. Information was power right now, and I had zero power and zero information. Watch and wait, that would be the smart move.

I paced around the base of the tree till I spied black hair and light reflecting from glasses. I stumbled over roots, stopping myself short of touching him. My hands itched to free Arty from his thorny bonds, but what would happen after? My belly filled with acid. What if I became entranced by touching him? I didn't know what to do. I sat as close to Arty as I could and waited. With my arms wrapped around my bent legs, I rocked and waited.

Other than the B-flat and the C of the bushes, I couldn't hear anything else. There were no humming insects or screams. I didn't hear footfalls. I was alone.

The girl stuck next to Arty whimpered. The tree pulsed and visibly moved in and out as if it was a beating heart and taking a breath like lungs. With every breath out, the girl next to Arty cried louder and the thorns around her breasts dug deeper. A branch appeared near her neck and wrapped around it with thorns, lashing around her neck. She screamed.

Nobody moved, and I was frozen in fear, transfixed. I couldn't move. How did I know the tree wouldn't lash out at me for trying to stop it? Her eyes opened briefly.

"Please, please," her small voice pleaded with me.

I watched the light in her eyes die. Her mouth was open with a 'please' dying on her tongue. She didn't blink, and the tree opened behind her. It split in two and drew her inside. I watched as the sickly pallor of her skin disappeared behind the brown of the bark, leaving behind only the bloody thorns that had been holding her in place.

My mouth hung open and soundless to the horror I'd witnessed. The shock of what I'd seen wore off, and I jumped up. The last thing in the world I wanted to happen was for me to die two feet from Arty and not having released him.

Zoe had barely laid a finger on Olive and the tree reacted. I tentatively stretched my arm out. The hum of the tree rose to greet me. My index finger made contact with his hand. I curved my fingers around his palm. The B-flat widened its resonance, and the branches and thorns vibrated. The creaking squeak of wood splitting open surrounded me as the tree pulled back releasing Arty. I grabbed his wrist with my other hand and dragged him away.

Are you kidding me? That's it? All I had to do was touch him?

Arty stood stock-still with milky-white eyes of enchantment. My hands shook as I ran them over his body, searching for injuries. Other than some bumps and bruises, he was fine—a mental zombie but fine.

I ran my fingers through his hair, combing it back from his face. I cupped his stubbly cheek. He didn't respond, and tears welled in my eyes.

What was I hoping for?

"Arty, wake up!" I shook his broad shoulders.

His eyes blinked, and his shoulders raised and lowered but nothing. The fire I'd been carrying around in my belly raged into an inferno. I raised my hand and slapped the side of his face. His head whipped to the side and returned to his original position.

"I'm sorry! I just want you back. Wake up please." My arms wrapped around his waist, and I buried my face in his belly. "Please, I can't do this without you. We're a team,

Tweedle Dee and Tweedle Dum." They had turned him into a dress-up doll. The only difference between Arty and my American Girl doll was that he was a boy.

I stepped away. I had to. We couldn't stay here. I'd take the Fae whammy off Arty later. We needed to get out of here. I grabbed Zoe's hand and then her sister's and led them to stand next to Arty.

The tree sounded like a bell in the back of my mind. I heard the Christmas song, "Ring Ding A Ling" playing in the back of my mind. It ran through my head, and I gazed around. That was it! I needed to create a song that sounded like bells or a metal xylophone; something with a metallic ring. If I could harness the sound the tree was putting off, maybe I could save everyone.

I began to hum "The Chorus of the Bells," but I couldn't remember the words. The tree rippled. It was vibrating with the sound of my voice. The tone apparently identified with the song, and the thorns retracted. The branches pulled back, releasing their captives. I grabbed the hands of the free and led them over to Arty. The tree's base was massive. It could've rivaled any sequoia in California, and they were thousands of years old.

In my mind, the song ended. I stopped humming. At that moment, every thorn lashed back, cutting into whomever they were still holding. I started again. Some of the words came back to me in different places.

My parents had never been much for Christmas music. My mother said it was everywhere, and it made her crazy. Now I wished I had listened closer. Every human that I freed from the tree, I pulled away as they stepped up. I moved as quickly as I could until there were thirty-eight people standing around the clearing. Every single one of them was dead in the mind. They were dead in their eyes; alive but no one was home.

I couldn't think of a way to free them, and I didn't hear anyone else coming. I stopped humming the bell song, and the tree vibrated deeply, rippling out from our location. I could almost make out a wave of sound.

I tried to think of what I'd heard Janice sing before he entranced Arty.

He used some nursery rhyme maybe. The only one I could think of was "Ba Ba Black Sheep." Maybe the words didn't matter, and it was all about the music and intent. Music was about swaying whoever was around you to your point of view and making them feel what you feel. I wanted every person here to be awake like I was. I had to think of a song that spoke of freedom, where you weren't beholden to someone else or enslaved by them. But I couldn't think of any songs like that. I didn't know those nursery rhymes. They didn't exist in my world.

Whatever it was, I'd have to create it. The ground rumbled to the point that soon I would stumble and so would everyone else. I couldn't risk anyone falling into the black shaft under the tree. For all I knew, it led to the center of the Earth. Hand-in-hand like a daisy chain, we walked over one of the bridges, reaching the edge's topiary garden. I gathered the kids into a tight circle.

Tapping my forehead, I walked around the group until I reached Arty again. I looked into his glazed eyes. Janice, he'd sung about home, his home. I was from Texas, the Lone Star State, and the only song that came to mind was the American national anthem. They sang it at the beginning of every football game, and it reminded me of home. I couldn't tear my eyes away from Arty. He loved the national anthem and watching the game. He always forced me to watch too.

"O say can you see, by the dawn's early light." I let it burst forth.

The ground shifted underneath us with the vibration elevating us. I saw the stones breaking away and separating. My ankles shifted back and forth like a surfer on a board. I fought to maintain my balance. Visually, it looked like we were still there, but I could tell there was a difference in level between where I was standing from where we had been.

I'd created a floating raft similar to what Janice used to bring me here. I kept singing a song of home, of America and Texas, of the flag that managed to stand through an entire battle, no matter how many times our enemies tried to take it down or destroy us. I held onto that idea, the idea that we could prevail, even in the direst of circumstances, humanity would prevail.

We rose into the air about three feet off the ground when Olive slipped as if to tumble over the side, pulling at Arty's arm. Arty's eyes lost their milky-white vacancy as Olive's arm yanked him off balance.

I couldn't stop singing, but my belly tightened. I missed a note, and our raft shifted until I regained my composure and carried on.

Arty released my hand and smiled at me, but he also turned the momentum of Olive's fall back around, flinging her onto our raft. He traded places with her before he disappeared over the edge.

My hand clawed at empty air. I wanted to scream at him, to save him, but I knew that if I stopped singing, everybody would be lost. My voice rose as my chest tightened and tears fell. I'd never heard clarity in my own voice or the beauty of my own songs. I always sang along with the radio and in the shower like everyone else. This was different though. I heard my own desperation as I raised my voice and sang those last few words, "The land of free and the home of the brave."

The world snapped, followed by a loud crack.

I suddenly wasn't looking at the garden of evil anymore. We were floating in the sunshine somewhere near my house. The circle of stones we'd been riding, they lowered themselves down onto the middle of the street.

We were surrounded by rotting corpses lying in yards and on sidewalks.

My zombie companions stood holding hands, and I couldn't think how to wake them up.

I walked over to Zoe and slapped her as hard as I could. Other than the red handprint on the side of her face, there was nothing.

I collapsed to the ground crying. Arty was gone. I made it out, but he wasn't here. My scream tore free. He'd woken up and fallen. I'd put Olive's hand in Arty's. Why? I tilted my head back, and my raw throat shrieked at the sky.

It was all for nothing.

I dug on nails into my palms and then beat my thighs with my fists. A warm trickle of blood filled my hands. I opened my palms, and they were covered with blood. All I saw were Arty's eyes as he sank from sight with his hand stretched out to me and his brows pinched. Blood was everywhere, and it filled my nose and met my eyes. My hands were covered in it. I rubbed them on my pant leg. The only thing I accomplished was rubbing the scabs off. The blood kept coming.

I desperately searched my surroundings with my eyes, which landed on Olive and Zoe. They stood together holding hands. They both wore their shy smiles of contentment.

They were together, and they had each other. I snapped my jaw shut, locking my teeth in place.

We have each other.

Arty wasn't gone. He was lost, and I had to find him.

I reattached Olive to my human chain and then grabbed her hand. I walked home with thirty-seven kids in tow.

I was on autopilot. I couldn't see where I was going through the blurry world of my tears. I instinctively I was facing the wide-open front door of my house. There were no bodies in front of my house. Hot tears rushed down my face again as I looked over at Arty's parents. His father's head was halfway across the yard. I wanted to scream, but I was afraid of who would hear me.

Carefully, I left all the kids in the middle of the street. None of them could see the bodies. I was sure they couldn't smell the stink of rotting human flesh. It was probably the most disgusting smell I'd ever encountered in my entire life. The number of flies was amazing.

Before I reached the tripwire to my house, I retched in the grass. There wasn't anything in my belly, but whatever was left was gone. I fell on my hands and knees. My hair fell into my face, and my braid had come undone. I wiped my mouth off with the back of my hand. I used my fingers to squeegee some of the puke out of my hair. I wiped my hands on my pants. My body was covered in a thin sheet of sweat and grime.

I didn't see any blood in the doorway, but the door was wide open. Clearly, someone had come in.

I carefully stepped over the trip line for the Claymore. I spied blood on the floor, just a little bit, but not enough for anybody to have died from. I forced my feet to carry me farther into the house one baby step at a time.

CHAPTER 26

I opened every door, closet, and cupboard. I went upstairs and downstairs. I went to the office and pulled back the safe, but it was empty. All the weapons were gone, and all the food was gone like someone had torn everything out of the cupboards, which hung off the walls. Arty's parents' freezer was standing open and still running, but it was empty. I stopped and absently close the lid.

There was nobody here. I wanted to sit down and cry, but I couldn't. They were probably dead. I went back to the gun safe and dialed the lock pin, my birthday, August 8, 2003. The door swung open without a sound, quietly since it was oiled. Inside, there was a note taped to the back wall.

"That room Arty and I were looking for. We found it. Come find us."

The room they were looking for at Sorenson's house. He'd found Sorenson's safe room or whatever they called it.

I crunched the note in my hand, listening to the crinkling of the paper.

I ran upstairs and ripped off all my clothes, hearing the threads tear from the seams. They had blood on them from the Fae, and I hated them. I grabbed jeans, a T-shirt, my own sports bra, and hiking boots, the ones Dad bought me earlier in the summer. I opened my nightstand and pulled out two LED lights, which I'd kept there in case the power went out. I put one in either front pocket and grabbed a little pocketknife and clipped it onto my belt loop. I threw on a belt and a couple of hooded sweatshirts, layering them over the top. It sounded stupid, but at some point in time, it was going to get cold. I didn't know if I was ever coming back here. I plucked my old backpack off the floor and dumped it out over the center of the bed. I pulled out a pad of paper and a pen. I went to the bathroom, and I grabbed a toothbrush. I threw that in the backpack, along with traveling packs of napkins, a bar of soap, several pairs of underwear, another sports bra, and five pairs of socks. I couldn't live without socks.

I glanced out the window, and then I looked down at the clock; it was four. I had a couple of hours until the sun went down. They hadn't caught my parents, which meant they'd be back looking for me. Maybe they did catch my parents and the note was a Fae trick. It could've all been a trap, every bit of it, either trying to trap me at Sorenson's house or trying to convince me to stay in the area. So they could trap me somehow. They knew I was gone, and they saw me take every single one of these kids. They would want us all back for their nefarious purposes.

I turned the water on in the sink, cupped my hands, and splashed my face. There was dirt and grime on me. I let the water washed it away, splashing and rubbing with my fingers. Whatever specks of dust disappeared with the water dripped off my nose. Finally, I stood and looked at myself in the mirror. My hair was a mess as it fell down all around my face.

I took both of my hands and moved my hair behind my ears. I didn't want to admit what I saw. My eyes had always been boring hazel, nothing exciting about them. I didn't have flecks of gold or all those various descriptions people gave. I had muddy hazel eyes, but when I looked in the mirror, that wasn't what I saw. I was no longer muddy boring hazel but a raging bright fluorescent green, all around the center with a dark chocolaty brown outer ring receding away. My skin had taken on the porcelain-perfect smoothness of Fae, and my complexion crystal clear.

My ears weren't round anymore, but they met with a slight point. I didn't look like an elf or anything. If I kept my hair down, no one would notice. Sure, I saw a little point. If I didn't know better, I would think it was wishful thinking. I pushed back from the mirror, letting my head rest against the doorframe. I watched the reflection in the mirror. My eyes locked on the frame and the numbers etched on it behind me.

I'd been the same height for the last three years. I hadn't grown an inch, not even a centimeter. I gazed at the door frame where my father had marked my height every couple of months from the time I was old enough to stand up. Notches had dates, and my last date was three years ago. I was clearly taller than that mark by a good inch.

How did you grow an inch in a couple of days? It's not possible.

I slammed my head back against the door frame.

"It's not fucking possible; none of this is possible." The sun chose that moment to peek over the horizon and flashed through the window, hitting the mirror. The full force of it blasted into my eyes, like someone took a needle and stabbed my cornea. The pain was excruciating. I had to cover my eyes and close them. I threw an arm over my face and slammed my fist into the mirror. I didn't want to see it. I retreated from the reflection.

There was nothing else I wanted or needed. It was all part of someone else's life. The old Sarah. I was the new Sarah, and none of this mattered anymore.

Down in the kitchen, I grabbed a couple of Ziploc bags and threw them in my backpack. You never know when you might need a Ziploc to keep your stuff dry or to keep something wet. It was one of those things my mother always said—Ziploc bags were good. Who cared if they polluted the environment when you were just trying to survive? If they meant the difference between life and death, I choose life.

My eyes trailed around the kitchen and landed on Arty's cell phone. It was still sitting on the kitchen counter. I unplugged it along with my backup battery. I snatched both along with the chargers. I shoved them in the front pocket of my backpack, and then I slung my backpack over my shoulder.

I didn't have any money, and I didn't have any ID. There was no one left to check for ID or to ask for money. It was all fake anyway. I marched out the front door.

I grabbed Olive's hand, and that was when it dawned on me what Janice had done. He'd whistled at Arty like he was a dog. I'd been too angry to pay attention.

I only knew one whistle, the one my father used for dogs. I didn't know why because we didn't have a dog, but he'd whistle for one and they'd come. I put my lips together and blew. Nothing happened. I licked my lips to try again, but my tongue wasn't in the right spot. The sound came out flat and reedy. I licked my lips again, pulling in a deep breath, and blew. The glaze in their eyes washed away. They collectively blinked, eyelids working like squeegees on a window. The milky film that made them zombies was wiped away.

My ears began to ache. I reached up, fingering the new tip on my ears that had formed. In the bathroom, it was small and slight, but not anymore. They all stood there looking at me. A cornucopia of voices rose with everyone asking the same questions. Where are we? Who are you? How did I get here? Where's such-and-such and so-and-so? Some of the questions sounded like they were in different languages, but they all gave way to weeping. The only laughter and happiness I heard, was Zoe clasping Olive. She barreled into me giving me a great big hug such as her little frail body could.

"You saved her, you saved me, and you saved us!" She looked around. "She saved all of us, the Fae had us and she saved us."

Many of them looked at me with disbelief. I shook my head. I didn't know what to say.

I hadn't saved them all. I hadn't saved Arty, or any of those other girls.

"It's getting dark. We need to leave the area. I have to go to a house down the street and check on something. When I get back, we'll all leave, okay?" My eyes searched the faces.

"Don't worry, Sarah, I'll watch out for them." Zoe's bright eyes glistened with her happy tears. "We'll all stay right here waiting for you."

"If I'm not back in twenty minutes, walk down the street until it comes to a T. Turn right and keep walking. Don't stop until you don't see another house. You'll end up in a warehouse district. Pick one and hunker down, but don't turn on the lights." I saw Zoe's sister clamoring at her whimpering. I turned away and headed down the street.

Phil Sorenson lay in his front yard with a big slash across his fat belly. His guts were strung out, and they'd been spread around. I guess the dogs had been at him. Probably King.

There wasn't anything to throw up, but my stomach starting to lurch. I dashed inside. I moved from room to room for a couple minutes, but I didn't see anything. There were no telltale signs of a secret room. Sorenson was too smart for that. He was always telling everybody how smart he was. Truth was he was smart, just not smart enough to keep himself alive.

The obvious answer for the entrance to his secret room would've been in his basement, but that was too obvious. The entrance to the basement would be easy to find? Me, myself, if I were going to put a secret entrance somewhere, I'd have it right next to an exit. That left a couple of options, front door, back door, or the windows. I wouldn't put my secret exit next to the front door. Most people barged in that way and also when you leave, they'd see you. Windows and doors on the backside of the house. I didn't even know if that was smart, but it was what I'd do.

I went through the bedrooms, but nothing looked even remotely close to a secret entrance. The only thing I found the least bit interesting was the china cabinet in the kitchen. It was one of those nice, old-style china cabinets. You know, like at your grandma's house. Filled with the stuff you weren't allowed to use; it was just there and you looked at it. Then somebody really important would come over, and they'd use a couple of things, which you weren't allowed to use because you were a kid. It had two sets of heavy wood French glass doors and drawers. The cabinet was six feet tall and five feet wide dark mahogany, and right next to the back door. The back door swung to the left, and the cabinet was on the right, which was strange. Usually, when you have a door next to a wall, the door would swing into the wall, not into the rest of the room because it cuts off room usage. The door had been rehung on the other side. He'd tried to hide the cutout by filling in the hole in the entire frame, and then he'd repainted it. The handle of the exterior door had actually been switched around along with the deadbolt.

None of that would do you any good if you couldn't close the door and lock it. All of Sorenson's plans were nothing but a big fucking waste of his time. I saw the dirt smudge on the wall right by the edge of the hutch. Of course, it was like Anne Frank. They hid their door behind a bookshelf; it was the entrance to the secret annex. Sorenson was smart, but he was unimaginative. The wall was smudged with three lines. They could've been fingers or knuckles, but it didn't matter. Somebody should've washed it off.

I reached over to where the smudge was, and I stuck my fingers behind the cabinet. It was pretty snug against the wall. There was enough room for my little fingers. So, I pulled. It swung away like it was on casters or ball bearings. It revealed a stairwell down into blackness.

I reached into my pocket and pulled out a flashlight. I shined it down into the blackness.

The words came to my lips unbidden. I didn't want to say them, but they were there nonetheless. I couldn't stop myself; I wasn't in control.

"Come out, come out wherever you are." I heard my voice ringing in my ears. It was like fingernails on a chalkboard. I'd heard Janice say the same thing right before he came to attack me and my family.

The slow cocking of a gun, a little click at the end as he locked the grip back into place.

"It's me, it's Sarah! Don't shoot me, please." Adrenaline jetted through my veins as my voice trailed off.

"What was the last thing Sarah's father said to her?" My father demanded.

A whimper filled in the background.

I coughed to clear the lump there. It was him; it was my father. "'I'll go get your mother. Stay with Arty; he'll protect you. Don't come back to this house no matter what.' Then you told Arty to take care of your girl and shut the door on us." Muffled steps came as someone crept up the stairwell.

"It is Sarah, isn't it?" He marveled.

I shook my head a little, up and down, hoping it would loosen my hair to make sure it wasn't showing my ears. My throat tightened. What if he rejected me? What if it was just him and Mom was gone?

My eyes burned with ideas and worry. The trembling started in my hands and worked its way up to my lips.

"Yes, Dad! It's me!" I choked on my words. They were alive.

The wrinkles around his eyes and forehead crinkled. He reached out and pulled me into the darkness, smothering me to his chest. I heard my mother's whimpering down at the bottom of the stairs.

"Get inside. Close the cupboard." Her words were desperate and pleading.

My father pulled back, and I looked up at him. The smile on his face reflected my own. I could've jumped for joy. He pulled me in, crushing me. His heart beat like Big Ben at high noon. I breathed in the moment. Dad always smelled of Old Spice aftershave. It was his everyday go-to, and I drank it up. The weight I'd been carrying, it lifted as if the act of embracing my parent had transferred it to him. For a moment, I was safe and loved. It was a child's dream.

"How did you make it out?" I whispered, into his shirt.

"We got lucky. Some gang must have been out looting and drew them away." My father smiled with his reply.

"But I heard an AR."

"I haven't shot my gun once yet. It was someone else's. We stayed in the wardrobe till sun up. I checked Vougher's house but you were gone. I checked every house on the street. I saw the shoes box with the dead cat. That was you right?" He kissed my forehead.

"Yeah, the Fae killed him. I should have gone back to the house. I should have looked for you. We should have looked for you. Arty would still be here."

"Come downstairs and get a shower and some food. You should rest. It will be dark soon. Where is Arthur?" The happiness of the moment was over and reality set in. Arty.

My lips began to tremble again as the vice on my chest squeezed every drop of joy from this moment. The heavyweight was back, bowing my shoulders down. It was mine, and I couldn't give it away. My father couldn't fix everything. He couldn't save Arty. But I could. "I have to go back. I left Arty there. I can't leave him there. We have to go." I wanted Arty to have this moment too, to feel safe and not be alone, to be loved.

I didn't know where it came from. I wasn't a hero. I liked a challenge, and I want to win, but I wasn't a hero. I didn't stick my neck out. That was how heroes worked. That was what my dad did, not me. I wasn't the one who ran around defending kids at school; that was somebody else. But Arty was gone; a Fae zombie.

Why did I say that?

"Sarah, I don't know how you got here or what happened to you. But wherever Arty is, you cannot go back there."

I stepped away from him. Fresh tears streamed down my face. I wasn't a child anymore. This wasn't my home. The bittersweet taste in my mouth robbed me of whatever happiness I could've had.

I heard a sharp intake of breath down the stairs. "Oh my god, look at her eyes!" I didn't have to look in a mirror to know what she meant; they were glowing. They had to glow. All Fae eyes glowed.

I clenched my jaw, none of that mattered. I pushed the pain of those words away. "No matter what I look like or what you think, I have to go back and save Arty. I don't care about anything else. I can't leave him there. The only reason he didn't make it was because he saved a little girl. I don't even know how he woke up to do it. But he did wake up, and I can't let him die down there, Dad." I was rambling. My eyes searched everywhere for the answers as my hands gripped the sleeves of my Dad's shirt.

Please let them understand.

"You can't go anywhere without a plan. Come downstairs, and we will think of a plan."

I pulled away, working my arms out of his grasp. My eyes found my mother down in the darkness at the bottom of the stairwell. If I went down there, I would never leave to save Arty. I would be cocooned in love, and my parents would talk me out of it.

That is my old life. The old Sarah, she's gone. I have to leave her life behind.

I swallowed back the rock lodged in my throat and pulled out of my father's arms. I turned so I could face them both.

I thought this moment would come at my dorm when they left me for college, that big moment when you both realize you're all grown up and on your own. I knew there would be tears. I never imagined the pain in my chest. My heart was being torn into a million pieces.

"There are thirty-seven kids up on the street that I brought out of the Hallowed Hills. We can't go downstairs and hide in the ground and try to make a plan. I have to find somewhere for everyone. All of those kids are scared. They don't know where they've been or how they got there. Some are injured, they've got cuts and bruises, and they're hungry." My father raised his hand and rubbed his forehead.

"There isn't enough room down here for twenty people, let alone thirty-seven kids," my dad said. "We only have a couple of hours till the sun goes down, and it's already curfew. We need to save ourselves. We will make a plan and save Arty. Tell your friends to hide in some of the houses around here."

I knew what Dad was saying. It was the right thing. You couldn't save everybody, but I'd just saved all those kids. I wasn't going to watch the Fae come and cull them all back. I shook my head and pulled away, stepping into the lingering light of the doorway. I wanted to hug my mom and feel her butterfly kisses on my cheek, but she faded back into the darkness. I couldn't drag her out of here. She needed the safety of this place. I didn't.

"You go ahead, Dad. You and Mom stay down there. Stay safe. I'll be back tomorrow. I'll be back." I assured them, as much as myself.

He shook his head.

I saw him reach for me. My mother called, "George."

"Don't try to stop me. I'll be back in the morning," I said. Before my father could say anything, I pulled back and then shut the cupboard door with shaking hands.

I went over to the drainboard and pulled up a washcloth. I dabbed some water on it and retraced my steps to the wall. I scrubbed the smudge marks off. I hurled the rag back into the sink, tears dripping from my jawline.

Dad was probably still standing there, hoping I'd open the door. That wasn't going to happen. He needed to take care of Mom. I knew he wanted to take care of me, but those kids needed me. I took a deep breath to settle the churning in my belly.

You can do this.

I'd brought them all out of Fae. They could suddenly die on the street or be recaptured and put back into that subterranean hellhole. I hesitated. I wanted to turn around, open that cupboard, and run down the stairs into their arms. I lifted my foot, unsure which way I would go. The image of Arty falling flashed through my mind.

I stormed to the front door, snatching Sorenson's truck keys off the wall as I went. He had a king cab, long bed. If we got really cozy, maybe everybody could fit. Maybe ten in the cab and then we could get at least twenty in the bed.

Just before I stepped out the front door, my mother called to me. "Sarah, you will come back to us, won't you?"

I turned back to face her. She was frightened with her face tear-stained and messy hair.

"Of course, Mom. It's just a game, right? I always was a great competitor. I'll come home with the medal for you. I promise." I replied, shaking my head.

She smiled tentatively and put her hand over her mouth. I saw the tears running down her face as she nodded her head. We moved to each other, and I clung to her. She sniffled and smothered me in tears. I snuggled deep into her arms, enjoying the peace it brought.

"It's not a game. Fae play for keeps." She said, her voice wavered, then her hands thrust me away, and she disappeared through the cupboard. I didn't think my mother was brave enough to leave the basement. She must've been really scared if she'd come out to ask me to come back. I stepped out onto the street and walked up to the black Ford pickup in front of Sorensen's house.

Why'd it have to be a Ford? Oh well, I just needed it to last long enough to get me to where I was going. I hopped into the truck, adjusting the driver seat so my feet could reach the pedals. I fired it up and rolled down all the windows to let the stuffy air out. After, I unlocked the doors. All the kids came streaming out from Mrs. Levine's house.

"Zoe, get them in the truck. We're leaving." I yelled out the window. I hadn't even asked Dad for a gun. It didn't matter. I felt the shifting of the vehicle as bodies climbed in from all sides.

Zoe squished next to me with Olive on her lap and some big jock on the far end. "Where we going now?" Zoe inquired with a light voice. It filled me with hope and dread.

"Somewhere to regroup. I'm Nick." the deep voice of the jock informed us.

I bobbed my head in agreement while casting a glance over my shoulder at Nick. He nodded his head in return. "We need a plan," I replied, then put my foot on the gas and turned right at the end of the street. We were headed to the industrial district. I knew it wasn't over. I still had to get Arty.

The end

Thanks for reading! I hope you enjoyed Trick of Fae.

Make sure to get your copy of the next installment of These

Hallowed Hills - Test of Fae

Take a sneak peek of Test of Fae.

TEST OF FAE
CHAPTER 1

No one here had seen me before. They don't know what I really look like. They don't know that my hair isn't black and my eyes aren't green. Every single one of them thinks this is me. That I look this way. Admitting to myself I'd been changed probably is the most difficult thing I have ever had to face.

Inside, I feel the same. I don't feel any different. I still feel human. But every trip to the bathroom, every glance at my reflection in the mirror, the window, or the shiny side of the car—all I see is me but alien me. I know what's causing the change, and I can't reverse it.

I can't go back to my parents' hidey hole. There isn't room for everyone. I have thirty-seven kids all looking at me—the new me, not the old me.

I dart my eyes around the warehouse, searching for Arty and hoping to spot his hair or his hunched shoulders. I catch myself looking at tables and different surfaces, seeing if he left his eyeglasses behind.

I could really use him. Arty isn't just my best friend; he's the perfect right-hand man: smart, strong, and always willing to do whatever I ask of him. The best part is that I never have to question whether Arty is on my side.

It doesn't matter what I do. If Arty wants to fight about it, he would later when we were alone. He wouldn't make me look like a fool in front of people. But Arty isn't here. Instead, I found somebody else to rely upon.

The juiced-up quarterback who jumped in the truck cab with Zoe and me. It's Nick. He's reliable, he steps up to the plate, and so far, he hasn't done anything to piss me off. He's big and beefy, and he's used to people doing what he tells them to do.

After the maze, the only person who knows what's going on, is me. Somehow, Nick got the idea I'm in charge. In his mind, I'm the top dog, and that makes him my right-hand man.

I don't know if Nick is loyal like Arty. What Arty and I had, took a lifetime to build, but Nick keeps everyone in line, keeps us moving and motivated. The Nicks of the world have their uses.

I hadn't sung anything since the moment I snapped everyone out of the enchantment in the middle of the street. To be honest, I'm afraid to sing now that I know I can create magic with it.

I sit in this dingy, filthy, grease-filled warehouse with closed eyes. I can hear its song. The rocks, every piece of metal, even the glass in the windows. They all have a rhythm, a vibration, or a tune, and they sing to me. Every now and again I feel the desire to sing back.

It has been two weeks since the maze, and we hadn't seen even one Fae. But I can feel them lurking in the background, one step behind our every move. My greatest worry now isn't just the Fae. I saw how easy it was for Janice to tame that dog, and I have seen pawprints all around the homes in my parents' neighborhood. My greatest fear is that the Fae might be using animals to hunt us. It means going out onto the street is dangerous. Even in the daylight, birds, dogs, cats, and squirrels are a threat, all enlisted to the Fae.

We don't want to draw the gangs' attention either since there are still gangs running around. I don't allow guns anymore; guns draw attention. The report of a gun carries, and the sound is even easier to hear if you're an animal. The last thing we need is a dog to follow the crack of a bullet back to us—no guns. Instead, we practice every day for an hour using bow and arrows, makeshift crossbows, and BB guns. A BB gun isn't going to kill anything, but if you can scare an animal off, it'll make it easier to get away. The animals are our real daylight enemy. They track you and then lie in wait until twilight to bring the Fae down on all of us.

I don't want to kill somebody's pet, but if it's a choice between me or somebody else's Mr. Wiggles. I'm sorry, Mr. Wiggles is dead.

"So, what are we doing today, boss?" Nick's inquiry pulls me out of my head.

"Same as we do every day. Go out. Look for food. Take only what you can carry. Meet back at the appointed place. Stick to the plan." I cocked an eyebrow at him.

He nods his head. It's plain he has something to say, especially when his nose snarls up to the side.

"Is this all we do? You know, scrounge for food and hope we don't get spotted by some Fae pet?" The toe of his boot kicks at a dirt clod.

I don't like his tone of voice, but he clearly has a burr up his ass. Rather than start an argument, I cross my arms and sit back, throwing my feet up on the table.

"All right, then. What's your idea?" I ask.

"We made a plan, it's a war, humanity against the fairies. We could go to the government and tell them what happened. We could take a whole division back with us." He's right to do all those things. Everything single one of them relies upon me. It means that I have to get us back into the Fae realm if the government doesn't decide to study me like a lab rat first.

"I got us out the first time. I'm not sure I can get back in. You don't even remember anything. The last thing you remember is some crazy, pointy-ear fucker was singing to you. Then your eyes went all milky-white, and you became a member of the Fae zombie clan. We aren't going to the government. I don't want to disappear into a black bag. And if you go to them, so help me. I will hunt you down to the end of my days. Stick to the plan, Nick!" In a flash, I'm up and leaning over the table with both hands planted into the surface.

He opens his mouth to say something. I put my hand up. "You're right, we should find some adults to take care of the littler kids. They need to be educated, loved, and coddled." I look around, knowing the only adults within five miles are my parents. I can't take anyone there. The rest of the adults are gangbangers and criminals, probably a few rapists too. "They aren't going to get any of that with us. I don't know how we would find good adults that are alive. I don't want to go over this again." I heave a sigh, blowing my bangs out of my eyes.

All of their parents are dead. I'm not going to dissuade them of the belief that mine aren't dead as well. My parents are safer if everyone thinks they are dead.

My head rolls to the side, creating a pop in my neck. My eyes slide around the warehouse. I focus in on one of the kids, Twitchy. He's good with electronics. So is his buddy, Doug, the super geek. I turn my head back to Nick, cross my arms, and change the subject. "Has Doug found anything on the radio?"

"They're still playing music. He says most of the news isn't worth listening to. The public service announcement to check in is still running." Nick gazes off to nowhere.

"We don't want to send a reply. You don't know who's on the other end of that radio. They will find us and take all the supplies or worse. I'm sorry, but I think we're just stuck with this for now. Our best bet is to keep organizing the softer teenagers to take care of the littler kids." He doesn't turn to look at me but nods his head. He stands up straighter and stomps off to the other side of the warehouse.

"Is he trying to get rid of us again?" Zoe is always nearby. The truth is she'd make a perfect spy. She moves without a sound. She's so tiny. I'm sure we could secret her away in a cupboard to eavesdrop on someone's conversations.

"He's not trying to get rid of you. He's trying to keep people safe. He knows we're not adults, and little kids need love and somewhere safe to call home. We're all so traumatized. I'm not sure we have it in us." I rub my forehead. I don't have all the answers.

"I love my sister. I help out with little kids as much as I can. You're right; they need love," her eyes plead with me.

"We're the adults now. Don't let Nick talk you into getting rid of us." Fear etches her face. The same fear grips me.

"Do you really think Nick has the ability to talk me into anything? Don't worry about it. Nick's not in charge. We stay together until we find a better option." My eyes follow Nick's movements across the warehouse.

Like Nick, I want to go back, but to save Arty. I'd only been in the Fae realm for a few days, but time had marched on, resulting in three months passing on in the human realm. It has been two weeks my time since I returned to the surface, and I can't figure out how much time had passed in Fae. A few hours?

What do they say about procrastination? You may delay, but time will not.

CHAPTER 2

All my plans are taking too long.

I keep running the picture in my mind. Arty's black hair in free fall, his eye's focusing on Olive and throwing her back on the platform. The last minute when our eyes met before he sank over the side and my stomach lurched. How did Arty wake-up? Everybody else was asleep. If Olive hadn't tumbled over the side, he'd still be here.

It's not even a choice I want to think about. Olive didn't deserve to be saved more than Arty. Arty would have wanted her saved before than him. She's little, with a whole life to live. Arty would want her to live. He was sweet like that.

I said it like he's dead. He's not dead; he's stuck underground with the life-sucking Fae, I think.

No one here is capable of withstanding the Fae. They would all become entranced, and it would be a big waste of their lives. Mine and Nick's plan is the only way, and I can't stay here.

I flip through the pictures on Arty's phone, most of them of me.

"Looking at the pictures of your boyfriend again?" I grit my teeth and shift my eyes to him. Nick grates on me sometimes by pushing just the right button.

"He's not my boyfriend. I've told you that; he's my best friend," I retort.

His dry laugh always follows. "I don't know any guy who has that many pictures of a girl that he doesn't want to bone."

"You're a real Shakespearean there, Nick. It isn't like that. Arty isn't into me, more like I'm his sister or something." I close my eyes. I can hear Arty's words before we were taken. He told me to save yourself. Isn't that what I was doing? No, you're procrastinating. Yeah, to save lives.

"Poor Arty, friend-zoned for all time. I'm sorry, Sarah! I'm not buying it. You're good-looking and available. You like him, and you hang out with him. He's your boyfriend whether you admit it or not." Nick crosses his arms, forcing his biceps to bulge and making them appear larger than they are and they are large.

"He's not my boyfriend. Kissing Arty would be like kissing my brother. Gross. We're friends, that's it. I literally lost my best friend. Could you leave me alone about it?" I grumble, shifting my eyes from him and back to the phone before pushing the off button and sliding it back into my pocket.

"I know you just lost your friend. We all lost somebody. You never once asked me why I was there or who I went with." The chiding tone of his voice mists over me like a cold fog and my head hangs as I run my fingers through my hair. Long, thick and unruly, my hair is a pain in the ass, but it covers the point at the end of my ears.

"I'm sorry! I never asked you whom you went in with. I didn't ask you why the Fae were holding you at the tree. Who was so important they tied your lives together? I didn't ask, not because I don't care." I chance a glance at him and then around the warehouse. "Everybody's got their own demons. I didn't think it was my business to pry into yours. Want to tell me? I'd be happy to listen." I turn my full attention on him.

He looks down and away, his shoulder rises as he draws in a breath. Then everything about him sags. "My sister. I have a twin sister. I'm Nicholas, she's Nicolette. I know, cheesy. If you knew my parents, you would've understood. I'm sure based on what you told me about the maze that she made it through. Nikki's really smart. She's the smarter of the two of us. Now you know who I'm going back for—you to get your friend, me to get my sister. I don't care if you're in love with him. All I care about is Nikki. She's in there, fighting for her life alone. I'm her brother. I'm supposed to be by her side, always." Obviously, his sister is the one in charge of their relationship. He'll do anything to save her. So, if it's a choice between Arty and his sister, he's always gonna choose his sister. Which is okay because that's kind of what I would expect. If it was my sister, I would choose her over somebody's friend every time. I would choose Arty.

I dart my eyes around. "Is this why you keep pushing me? You don't want to be responsible so we can go back and save Nikki?" I tap my hands together, lightly letting the tips of my fingers meet.

"Yes, that and frankly I'm not ready to be micro-dad. Some of these kids, they look up to us like we're supposed to be their parents. I'm not ready for that. I'm not sure I would ever be ready for it. Until a couple weeks ago, the only thing I wanted to do was play football and get into a good college. That's it." His words come out hard and pleading at the same time. "I wasn't thinking about anything else other than girls. Now all I can think about is Nikki, killing Fae, and getting revenge." His right fist smashes into his left hand, flexing the muscles in his upper body at the same time. Nick likes to put on a show of strength. For a moment there, the bravado vanishes and I see the real Nick. The guy without all the brawn and he is hurting and alone. Just like the rest of us. I stand up, keeping my eyes on his, I pat his arm, and turn my mind away from all our losses.

I know how he feels. Before all of this, the only thing I was worried about was finishing high school and who I'd go to prom with.

It had all been so clear when I spoke to my parents. I had to go back in the Hallowed Hills and find Arty. But the longer I think about it, the more I realize it won't be that easy. What if he's dead? The what-ifs play a broken record in my head. There is only one way to make them stop. That is why Nick and I made our pact.

If you've enjoyed what you've read here please give it a little love and leave a review or feel free to follow me on Amazon Or send me an email slmason1889@gmail.com or follow me on Instagram @s.l.mason_author

For the most up to date information on the Killing Gods Universe or These Hallowed Hills visit:

Quickquillpublishing.com

www.ingramcontent.com/pod-product-compliance
Lightning Source LLC
Chambersburg PA
CBHW051558100726
47898CB00001B/137